THE BOOK OF EXTRAORDINARY AMATEUR SLEUTH AND PRIVATE EYE STORIES

Published by Mango Publishing Group, a division of Mango Media Inc.

Cover & Layout: Elina Diaz

Mango Publishing Group
2850 S Douglas Road, 2nd Floor
Coral Gables, FL 33134 USA
info@mango.bz

For special orders, quantity sales, course adoptions and corporate sales, please email the publisher at sales@mango.bz. For trade and wholesale sales, please contact Ingram Publisher Services at customer.service@ingramcontent.com or +1.800.509.4887.

The Book of Extraordinary Amateur Sleuth and Private Eye Stories: The Best New Original Stores of the Genre

Library of Congress Cataloging-in-Publication number: 2019944136
ISBN: (print) 978-1-64250-078-3, (ebook) 978-1-64250-079-0
BISAC category code FIC022100—FICTION / Mystery & Detective / Amateur Sleuth

Printed in the United States of America

THE BOOK OF EXTRAORDINARY AMATEUR SLEUTH AND PRIVATE EYE STORIES

The Best New Original Stories of the Genre

Edited by Maxim Jakubowski

Mango Publishing

CORAL GABLES

Table of Contents

Introduction

Maxim Jakubowski

With all due respect to police officers and eminent official representatives of the law, it can easily be argued that the amateur sleuth, whether intentionally or not (or dutifully employed as a private investigator) has for almost two centuries now been at the fulcrum of mystery fiction.

As far back as Edgar Allan Poe's "Murders in the Rue Morgue," which the dogged Chevalier Auguste Dupin solved, and the immortal exploits of Sherlock Holmes, the heroic detective with an eye for the truth and the intellectual patience to solve the most challenging of conundrums and baffling criminal cases has dominated the often-bloody pages.

The list of classic amateur sleuths is endless, ranging from the cozy, but nonetheless impeccable, credentials of Agatha Christie's set of Hercule Poirot, Miss Marple, and the lesser-renowned but seductive duo of Tommy and Tuppence, through to a whole cohort of Golden Age sleuths like Margery Allingham's Albert Campion, Dorothy L. Sayers' Lord Peter Wimsey, Ngaio Marsh's Roderick Alleyn, S.S. Van Dine's Philo Vance, Erle Stanley Gardner's Perry Mason, and more realistic treks through the mean streets with Raymond Chandler's Philip Marlowe and Dashiell Hammet's Continental Op and Sam Spade.

And, more recently, Lee Child's Jack Reacher, Colin Dexter's Inspector Morse, Jeffery Deaver's Lincoln Rhyme, Sara Paretsky's V.I. Warshawski, Sue Grafton's Kinsey Milhone, and so many others have joined the ranks.

The figure of the lone investigator as a servant of the truth is one that is inherent to crime and mystery fiction. Readers never tire of watching brain and brawn crack open the most difficult cases, brushing away red herrings with every new twist of the plot, seeking a resolution amongst the forest of confusion that crime elicits.

Our second volume in Mango's series of collections presenting the best in the field follows in the footsteps of the *Book of Extraordinary Historical Mystery Stories* and highlights some of the more original and brilliant amateur sleuths and private eyes conjured up by the fevered imagination of many of the genre's leading US and British practitioners of the art of the criminous short story. Each protagonist is both unique and fascinating, some created for the occasion and others established characters that have appeared on a regular basis in the respective authors' previous novels and stories, but each tale is brand new and specially crafted for this anthology.

I hope they and their exploits have you scratching your head (or other parts of your anatomy...) and enjoying the way their gray cells are put to work as they resolve puzzles and uncover the truth behind our seventeen new sets of often fiendish mysteries.

The Asphodel Meadows

Alison Joseph

The woman on the stairs had uneven pale hair and a glassy, bitter stare.

"Maybe you'll last longer than the previous tenant," she said.

Sister Agnes fixed her with a look. "Maybe I will," she said.

The woman tilted her head, gave her an empty smile, and went on her way, her limping tread echoing on the staircase.

***

"What on earth did she mean?" Athena turned away from the window, silhouetted against the spring sunlight. "Really, sweetie, those nuns should have moved you into somewhere safer. An ex-council flat in a rough part of South London, with weird women hanging about on the stairway muttering curses—"

"It was hardly a curse—"

"Just because they claim they're doing up your old place—"

"The roof was leaking."

"These riverside views—they could at least have chosen the fashionable bit—"

"And anyway, it was either that or moving into the community's house in Hackney."

"Oh no. You? Living with a load of nuns? Out of the question."

Agnes laughed. "Athena, I am a nun."

"Yes, but you're different. You have standards. Mind you, those old jeans have seen better days. And your hair, I mean it's okay keeping it short, but, you know, with all that gray… All I'm saying is, a decent cut and color, you'd be back to normal in no time."

"I'm not sure my fellow sisters would see it that way."

"They just don't have a best friend to tell them, that's all."

Athena went back to unpacking boxes. She wore a navy tailored skirt, a blue blouse. Her long black hair fell in measured waves.

"Do you really read this stuff, kiddo?" Athena held a book out to her.

"Some of it, yes. Some of it I just kind of absorb without taking it off the shelves."

"The last thing one finds in writing a book is knowing what to put first..." She peered at the spine. "And do we find out who dunnit?"

Agnes smiled. The room was bare, with cream-painted walls. But the new paint couldn't hide the 1970s functionality, the low-ceilinged meanness of the space.

"And a new job too," Athena said. "It's like a midlife crisis that you haven't even chosen. It's not for me to criticize Father Julius, but for him to insist you go and work in that hospice up the road and then bugger off on retreat—"

Agnes laughed. "The job is all good. And Julius needed a break."

"I mean, some of us could really do with sitting up a Welsh mountain with a load of shaven-headed Buddhists. Me, for example, it would barely touch the surface of my sinfulness. But him... I'd have thought he'd be holy enough." She went back to the boxes. "Ooh—this is pretty. Where did you get this?" Athena held up a square of thick paper. "A drawing," she said. The pencil lines showed three tall flowers, with thick stems and rows of tiny petals. "Asphodel, isn't it? I remember it from Greece."

Agnes took the paper from her, held it in her hands. "That is so weird," she said.

"What?"

"Heavens. I'd forgotten all about this."

"What's weird?"

"It's just—the boy who drew this for me—years ago...in Provence..."

"A boy?" Athena sat back on her shiny navy heels.

"I was sixteen," Agnes said. "Living with my parents..."

"Before I knew you, even. Aeons ago."

"Olivier." Agnes touched the creamy paper. "That was his name. I just heard from his cousin, like—yesterday...day before...I'd not even thought of him forever, and then I get this email from Jean-Yves...and now you've found this. Weird." She looked up. "He was English. Oliver. Though all the locals called him Olivier. He was staying with his aunt. He was very shy. Lonely. Both of us. That's what this is…" She gazed down at the paper in her hands. "The Asphodel Meadow, he called it. We used to take refuge there. And now—"

"Oh sweetie. Look at you. Bad news."

"He died. Last month. His cousin tracked me down, thought I should know. They had the funeral back there, in Marseilles, where he lived. His aunt is still alive. Oh, God, I don't know why I'm crying…"

Athena laid a hand on Agnes's. After a moment she said, "The Asphodel Meadows. In Greek mythology—it's where ordinary people go, after death. The Elysian Fields, that's for heroes. But for the likes of us…" She gave a brief smile. "Unless we're headed for hell. Always a chance, I suppose, for you and me."

They listened to the silence, the soft rumble of the London traffic.

"He was lovely," Agnes said. "Kind of vulnerable. Sensitive. He didn't seem to have parents. Never mentioned them. We used to talk about English novels. And heroism. And cheap wine. And smoking. He used to draw a lot. Characters from myths and legends. Odysseus, was it? Someone who visited the underworld."

"And flowers. For you."

Agnes dabbed the tears from her eyes. "He was found dead in his flat. Heart disease, apparently, though it would have been treatable if he'd bothered to look after himself."

Athena traced the lines of the drawing with a pink-painted nail. "You might have married him," she said.

"He asked me once, as a joke. Both of us being half-English, as he put it."

"You'd have swerved being a nun."

Agnes shook her head. "Whatever path I took to get here—this is where I'm meant to be."

***

There was no sign of the woman on the stairs. Out in the street, Athena gave Agnes a hug. "You look after yourself," she said. "I'll be back tomorrow. For more unpacking. And more tales of lost loves."

Agnes walked away from the river, toward the City. She glimpsed the church of St. Mary Magdalen, sat squarely between the soaring concrete and steel, as she approached the hospice. A chaplaincy job, arranged by her friend Father Julius, who'd persuaded her Order that she needed a change.

"You'll love it," Julius had said. "Helping people from this world to the next—just your kind of thing."

"You make me sound like a serial killer," she'd said.

"No, no," he'd replied. "We leave the heavy lifting to Him up there. All you have to do is lighten the load."

***

The hospice was a clean, sleek building in red brick and glass. The wide, low windows shimmered in the late afternoon sun.

"The thing is, Sister…" Donald MacBride was sitting in his usual chair, watching the buses go by, the trees coming into leaf. "It's a question of what happens next. All this…" He gestured to his chest. "This is going to be empty of me, I can understand that. But then, where will I be? What happens to the me of me?"

Agnes smiled as she took a seat next to him.

"You'll tell me it goes on somewhere, won't you? You being a nun and that."

"Well…"

"Heaven, Hell, or that other one. The in-between one."

"Purgatory," she said.

Donald had a brightness about him that his illness had so far failed to diminish, and a feathering of silver hair. He wore a tweed jacket over his thin frame, sharp-creased trousers.

"That's the one," he said. "Purgatory. Where we atone for our sins. I'll be there a long time, I tell you."

"Not you," she said.

He looked up, and a shadow crossed his hazel eyes. "I'm seventy-two," he said. "I feel I've lived a long time. Those flats," he said. "Across the road there. I remember them being built. My father, he worked on the sites. Came over from Ireland, made a life for himself. Carpenter, he was, in the end. Like me." He fell silent, his gaze fixed on his hands in his lap. "I've had a happy life." He raised his eyes to her. "I have no complaints."

"So—"

"Sister. I'm terrified. I've sinned, Sister. So many sins."

"Donald," she began. "If our faith speaks of anything, it speaks of forgiveness."

He shook his head. "Where do I start? I stole from the shop there. Cigarettes. Me and my little brother, Jason, we used to sell them in the school yard. On the days we went to school, that is."

"That's not a sin—"

"I lied. To my sister. She was seeing a man, we were older by now, he was from the Island, down by the docks. Baz, they called him. Connie adored him. I never liked him. I told her he'd been speaking ill of her, told her he'd been calling her the names men call women when they feel they can't own them… She believed me, called it off. She was heartbroken at the time."

"But were you right about him?"

He gave a brief nod.

"Then—that's not a sin," she said. "Or rather—it's doing the wrong thing for the right reasons," she added.

"And I killed a man," he said.

Outside a siren passed, a loud pulse of blue light.

"You…"

"You heard me," he said.

Silence hung in the air.

"What happened?"

"You'll call it doing the wrong thing for the right reasons," he said, with an almost-smile. "I went armed. I knew what I was about. A kitchen knife. I cornered him, there was an alehouse where he always drank, down by the river there, it's all done up now, full of City boys. I challenged him. We went outside. And… I stabbed him." He held his hand out, and Agnes saw the shake in his long carpenter's fingers. "Even now, I feel it, the way the knife went into him, there, between his ribs. The smell of it. The slicing of it. It wakes me at night, even now."

"And he died?"

He nodded. "He stumbled. Tried to walk away. But the river was just there, the tide high… He fell." He clutched his hands together in his lap. "The band was playing that song. That one that goes, 'At last I am free…' I can't listen to it now without the smell of blood."

Agnes sat silent.

"He was found, three days later. Washed up. Downstream." He looked up at her. "Your God ain't going to allow me through the pearly gates. Not with that on my record."

"Did no one—?"

"No one knew it was me." He shook his head. "You'd call it getting away with it. It was dark, that night. I threw the knife into the river. It was never found. And in any case, Victor, he had so many enemies." He shrugged. "The police did what they could. Time passed. He had a pauper's burial." He gave an empty smile. "Getting away with it," he said.

"Why did you kill him?"

"I had to." His gaze was steady. "My little brother. Jason. Good as gold, everyone adored him. And because of Victor, he died. We were all mates, to start with. We all worked together, on the sites. We did a big contract, Mermaid Court, up toward the City there. In the boom times. And out of that, Jason, he bought a garage, out by the Salter Road. Did very well. Limos and that. And Victor, he went into property. But then, Victor's company, he bought up the site where Jason had his garage. And then Vic, he puts up the rent, drives Jase out of business." He stopped, took a breath. "He lost everything, my brother. He was a proud man, proud of his business, and to be ruined like that…" A small shake of his head. "He killed himself. Put a noose around his neck. He was found by his mechanic, hanging from the rafters." He smoothed his hair from his forehead.

"We never got over it. My sister, she moved away. My Mam, she didn't live much longer after that. Broke her heart, it did. And me… left here. On me own. Victor kept away. But then, about a year later, there was the night when he appeared. At the bar there, flashing his money around. And—I'd been drinking, I admit it. And I went out of the pub, walked along the riverbank, frosty sky, you could see all the stars… and it all became clear. Like it was written up there, in the heavens. And I went back. I went armed. You know the rest." He leaned back in his chair, settled his breathing.

"At the time, I thought I'd been lucky. There was a charm he wore—we all had one. A silver mermaid, we had them made after the Mermaid Court days. He wore his round his neck. But when he was fished out of the Thames, it was nowhere to be found." He gave a thin smile. "I said to myself, at least the water spirits are on my side. At least I've got away with it." The smile faded. "But I was wrong. It's been a life sentence."

His gaze drifted to the window. "There was a woman I loved. Annette. She knew I'd done it. She kept her silence, but she knew. And after that, she kept her distance from me too." He turned back to her. "That prayer," he said, suddenly. "We used to say it when I was little, me and my Mam. Me kneeling by my little bed… 'Now I lay me down to sleep. I pray the Lord my soul to keep…' " His eyes watered. "I used to kneel there with Jason. Saying those words. I know he's up there, with our Mam. But me—I can't say those words no more." He stared at his fingers. "Human flesh," he said. "You'd be surprised. The way it fights against the blade." He leaned back in his chair, closed his eyes.

Agnes brushed his fingers with her own. "The God you prayed to, as a child. You could still pray…"

He opened his eyes. "Who's going to hear?" He shook his head. "No," he said. "Whatever place I might have had up there with all the saints, I gave it up in that moment. There's a place for me in Hell. And it's a hell I've made my own."

***

Agnes left the hospice, walked through the twilight, the hurrying crowds. Julius's words in her mind, that it's about lightening the load. But that poor man is carrying a dead weight, she thought. A heavy, heavy weight.

At the entrance to her block of flats stood the odd woman. She seemed even more threadbare and unkempt. She raised her hand, wagged an accusatory finger, then turned and walked away.

The flat was chill and dark. Agnes switched on lights, heating. She poured herself a glass of wine, marveling that there was any left in the bottle.

She pulled a book from the shelves. "We look for clues for the workings of God around us," she read. "But the nature of faith means that we won't know the clue until it comes to us, and even then we won't know it as a clue."

It's the sort of thing Julius would say, she thought. It's the sort of thing he says when he accuses me of creating a mystery yet to be solved. *Don't tell me,* he says, *you've got that shivery feeling you claim to get when you sense a truth waiting to be revealed.*

She picked up the asphodel drawing. "When we've escaped," Olivier used to say, "that's when my life will begin." And he never got further than a one-room flat in a deprived suburb of Marseilles.

Beginnings and endings. Her eyes welled with tears as she placed the picture on its shelf.

***

She woke to early slanting sunlight through the thin blinds, and a feeling of having slept very deeply. The clamor of the day, a motorbike's roar, the magpies calling, the to and fro of a police siren.

The siren got louder and louder and then stopped. The courtyard flickered with blue light.

Agnes pulled on jeans and a fleece and stumbled out to the staircase.

The street was blocked with cars, police, ambulance. The woman was standing by the railings, watching.

"Another ghost," she said. "Another unquiet spirit." She turned to Agnes. Her hair was awry, her shabby raincoat unevenly buttoned. "They found a man in the river this morning. Drowned, last night. Kids, they found him." She screwed up her eyes. "They say you're a nun."

"I am," Agnes said.

"Don't look like one. Don't they wear them things, you know. Black and white."

"Not always," Agnes said.

"Jesuit, are you?"

Agnes blinked. "Ignatian. Yes."

"Ah." She screwed up her eyes. "Witches the lot of them." She jabbed a finger at her own chest. "Mary. Named after Mary Magdalene. See the church up there? They say I was found in the doorway. Little baby, left there in a basket." She turned back to the activity in the street. "All lies," she said. "Had a ma and pa. Rubbish at it, both of 'em. If I was dumped in the doorway, it's because they'd forgotten all about me. Now look—" She pointed toward the ambulance. "Don't know what they think they're doing with that. A hearse, that's what they need." She gave a short laugh. "The kids thought it was a coat, floating in the river." She turned back to Agnes. "Happens more often than anyone knows," she said. "But then, people like us, no one cares if we live nor die. Not you," she added. "You've got all them saints to keep an eye on you." She gave a brief, cracked smile. "Funny thing is, the man they found. He was wearing a mermaid round his neck. You'd think a lucky charm like that, you'd think she'd have kept him safe. Like you and your holy spirits." She tapped Agnes on the arm, then turned and stomped away.

Agnes watched for a while longer. The ambulance started its engine, drove off into the traffic. The police cars dispersed. She was aware of a cold, shivery feeling.

***

"Coincidence, sweetie." Athena placed two mugs of coffee on the low pine table. "Another one. Sometimes I think we're just figments of someone's imagination…our lives all mapped out by some greater intelligence."

Agnes stirred milk into her coffee. "God, perhaps."

"Oh, I wouldn't go that far." Athena sipped her coffee. "But Asphodel Meadows. And now silver mermaids… And you say the witch on the stairs knew all about it?"

"Not a witch. She's named Mary after the saint, Mary Magdalene."

"Isn't she the one who had seven devils cast out?"

"Heavens. Fancy you knowing your Bible after all."

"Just the interesting bits." Athena bit into her croissant. "Saint or witch, it explains her knowing all about weird drownings." Athena licked her fingers. "At least you've got decent jam in your austerity kitchen."

***

That afternoon, Agnes was back at the hospice. She talked with a man in his nineties, a gentle soul whose gaze was shadowed with the horrors of Auschwitz. A woman of thirty-nine whose blood cancer had finally caught up with her, with her smart red suit, her black hair plaited in cornrows, her jolly stream of visiting friends. And now, as the sky grew pink behind the half-built city towers, she sat with Donald.

"A drowning," Donald said. "Last night."

"You heard?"

"The nurses were talking of it."

There was a silence.

"Donald," she began. "They say this man was wearing a silver mermaid round his neck."

Donald levelled an even gaze.

"They're not very… I mean—it's a rare thing, isn't it?"

"Well, that's a strange thing," he said. "Four of us. All on the sites. Victor, me, and Jason. And Scott. He was the fourth. But he married a Spanish girl, went off to live in Madrid." He shrugged. "Maybe mermaid charms aren't so unusual. Maybe they're two a penny."

"And they don't protect from drowning either."

He managed a smile. "A river death." Donald's eyes followed a passing bus. "Passing into Lethe." He turned back to her. "The river of forgetfulness. But me—what frightens me, when I pass from this world to the next—they won't let me forget."

Passing the church, under the gathering clouds, she saw a figure hunched in the shadows, realized as she approached that it was Mary Magdalene, idling by the gate as if in waiting.

"This dead man." She took hold of Agnes's sleeve. "They're saying he'd been drugged. Then dropped in the river."

"How do you know?"

"Gossip. That's all. Nothing better to do with my time. And these days, it's all caught on camera, isn't it. They're looking for a woman, they're saying." She dropped her grip, pointed at the churchyard. "There. That's where they say I was found."

Agnes saw the arch of the church doorway, shadowed by the sunset.

"And it isn't true?"

Mary Magdalene shrugged. "Who knows? I had a father who loved drink more than anything, and a mother too busy with her rage to care. Also…" She hesitated, and for a moment the brittle smile softened. "Also, here." She took Agnes by the arm. "Look." She pointed, to a small patch of earth, dotted with flowers. "It's where the babes are laid to rest."

Agnes looked at the rows of primroses and violets, laid out as if newly planted.

"The local women come here," Mary said. "Those tiny souls are cherished here." She relinquished her grip.

"And you?" Agnes said.

She shook her head. "No motherhood for me," she said. "You and me—we have that in common, at least."

***

Back home, Agnes made an omelet for supper, a tomato salad. She sat and looked at the drawing on its shelf. She thought about Olivier, how they'd spray cheap perfume so no one would know they'd been smoking when they got home. Neither of them saying out loud that there'd be no one back home who cared.

There was a knock on her door. Mary Magdalene, she thought, as she got to her feet. With more tales from the graveyard—

A woman stood in the doorway. She had tired blonde hair, a thin raincoat roughly belted, worn flat shoes.

"Sister Agnes?" she said. "I'm Annette Bradshaw. I—I hope you can help me. I need to see Donald."

Agnes settled her on one of the armchairs, made a pot of tea.

"I'm sorry to track you down like this." Annette hung her coat over the back of her chair. "But I didn't know who else to ask. And that woman out in the street told me which flat was yours. She seems to know everything."

Agnes handed her a mug. "Mary Magdalene. She says that's her name."

Annette managed a small smile. "I care about him, you see." Annette had a direct blue gaze. "I know he thinks I'm keeping away, but—but he's a good man. A good Catholic man. He deserves to die in peace. It was the nurses there who said you were visiting."

"He's afraid of Hell." Agnes brushed dust from the arm of her chair. "He says he's sinned."

"I was there." The words tumbled from her. "I saw him leave the pub, I knew that awful man was having a smoke out on the terrace. I knew that Donald was going after him. I went out too, I think I thought I could stop him… I was too late." She gave a little shiver.

"And now a second drowning," Agnes said.

"Yes, I'd heard." She had work-roughened hands, bitten nails.

"Mermaids," Agnes heard herself say.

Annette shot her a glance.

"A silver mermaid charm, worn round the neck."

The blue eyes were fixed on her.

"It seems odd, to me. Both men, wearing such a thing. A coincidence."

"If you believe in coincidence." Annette shifted in her chair.

"And you don't?"

Annette looked up. "When I was small, I was taught that God loves me. That he loves us all. My mom, that's what she told us."

"But mermaids—"

"Faith," she said. Her voice was sharp. "Not coincidence. If anything's laid down, it's laid down by the good Lord." She curled a lock of hair behind her ear. "A good Catholic woman, my mom. A wonderful woman. I always thought I'd be a mother the way she was."

"And—?"

She shook her head. "It wasn't to be. Too late for me now." Again, the fierce blue gaze. "Sister—I need to see Donald. I want to make it better for him."

She got to her feet, gathered up her coat. "That song," she said. " 'At last, I am free…' They were playing it, that night. That's what I want for Donald. I want him to be free."

***

The rain continued through the night. Agnes, up before sunrise, headed to the Community House in Hackney for Lauds. The nuns murmured the liturgy in the pre-dawn quiet. "Look upon my adversity, and forgive me all my sins…"

Afterwards, the bus tires swished in the London rain. She got off the bus at the church, walked through the churchyard. She looked at the dotted rows of pink and yellow, drooping under the gray sky. A lone woman stood there in smart coat and leather boots, her umbrella splashing rain as if the whole sky was weeping for the mothers living still, mourning still.

She was early at the hospice. She found Donald in his room, dressed and tidy, but looking tired.

She pulled up a chair next to his. He reached to his bedside locker, opened a drawer.

She saw, lying in the palm of his hand, a silver mermaid figure.

"It's beautiful," she said.

"Derek," he said. "He made them for us. Silversmith at Hatton Garden, he was. We knew him from school. Went into his dad's business."

"Donald—why would Scott have come back?"

He gave a weary shrug.

"And—who would want him dead?"

He glanced up at her. "If it is Scott."

She held the mermaid between her fingers.

"So—there were four of these?"

He gave a nod.

"Victor's is at the bottom of the river," she said. "And Scott's—if this man is Scott—is with the forensic boys, I imagine. That leaves Jason's," she said.

"No one ever found it," he said. "We asked…when they—when they took him down. He'd always wear it. But…" He closed his eyes.

She spoke again. "Annette came to see me," she said. "Last night. She wants to visit you."

His eyes flicked open. "She does?" He straightened up, grew taller in his seat.

"She's waiting outside."

She led him out of his room, into the lounge area. Annette was there, walking toward them in pleated skirt and heels, her hair freshly washed.

Donald got to her first, took hold of both her hands. "Annette," he said.

"I had to see you," she said.

***

Agnes left them alone. The rain had eased, and she went out into the morning, and the birds sang loud as the sun broke through the clouds.

She walked to the graveyard. The green buds on the trees sparkled with raindrops. She thought about the clues that come upon you when you can't see that they are clues.

She was aware of the click of heels on the stone path. She turned to see Annette.

"Thank you," Annette said.

"Was it okay?"

"It was more than okay," she said.

They walked, slowly. They looked at the rows of flowers, fresh in the morning light.

"The Asphodel Meadows," Agnes said. "In the old stories. Where souls of ordinary people go. Only—here, it's just London flowers. For London souls."

Annette paused, staring down at a patch of earth, a tangle of weeds between the well-tended borders.

"Forgiveness," Annette said. "That's what we talked about." She looked up at Agnes. "He is so frightened," she said. "A brave man like that, a proper sort of bloke, to see him quaking with the fear of Hell…" She bit back tears. "If only I could help."

Look upon my adversity. The words sounded in her mind. *Forgive me all my sins*.

"You could tell the truth," Agnes said.

Annette's expression hardened. They stood silent by the graves, as the sun went in and the clouds gathered overhead.

"I think," Agnes said, "I think you have Jason's mermaid charm."

Annette's eyes filled with tears. After a while she said, "Ordinary souls." She waved a hand toward the graves. "Is that what you said?"

Agnes looked at the spread of thistle and dandelions. She looked up at Annette. "You—your—"

"My baby," she said. "Our baby. Mine and Jason's. But not ordinary. He was the most perfect baby in the whole world."

"He's—he's here?"

Annette gave a small nod. She took a few steps, pointed at a space where a ragged rosebush drooped by the old stone wall. She seemed to crumple, as Agnes caught her by the arm, led her to a damp wooden bench.

She sat, breathing, her hands over her eyes.

"It's not Donald," Agnes said. "It's not Donald who needs the dead weight of sin to be lifted from his shoulders. It's you."

"I tried to tell him." She took her hands from her face. "I said to him, the angels are waiting for you. It's me who's banished. Exiled from my baby…" Her voice cracked.

"And—Jason?"

"I loved him. We were going to get married. And then—"

"He died."

She nodded.

"Victor stole your child's father."

Another nod. "I lost the baby. The shock of it…"

"It wasn't the knife wound that killed Victor," Agnes said. "It was the person who led him to the water, who pushed him in."

Annette's blue eyes were fixed on her. "Donald was drunk. He doesn't realize how drunk he was. Sure, he pushed the knife into Victor's side. But it was a flesh wound. The guy wouldn't have died of it. And Donald saw him stumble toward the river. But what he didn't see, because he turned and fled, was me. Hiding in the shadows. Taking hold of an injured man, a man stumbling, from drink, from shock. Leading him to the water's edge. A push. That was all it took. It was high tide. The water spirits were on my side. One minute he was standing on the embankment. The next, splash. Into the waves, the darkness." Her voice was level now. She went on. "But as he fell, he turned to me. As if to call for help. His mouth open in an *O*. His eyes pleading. As if I was there to be his savior, not his killer. And then, splash. Gone."

"Donald said..." Agnes began. Suddenly there it was, all of it, laid out in front of her. "Scott came back. He found you. He knew the whole story."

"He was broke. He wanted money. He came back thinking I'd pay up to keep my secrets. I just wanted it all to go away. We went drinking, Sunday night. I spiked his beer. Led him to the river. But it's different now. They can see so much. CCTV, you know. It's a matter of time until they catch me. I know that now."

They sat in the rain, gazing at the rosebush.

Agnes touched Annette's arm. Annette reached up and grasped her hand tight.

***

Two days later, Annette was arrested. She pleaded guilty, and was remanded in custody.

"Donald still won't have it," Agnes said to Athena, as they arranged the last few books on the shelves. "I keep saying to him, you fought the man who'd caused your brother's death. That's your only sin. You have nothing to fear apart from death itself."

"Which we all bloody fear," Athena said. "Don't expect me to be all noble and peaceful about the ending of this life. And anyway, I can't die yet. Chanel have just brought out a fab new range of anti-aging skincare products."

"He says he wishes he could take the blame for Annette."

"Sweet."

"She won't have it. She seems relieved it's all over."

"Is Julius back? What does he say?"

"He is back. He just said it was typical of me to find the mystery that no one else could see."

"Ah. Bless."

"I'm not sure it was a compliment."

Athena picked up the Asphodel drawing. "You should frame this, you know. Look after it properly."

Agnes shook her head. "I know what I'm going to do with it."

were also unreal, as if they had been lifted from a cheap detective novel, the kind of novel that the members of the Reconstruction Club claimed to despise but in fact relished in secret, translated from French and sold only in one bookshop known to them, and that down a Norwich alley that had an unsavory reputation.

Beastly poured tea for all of them and then served himself and stirred sugar lumps into the brew with a sour expression.

"Any ideas?" he asked.

Rufus shrugged. "The facts of the case, if they have been reported accurately, and there's a good chance they haven't, would indicate either that the murderer is a lunatic or that the victim was killed in an accident that only has the semblance of murder, an accident too unlikely to be considered as tragic and thus interpreted as a symbolic act and the result of a murderous impulse."

"If only we had the resources to take a trip to Paris!"

That came from Diggs, the baker.

He was perhaps the most financially successful of them all, yet without exception they were lower-middle-class gentlemen, bound to their trades as if by shackles, not poor by any means, but with little surplus income to fritter away on foreign travel and other such inessentials. None of them had been to Paris. Everything they knew about it came from books, newspapers, and radio programs. Rufus, a shipping clerk, worked with the names of distant locations every day, but not with the places themselves, and Paris wasn't one of those names anyway.

"We will do things the way we always do them," he replied.

Diggs nodded. "That's for the best."

"We reconstruct, we don't replicate," wheezed Jaspers.

"Indeed," said Beastly.

Rufus finished his tea, wiped his lips with a handkerchief. "My friends, it seems no great hardship for us to turn Norwich into Paris for a few hours or so. But it will be easier and smoother if we repair to a spot just *outside* our noble city for the task of reconstruction, when the time comes."

"Which spot exactly?" the others wanted to know.

Rufus smiled; his free hand delved into the spacious pocket of his jacket, and he groped for the briar pipe there. He lifted it out and, just before inserting it into his mouth, said in a casual tone of voice:

"There are many windmills in our county and several are very close to Norwich. Of course, most are defunct in this day and age, but the one at Little Melton is large, powerful, in fine condition, and it turns."

"I cycled through the village last week," said Gertie.

"Then it's settled?" asked Rufus.

They all nodded, even Jaspers, who winced as he did so.

"Next weekend, gentlemen?"

"Saturday or Sunday?" asked Chunder.

They briefly debated this point and decided finally that Sunday was the more suitable day. It was nearly always a Sunday when they performed the reconstructions that gave their club its name and character. Sometimes one or two of them would be free for an attempt on a weekday, and they wouldn't worry about including the others. It depended on the nature of the crime.

Certain crimes required more participants than others. This Paris murder fell into the "more" category. It would be best if all seven of them were free. As Rufus chewed his pipe, which he never lit or even filled, he tried to imagine how it would be when they all embarked for Little Melton, which was only a few miles beyond the western edge of Norwich, and stepped off the bus together.

The driver would be sure to make a joke, the other passengers might be amused, bewildered, or even disgusted, but his colleagues had no inkling of this yet, for Rufus was a man in the habit of making plans for them and keeping those plans to himself until the day of truth dawned. He smiled.

A smile that expressed itself in the shifting of the pipe from one side of his mouth to the other. But his colleagues were no fools. They knew Rufus was capable of some monstrous decisions, and they respected him for it. Any price to pay was worthwhile in the fight against crime. They were amateurs and had much to prove to themselves, if not to outsiders, and they had been toughened by the war anyway, by the epidemics that had followed, by the responsibilities of British life at a time when politics was in a state of radical transition. Monstrous decisions could be just what was required as the Empire began its long decline unnoticed.

"Now," said Chunder, consulting his wristwatch, "it's time for me to be off too. I will be back here next Sunday at what time?"

"Early," replied Rufus.

He spoke with the pipe still between his lips and the word came out of the empty bowl as if from a very distant megaphone with a slightly whistling quality, as if taken and twisted a little by the wind.

"Seven o'clock in the morning?" asked Chunder.

Rufus nodded, and his nod included them all. This was the most important task of this particular convocation. It was highly unlikely any of them would see each other again before the scheduled date. Only Diggs possessed a telephone. Communication was the biggest obstacle in the smooth running of the club, and yet the club operated well enough as it was, having solved many crimes in its particular way. Chunder put on his hat and went out the front door.

"Anyone else have a pressing engagement?" asked Rufus.

"Not me," said most of them.

"I promised to take the wife to visit her mother in Yarmouth," said Beastly, and he also picked up his hat from the little table that served in lieu of a hat stand, but he was less eager to cram it down on his head than Chunder had been. It was obvious that he wanted to linger, to hear what else Rufus might have to say. Rufus wasn't the leader, a notion that would have embarrassed him and them, but somehow he had evolved into the role of an oracle or consultant.

"Don't keep her waiting," was his only remark.

And Beastly went off too.

The five who remained formed an irregular circle, there in the front room of that cramped but mostly empty house in Livingstone Street, a building that had been left to Rufus by his aunt, who had never liked it and never had a use for it, and that's how it ended up as the base for an association of sleuths of limited means but sharp minds, all of whom abided by the ideals of modelling an event or incident in order to learn a revelatory truth about it. Rufus said:

"It wouldn't be the first time that a person was killed by the sail of a windmill, but this fact doesn't mitigate the awkwardness of what happened. The windmills in Paris aren't strictly functional, for one thing."

"Not now, but once they were, and they are certainly the same structures in terms of sheer power as before," said Diggs, who as a baker had a particular interest in such things, and when he felt the pressure of all eyes upon him, he added, "I mean that the internal workings are serious machines."

"Dangerous if a person fell into them?" said Gertie.

"Would grind a man to sludge."

"But no one fell into anything, and there's the problem," declared Rufus, and with a grotesque lunge he snatched the newspaper Pollard had left for them, rolled it up as Pollard had rolled it, then began whirling his long arms in front of him, mimicking a windmill but with only two asymmetrical sails. The effect was disturbing, the pipe at the end of one arm, the newspaper at the end of the other, and Rufus making a series of clanking noises at the back of his throat.

Then he stopped. There was no applause, but Jaspers coughed.

"Very good," offered Gertie.

"The victim," persisted Rufus, jamming the pipe back into his mouth and letting the newspaper fall to the floor, "was snatched up by one of the sails and spun round and round and then hurled away over a roof. He was found in a courtyard, mangled, broken, barely alive, and with his dying breath, he was unable to give an explanation for what had happened. Which means?"

"He didn't fall *into* anything but *onto* something," said Diggs.

"A cobbled surface," finished Gertie.

"The sails of windmills are usually situated high above the heads of anyone who might be passing them. The clearance is considerable. People have reported feeling a rush of wind, but it's very rare to be clobbered on the skull by one. It has occurred in a few instances, yes, and in the old days when riders on horses were more common, the risk of passing under one was greater."

"But this victim wasn't on a horse of any kind."

"Thank you, Jaspers. Quite so."

Gertie turned to Diggs and asked with a smirk, "And how do *you* know anything at all about the windmills of Paris?"

"From books." The baker was unashamed.

They all knew what kinds of books, they were men, but they had strong loyalty to each other, they were discreet, they were all readers of those books, and the inside of the bookshop that supplied them was more familiar to each of them than the interiors of any of the city churches. Rufus made a gesture of support. "Expand," he said, and Diggs gave them a brief lecture on the topic.

"The windmills of Paris were like the windmills one finds anywhere. Some grind corn into flour, others operate pumps to drain soggy land. As Paris grew, as centuries passed, many of the windmills were dismantled, just as they were

"Great view," as he gestured at the spread of Norwich.

They agreed. He shielded his eyes.

The sun was weak but there was glare from the low clouds, a bright haze that was reflected off the cleaner buildings of the city. It was as if Rufus was observing a scene after it had been treated in a photographer's studio, the contrast levels high, the grimy houses among the brood below much more in focus. He tried to pretend he was above Paris, looking down on the City of Light. The cathedral in the distance could be the Eiffel Tower, conceivably, but what about the other landmarks, the Arc de Triomphe or the Sacre Coeur? It was less easy to imagine those. He squinted to the west and at last he found what he was hoping to see.

The windmill of Little Melton. A tiny dot, irregular.

No, that was a tautology.

And a logical contradiction. All dots are tiny. None are irregular.

Don't lose your mind, he warned himself.

But it was the windmill, for sure, and he might as well be sitting on the balcony of the highest room in a tall apartment block on a fashionable boulevard and scrutinizing the Moulin Rouge in its niche near Montmartre. That was the effect he wanted. With a sigh of satisfaction he looked down at the canvas bag he had left on the pavement and asked the worker nearest to him, "If you wanted to pull that thing up here, how would you do so, in the most efficient way?"

"Rope and pulley, of course," came the reply.

And the fellow indicated the pulley that was attached to a steel bar above them, a rope of rough fibers coiled next to it.

"And it wouldn't require too much force, would it?"

The worker rubbed his chin.

"What sort of a question is that, if you don't mind me asking? It requires as much force as necessary, no more and no less."

That was a good answer.

Rufus climbed back down, the pipe still between his lips. When he reached the ground, he shouldered the bag, lumbered on. He was a bachelor, just as Jaspers and Gertie were, and his house was no bigger than the one in Livingstone Street, but it was furnished far more comfortably. He emptied the bag on the floor of his bedroom upstairs and sorted through it. Bevins had done well. These costumes were very good indeed. And the various sizes seemed right.

Well, that remained to be seen, on the appointed day.

The week passed, the weather improved slightly. When Sunday came, Rufus was up very early indeed, and he managed to carry the bag by himself to the clubhouse. It was still only six thirty when he paused in front of the door to fumble with his key in the lock. The metal plate he had fixed on the brick above the door was dull and the sign engraved on it was difficult to make out.

It was an equals sign, the official symbol of the club.

Yet Rufus now realized that it ought to consist of two wavy lines rather than two straight parallels, because reconstruction wasn't exact equivalence. Reconstruction was an approximation. Was it too late to alter the plate? Maybe he would get round to it one day. But who else would care?

He expected to be the first to enter the house, but Jaspers was already there, on the sofa, on the comfortable side. Rufus frowned.

"What time did you arrive?"

Jaspers smiled weakly. He looked very ill.

"I never left. I've been here since the last session. I was too weak. I managed to go to the kitchen a few times, drink water, and heat up soup. There are tins in cupboards, but they are very old. Hideous, awful."

He grimaced, and Rufus made a decision. "I don't think you should come with us to Little Melton today. You haven't recovered fully. Don't push it, dear boy. I brought a costume for you, but you don't need to wear it. Five will be enough. There are five strapping fellows who will fit the bill."

"Costumes?" gasped Jaspers.

"I plan to dress you all as girls, dancing girls."

"Ah, that's a novelty."

"Have you been following the newspapers since I last saw you?"

"I haven't been able to."

"Of course not! How idiotic of me. The victim has finally been named. A certain Jean-Marc Duclos. He was the accountant of the *Moulin Rouge* cabaret. Now that is the interesting detail, as far as I'm concerned. The accountant. Why would anyone in their right mind wish to murder an accountant? Not as a crime of passion, not because of love, but surely for reasons connected with money. And I don't mean robbery. His wallet was still on him when he

Beastly gasped, "I certainly would welcome the help."

"Me too," puffed Pollard.

"String us up," wheezed Diggs and Gertie.

Chunder was too exhausted to make any remark at all, but Rufus kept urging them on, and they kicked as hard as they could, but it was clear that the legs weren't going up as high as before, that they were gradually sinking. Then Rufus took his pipe out of his pocket and gestured with it.

"I am Monsieur Duclos, and I have been employed by the manager to take care of the accounts. But I am growing uneasy. I begin to note that my employer is unethical. He employs dancing girls and in order to maximize his profits he works them far too strenuously. He overworks them. Conditions are terrible. They are exhausted, but he won't let them rest. He arranges for their legs to be operated mechanically, yanked up and down by strings connected to the axle of the revolving windmill in the roof over their heads. These strings dangle through holes in the ceiling. The unscrupulous rogue is therefore able to make a lot of money by working his girls longer than he should, harder than he should. And the audiences never notice. It's too dim in there, smoky, and the patrons are often tipsy. The strings are never detected. But I know about them and it makes me shudder. And one night—"

"We've had enough," said Pollard, and he stopped dancing.

The others stopped too. Rufus added:

"No strings attached, that's why you were able to stop. Imagine if you hadn't been able to rest when you desired? Imagine if there were strings tugging your legs up and down, up and down, against your will?"

"Heinous," said Beastly.

"Yes! And eventually Duclos thought so too. He decided to do something about it. He resolved to report his employer to the police. But his employer had never trusted his new accountant. He had taken measures to silence the fellow if Duclos ever made a move against him. The accountant was being carefully watched. He left the club in disgust, intending to make his way to the nearest police station. A thug on the top of the windmill was ready, a thug who worked for the same employer. Down came the noose, it snared Duclos, the other end was already attached to the windmill, and off his feet the accountant was lifted, spun around a few times, then the cord broke and he was catapulted right over a house."

"But who was the employer?" Diggs asked.

"I don't know yet. But we can find out easily enough. We know that *he* was the murderer and that means our reconstruction has been totally successful, agreed? Yet there is something vital still missing."

"What?" wondered Gertie.

"This!" cried Rufus, and on a wild impulse he ran at the windmill. His momentum carried him up the side as far as the tip of one of the swooshing sails and he reached out and grabbed hold of it with one hand.

Up he went, the pipe still between his lips, laughing.

Or was he in fact screaming?

It was difficult to tell. All five chorus girls watched him. The shriveled man too. He went up and came down, then he went up again. He was talking now, but because of the rotation his words were difficult to interpret, loud one moment, quiet the next. Then he bellowed, "I am the murder victim." They all heard that clearly enough. He abruptly released his grip on the sail.

He arced through the air, landed on a tree.

There was a splintering sound.

One of the broken branches had impaled his arm. His legs were at an unnatural angle. Blood dripped from his torn face. He was mumbling to himself. Not until the others had retrieved him from the damaged tree was it possible to work out what he was saying. "It remains unproven, but I think we have done our best. I am satisfied with today's results, gentlemen," were his words. They carried him to the road and waited for a bus going to Norwich.

"No need for hospital, no need for doctors," he muttered.

It was unmanly to disregard his wishes.

The bus came and they boarded it.

Nobody laughed this time, not even the driver.

As solemn as nurses, they bore his wrecked body along Livingstone Street and into the little brown brick house. They sat him on the sofa next to Jaspers. Then it was time to change back into their normal clothes. Beastly made a vague promise to return the following day to brew tea. Then they hurried out, all five of them, keen to make the most of the remaining day.

Another case had been solved. The club was flourishing.

Rufus and Jaspers were left alone.

They sat in silence.

The Mystery of the Missing Vermeer

Eric Brown

The moon-faced little man in the Harris tweed overcoat was acting oddly, which in itself was not remarkable. The Pig and Whistle was known for its eccentric clientele.

I'd just finished a shift at New Scotland Yard and had nipped in for a quick pint before heading home. The tavern was one of my favorites in London; it was quiet, for one thing—no piped music here, or noisy gambling machines. The only sound was the murmur of drinkers and the somnolent tick of the grandfather clock.

I was contemplating a second pint of bitter when I noticed my neighbor at the bar. He was staring across the room with an expression of intense concentration. From time to time, he muttered to himself and wrote something in a notebook.

I cocked my head and listened.

"Eleven feet seven and three-quarter inches," he murmured, and applied pen to paper.

He turned his gaze to the row of single malts behind the bar. "Three feet three and a half inches," he said, and meticulously wrote down this figure.

Next he gazed across at the grandfather clock. His face was rather bland and bookish—the mild countenance of a librarian, perhaps. "Nine feet seven and a half inches," he said.

He looked up and caught me squinting at his notebook.

"Forgive my curiosity," I said. "But what on earth are you doing?"

Far from being annoyed, he seemed to welcome my interest.

"Not at all," he said, offering his hand. "James Henry Murgatroyd, by the way."

"Jeffrey Mallory," I said.

"Delighted to make your acquaintance, Mr. Mallory. As to what I'm doing… Well, sir, we all have our special and peculiar abilities, don't we?"

"Some more than others," I allowed.

"And I," he said, "possess a talent which I refer to as 'acute spatial estimation.'"

"Acute Spatial Estimation," I said, giving each word the capital letter it deserved. "And what's that, if you don't mind me asking?"

Mr. Murgatroyd laughed good-naturedly. "Not at all," he said. "I have the odd ability of being able to estimate, with extreme accuracy, the distance between any two given objects."

I stared at him. "That's… quite some ability," I said, trying to keep the sarcasm from my tone.

"Oh, it's a useless talent for the most part," he admitted. "I found it helpful when I worked as an estate agent—estimating room sizes, you see—before a weak heart enforced my early retirement. Now, though, it's merely a hobby."

"A hobby?"

"Or perhaps a better description would be a compulsion. You see, I cannot go anywhere without finding myself estimating distances. I find it most satisfying to estimate the precise measurement between myself and any given object, but I can just as well judge the distance between any two points, provided they are visible."

"Remarkable," I said.

"Yes, isn't it?" Mr. Murgatroyd beamed. "A strange talent, and one for which I make no great claims. It is merely a freakish ability of the old gray matter."

I decided that a second pint was in order, and asked if my new acquaintance might like a drink.

"Why, that's very kind of you. A half of milk stout would be most welcome."

Our drinks recharged, I said, "If you don't mind me asking, how accurate are you with these estimations?"

"I don't mind at all, sir. And I can report that I am accurate to within a hair's breadth either way. And if you doubt that claim, then I can prove it."

"You can?"

From the pocket of his overcoat he withdrew a small rectangular device resembling a mobile phone. He pressed a stud on its side and passed the device to me.

"What is it?" I asked, examining the black box with a tiny inset screen.

"A laser measure," said Mr. Murgatroyd, "much used by estate agents these days. You merely direct it at an object across the room, press the stud, and the distance of that object will appear on the screen, in either metric or imperial measurements. I have it set to imperial because, as my friends like to point out, I am somewhat old-fashioned. Go on, try it."

I pointed the device at a painting on the far wall and pressed the stud. A wire-thin red line vectored across the room. *Twelve feet six and three-quarter inches*, the screen read.

"Now, let me see..." Mr. Murgatroyd said, his gaze shuttling between my hand and the painting. "Twelve feet six and three-quarter inches."

"Astounding!" I said.

I pointed the laser device at the taproom door and pressed the stud. The measurement came up (*nine feet three and a half inches*), and I looked at Mr. Murgatroyd.

Instantly he said, "Nine feet three and a half inches."

I laughed in astonishment. "Spot on!"

Mr. Murgatroyd beamed his delight. I guessed that he rarely had the chance to exhibit his peculiar ability.

"It's a talent that doesn't, since my retirement, have much practical use," he said, pocketing the measuring device. He looked at me and his eyes twinkled. "Until now, that is."

I was intrigued. "Until now?"

"Now, you see, I very much hope that my ability will enable me to solve a crime."

I sat up, my professional interest piqued. "A crime?"

"None other than the theft of Vermeer's *The Milkmaid* from the Fortescue Gallery."

I smiled to myself. "And good luck to you, Mr. Murgatroyd. A team's been working on the case since it was nabbed last week, with not a sniff of a clue. And I should know. I work at the Yard—Detective Inspector Mallory, in my official capacity—and I know the DI leading the investigation. Ballamy's at his wits' end trying to solve the case."

I looked at the little man, who was smiling in a rather self-satisfied manner. "But what makes you think...?" I began.

He took a prim sip of his stout and set the glass precisely upon its mat. "I visited the museum a month ago," he said, "expressly to view the Vermeer. I am an aficionado of the arts, Mr. Mallory. I make a tour of the London galleries every month or two, now that I'm retired. Yesterday I returned to the Fortescue, and the room from which the Vermeer was stolen. I noticed nothing untoward at the time—other than the glaring blank wall which the painting had occupied. But I came away from the gallery with an odd sense of something not quite right."

"Not quite right?" I echoed.

"It was only when I returned home that I began to wonder. I must admit that I spent a rather sleepless night, and this morning I decided that I would return to the gallery and find out if my supposition was correct. I came here for a pork pie and a half of stout, by way of fortification, before I set off for the gallery—which I think," he said, draining his glass, "I will do now, if you will excuse me."

I quickly finished my own drink. "If you don't mind," I said, "I'll come along with you."

I couldn't fathom how his strange ability might help to solve the riddle of the theft, but I was curious—and I must admit that I'd taken a liking to the little chap.

"By all means. You can be my Watson," he said, and chuckled to himself at the irony of having a detective inspector accompany him as his "Watson" to the scene of the crime.

We turned up our collars against the biting January wind and left the Pig and Whistle.

***

The Old Masters room was long and low, with a dozen paintings mounted on each of the long walls. Vermeer's *The Milkmaid* had hung by itself, in pride of place, on the wall at the far end of the room.

The museum was busy that afternoon with genuine connoisseurs of the arts, those wishing merely to escape the winter chill, and a sizeable contingent come to gape at the space where the painting had once hung. I found it indicative of the artistic appreciation of the British public that the bare wall was attracting more viewers than had Vermeer's masterpiece.

Mr. Murgatroyd stared around the room, examining the walls and ceiling with the attention of a short-sighted blackbird.

"What exactly are you looking for?" I asked, as we walked to the far end of the room and halted before the empty wall.

"Security cameras," he murmured.

I recalled what Inspector Bellamy had told me. "Apparently this room doesn't have them," I said, "though there's one in the corridor outside."

"Hmm," he said. "Very interesting."

He examined the space where the Vermeer had hung, staring at the wall as if the masterpiece had still been *in situ*.

After a minute or two, he nodded to himself and made his way from the room. He peered up and down the corridor, at last spotting the security camera situated high on the opposite wall.

He tapped his chin, frowning. "It's a pity," he said, "that I don't have access to the footage from around the time the painting was stolen."

"Bellamy's team has studied every last second," I said. "They didn't see a thing."

"Nevertheless," said Mr. Murgatroyd, "I would like to form my own opinion."

I had an idea. "Come with me," I said, and escorted him to the director's office.

***

Director Amelia Shaw was a tall woman in her forties with a careworn face and a habit of worriedly running a hand through her long auburn hair. I showed her my police ID card, introduced Mr. Murgatroyd as a "specialist consultant" (he positively glowed at the accolade), and explained that we were following up various leads pertaining to the theft of the Vermeer.

"Such a mystery," she said, "and all the more embarrassing for the painting being on loan from the Rijksmuseum."

In due course, she led us to a tiny room in the basement of the gallery. A security officer listened attentively to Director Shaw's instructions, then walked his fingers along the rack of DVDs until he found the relevant disc. He inserted it into the player and pressed "fast forward."

"The theft took place between closing time on the Friday evening, six o'clock," he told us, "and seven the following morning, when the painting was found to be missing. I'll stop it here, at a little before six p.m. There's the last of the punters leaving the room."

I squinted at the grainy image. "You can't actually see into the room where the Vermeer hung."

Director Shaw said, "As there are no windows in the room, all we need to survey is the entrance in order to cover all comings and goings."

"And no one came and went during the specified hours?" Mr. Murgatroyd asked.

"Nobody other than a couple of porters," said the director.

The security officer fast-forwarded until the numerals at the top right corner of the screen indicated twenty-two minutes past six. The porters moved along the corridor, pushing a trolley bearing what appeared to be a big painting wrapped in a protective covering, and turned in to the Old Masters room.

"What's that?" I asked.

"A painting that had just been restored," Director Shaw said. "The porters delivered it just after closing time, to be hung first thing in the morning."

"It's very large," Mr. Murgatroyd commented.

"*The Vendramin Family* by Titian," she said. "Nine feet by six, but it appears larger because of the protective packaging."

The security officer fast-forwarded, then pressed "play" just as the two workmen were pushing the empty trolley out of the room and back along the corridor. I glanced at the digital clock on the screen: six fifty-four. They had been in there for just over thirty-two minutes.

More than enough time, I thought, for them to have taken the Vermeer from the wall.

The trolley they were pushing, however, was empty but for the folded bubble wrap and hessian sacking that had swaddled the Titian.

"So the porters couldn't have had anything to do with it," I said.

"Your lot looked into that," the officer said. "They wondered if the canvas might've been cut from its frame and rolled up." He shook his head. "But whoever nabbed the painting also took the frame. And they"—he indicated the porters—"obviously haven't got the frame about their persons."

I had him freeze the image and examined it closely. There was no way the porters might have concealed the frame on the trolley or beneath their work coats.

"Isn't it unusual to take the frame as well as the canvas?" I asked the director.

"That entirely depends on who is behind the theft," she said. "An art lover wouldn't want the canvas damaged by having it cut from the frame."

"And the porters were the last to enter and leave the room?" Mr. Murgatroyd asked.

"That's right," the director said. "The museum was locked up at seven when most of the staff left the premises."

"Most?" I asked.

The security officer nodded. "My colleague was in here for the night shift," he said, "monitoring the cameras. He noticed nothing amiss until seven the following morning, when an attendant made the discovery."

He fast-forwarded until just after seven that morning, and we watched the image of a uniformed attendant enter the room, then rush out again seconds later, clearly agitated.

I asked Director Shaw if I might interview the porters that afternoon, and she assured me that they would be only too glad to assist the investigation.

***

She showed us to her office on the ground floor of the museum, then left in search of the porters.

"As a matter of interest," I asked Mr. Murgatroyd as we waited, "how old were you when you became aware of your odd ability?"

"Now, that would be when I was just six years old," he said. "My father was in the habit of making things for the house—shelves and cupboards and the like. He was always measuring up pieces of wood, and I became fascinated with his tape measure—it was one of those big retractable things in a leather case like a discus. Whenever he wasn't using it, I'd borrow it and measure anything and everything—and the distances between things."

"Ah..." I said.

Mr. Murgatroyd shrugged modestly. "I suppose I became adept at estimating distances from habitually measuring objects and the like."

"That might explain it," I agreed.

The door opened and the porters, William Evans and Douglas Wainwright, slipped into the room. They struck me as being dead ringers for Laurel

"Impossible!" I cried. "Why, you've seen the footage yourself. There's no way they could have stolen the painting!"

Mr. Murgatroyd smiled at me. "But as I explained," he said patiently, "the painting has not been stolen… yet."

***

One hour later, after I'd phoned the Yard and impressed upon Inspector Bellamy the need to meet us at the Fortescue, four of us stood in the rather cramped confines of the porters' storeroom: Mr. Murgatroyd and myself, Director Shaw, and Detective Inspector Bellamy. Two plainclothes officers loitered in the corridor outside.

The security officer had been sent to find Messrs. Wainwright and Evans and tell them that their presence was required in the storeroom.

Mr. Murgatroyd was showing a marked interest in a large map of the world which hung on the wall. "Very interesting," he said. "You will note, my friends, that the map occupies the wall abutting the Old Masters room."

Detective Inspector Bellamy looked dubious. "And this is significant?" I think he was more than a little disgruntled by Mr. Murgatroyd's claim to have solved the case.

"Highly," said Mr. Murgatroyd.

"If you would kindly explain–" Bellamy began, only to be interrupted when the door opened and the porters rather warily entered the room.

"Gentlemen," Director Shaw said, "I am so glad you could join us. Mr. Murgatroyd, here, would like a word."

Wainwright and Evans looked from Mr. Murgatroyd to Detective Inspector Bellamy; they seemed more than a little apprehensive.

Wainwright found his voice. "How can we help you?"

Smiling, Mr. Murgatroyd reached out and lifted the map from the wall, laid it to one side and, with a flourish of his right hand, said, "Now, I wonder if you might explain… *this.*"

We all stared at the wall, or rather at the place where a great patch of plaster had been removed, along with perhaps a dozen bricks.

"Run!" Evans cried. He flung open the door and bolted with Wainwright hot on his heels and Inspector Bellamy in close pursuit.

We heard the sound of a scuffle from the corridor, followed by a cry. By the time we emerged, the plainclothes officers were in the process of handcuffing the porters.

"Good work, men," Bellamy said. "Now," he went on, turning to Mr. Murgatroyd, "if you wouldn't mind explaining exactly where the blazes the painting is?"

"Not at all, Inspector," Mr. Murgatroyd said. "If you would care to follow me."

***

In the Old Masters room, Mr. Murgatroyd told Director Shaw and Inspector Bellamy how his peculiar ability had assisted him in solving the mystery of the missing Vermeer.

"When I left the gallery yesterday," he said, "I had the distinct notion that something was not quite right about the room, compared to when I had seen the painting a month ago. When I returned here today, I knew what was wrong. You see, the Old Masters room is smaller than it had been."

Inspector Bellamy looked incredulous. "Smaller?"

"Or, to be more precise, the room is *shorter* by some four inches."

"But..." Director Shaw began.

"So, of course," Mr. Murgatroyd went on, "I suspected that this had a bearing on the disappearance of the Vermeer."

"But how?" Bellamy sounded exasperated.

"This was a very clever, I might say ingenious, heist," Mr. Murgatroyd said, "though technically it was not a heist in the accepted sense of the word. Rather, it was a *concealment*."

"A concealment?" Bellamy repeated.

"Exactly," Mr. Murgatroyd said. "You see, when our friends Mr. Wainwright and Mr. Evans trolleyed the Titian into the room that Friday evening, they also brought with them, hidden behind the swaddled painting, a screen in four parts—a screen got up with the same maroon flocked wallpaper, magnolia cornices, and picture mounts as the other three walls. Now, during the thirty-two minutes and fourteen seconds they were in the room, they unwrapped the Titian, set it to one side, then unfolded the false wall and secured it in position, four inches in front of the wall bearing the Vermeer."

"Good God!" Bellamy gasped, staring at the empty wall.

"To all appearances," Mr. Murgatroyd went on, "it would seem that the painting has been taken from its mount. Now, when I learned that the porters' storeroom was next door to the Old Masters room, everything became crystal clear."

"Ingenious!" Director Shaw said.

"And as we have just discovered," Mr. Murgatroyd finished, "Mr. Wainwright and Mr. Evans have already started removing the bricks from the wall in the storeroom in order to gain access to the Vermeer—working against time before another painting is hung and the wall is found to be false."

Inspector Bellamy stepped forward. "Do you mind if I…?" he asked the director.

"Be my guest," she said.

Bellamy regarded the false wall. It was some eight feet high by twelve wide, and the porters had done a fine job of matching the flocked wallpaper with that of the other walls. I certainly was unable to tell the difference.

Bellamy reached out and tapped the wallpaper. The wall appeared sturdy enough, though a satisfyingly hollow sound reached our ears.

As we watched, Inspector Bellamy moved to the corner of the room and inspected the intersection of the false wall with the outer. He looked back at us. "Now, how to go about this?"

"I have an idea," I said. "Back in a jiffy." I hurried to the porters' storeroom, found what I was looking for, and returned with two claw hammers.

"These should do the trick," I said, passing one to Bellamy.

We took up positions at each end of the false wall and, with the claw ends of our hammerheads, began work. Within a minute, I had made a hole large enough to insert my hand.

Bellamy had excavated an even larger aperture in the ply-board. "Clever…" he said, peering into the hole. "They even knocked up a four-by-three timber frame to give the wall solidity. If we give it an almighty tug, on the count of three…"

"Stand back!" I called to Mr. Murgatroyd and Director Shaw.

They retreated to the middle of the room and watched the operation with some apprehension.

"One, two, three… Now!"

We tugged in unison and, as the wall came away from its nailed moorings, we scurried away and joined Mr. Murgatroyd and the director.

The wall fell slowly forward with a *whumph* of displaced air to reveal, hanging in pride of place in all its splendor, Vermeer's *The Milkmaid.*

"Well, I'll be…" Bellamy said, allowing himself a rare smile.

"I think," I said, "that this calls for a celebration. How about a drink at the Pig and Whistle? We'll raise our glasses to Mr. Murgatroyd's Peculiar Ability…"

The little man beamed. "I'll drink to that," he said.

The Chocolate Underpants Caper

Mary Harris

I'm an officer. A grievance officer. Dana Gore, assigned to Local 221, American Authors Union. All the doo-doo that agents, editors, and publishers dish out to writers ends up on my shoes. Usually, doo-doo happens because writers can be idiots. They don't ask for contracts. They don't read contracts if they get them. They sign contracts without any forethought or advice. Then the doo-doo hits the fan and they run screaming to me.

It was a dark and stormy Monday. I knew it was a deep-doo-doo case when he burst through the door and thrust a handful of papers onto my beat-up metal desk, shoving the keyboard askew.

"You know what they did to me?" he yelled.

I saved the book I was trying to write, made sure my blouse wasn't gaping, and pointed to the rickety guest chair.

"Sit."

He sat. I studied the contract. It made for sad reading. Mr. Walter Dunphy had signed away his latest children's book to Edacity Publications. For years, he had existed meagerly on cutesy plots featuring baby animals and itsy-bitsy toddlers, using carefully researched language structures appropriate for his target market; then he gave up and dashed off a stupid little book about an eight-year-old boy who wouldn't wear underwear but always saved the day.

It hit the *New York Times* bestseller list. TV-Land was working on a cartoon spinoff. A multinational toy company contracted to produce the doll, clothing (sans underpants), and coloring books. There were rumors of Hollywood interest. All these goodies normally bang more bucks into the writer's pocket. However, the contract was a standard boiler-plate confection from the early '60s. Poor old Wally was fifth in line at a cash cow with four teats.

I waved the papers at him. "Did your agent approve this?"

"Don't have one. Why should somebody get fifteen percent of my blood, sweat, and tears?"

"Because now you're getting one hundred percent of bupkes. Did you get legal advice before signing?"

Dunphy hung his head in his hands. "No," he mumbled through thin fingers.

"Did you talk to an Authors Union contract advisor?"

He shook his head, thin gray hair creating a sad halo.

"Right. So what do you want me to do?" I asked.

He bolted from the chair. It teetered, then settled back into its usual slump. "I want my rights! I want what's mine! They're making a fortune off me!"

I pointed to paragraph 15, subclause H. "You get 10% of the publisher's 50% for sub rights, triple net."

"I don't even know what that means!" he screamed.

I opened a battered drawer and took out a pamphlet, ignoring the metallic screech as I shoved the drawer closed.

"Here. This explains everything."

He glanced at the pamphlet, his sweaty fist creating inky smudges. "But what are you going to do? I'm a Union member! You have to help me." He ended on a whimper and collapsed onto the chair. I hoped the slightly bent legs would hold.

"Help you do what? You signed away your rights for a mess of pottage. A really small mess."

"Can't you threaten them? Don't you have a gun? Can't you break into their office and steal the contract?"

I looked at him. "Are you crazy? I wouldn't do that for one of my *own* books."

"What *will* you do? I pay my dues. I'm entitled to help!"

Entitlement. I've heard it all. One co-author screws another. The agent hangs onto royalty checks for a year or more, but never passes along any interest. The publisher grabs e-rights by shoving them into an obscure paragraph about foreign language reprints in Guam. They all feel they're entitled to a bigger slice of the pecuniary pie because they've worked harder than anyone else.

"You're entitled to a fair contract. You're entitled to on-time royalty checks and statements. You're entitled to a decent promo budget. Heck, you're even entitled to get paid more than twice a year. Which will never happen. But you have to do the spadework first." I shoved the contract and letters across the desk. Several pages drifted to the floor.

"I was so happy to make the sale I never…the contract looked so nice, with my name on it and everything… You don't know how long I've…"

"Sure I do. Been there, written that. Which is why I got into this biz." I tossed a card at him. Handled carefully, the lettering wouldn't smear. "I got ripped off one too many times. Discovered the Union could help me level the playing field. Now, when I negotiate a contract, I avoid those nasty little clauses which give a year's worth of work a dollar value less than minimum wage. And I help other writers avoid the same potholes on the road to committing literature."

He stared at the card. "Then you're getting paid by the Union to help me!"

"Hold on there, scrivener. We're volunteers. I'm paid squatta. I'm lucky to get reimbursed for phone calls and stamps."

He looked around my office. A dingy room with a toilet down the hall that no self-respecting vulture would use, the single window permitted a narrow view of a brick building assembled by architecturally impaired nineteenth-century immigrants and allowed the gentle odors of uncollected garbage to waft in. The best attractions, however, were its low rent, paid in cash to a small furtive man on the first of every month, and its distance from my home, where several children and one husband felt it their mission from God to interrupt me every time a story took life or a deadline became imminent.

I pulled a file folder from another screeching drawer. Got to remember to bring the WD-40 tomorrow, I thought. The noise, however, drove the dingy pigeons from the windowsill.

After scanning and printing his papers, I handed Dunphy his originals. "I'll take another look," I said. "You'll hear from me. But I'm not promising anything."

Anger warred with gratitude on his face. "Those greedy encephalic spawn of hell better pay up! Thanks for your help." He shambled out of the office. I accessed my novel again and tried to coax the muse back to my shoulder.

***

Tuesday morning was already hot as I climbed the three flights to my office. A well-fed, elegantly clad gentleman waited outside the locked door. He flourished a business card while I pulled out my purse-sized Mace keychain.

"I'm Arthur Razewell Delahanty. Attorney for Edacity Publications. You must be Ms.," he peered at the inset window, "An Gor."

"What?" Several more flakes of gold lettering drifted off the rippled glass, further reducing my name. "No," I replied. "It's Dana Gore. But that's okay, Art. Easy mistake."

We entered and I waved him to the folding chair. He glanced at it, then stood next to my desk and snapped the card down. "I'm here regarding Mr. Dunphy's unfounded complaints in re Edacity."

I pulled out Dunphy's file. Delahanty's head craned over my arm. "Don't hover, okay, Art? Makes me nervous."

He moved away, still trying to read my notes. "Actually, the name's Arthur. Or Mr. Delahanty. I've never been called Art."

"Nor has anything your employer puts out. Let's get right to it, Art. What are you offering?"

He plunked down his tooled leather briefcase and abstracted papers. "According to the contract, Edacity owes Dunphy nothing." He patted the signature. "It's all legal and ironclad."

"Did anyone talk to Mr. Dunphy about this contract? Before he signed it with his blood, I mean."

Delahanty's nostrils flared. "I spent time with him going over various terms. An inordinate amount of time, I might add. For which he did not pay."

I totally revere the English language but don't object to ending sentences with prepositions. Especially when, spoken correctly, they're uppity. Ergo, I wanted to give Art what for.

"So he signed upon your advice and direction, huh? Sounds like a conflict of interest to me."

I typed in a website address and stared at the screen. "According to the database, you've been sued over twenty times. And lost. Ouch. Big time. 'Legal' and 'ironclad' might not be the best words to use, Art. Coercion, duress, misdirection, ethically challenged, those are the words which occur to me."

"You a lawyer?"

I grimaced. "Mom didn't allow such creatures in the house. And I was raised to respect my mother."

"Those contracts were different. And we didn't lose." He shuddered. "We settled. And my ethnicity has never been called into question."

"These cases don't look like they're distinguishable from Mr. Dunphy's. So what are you willing to settle upon him?"

A look of cunning flitted across Delahanty's face. "Are you empowered to negotiate binding terms for him?" He glanced around my office. "Your time must be valuable. We'd be willing to pay a substantial—" A pigeon lit on the windowsill, deposited a juicy load which hit the floor with a splat, then flew off. "A nominal amount for your services."

I smiled. "What's a nominal amount, Art?"

He quickly checked a printout. "Say, five thousand."

Seeing my face, he added, "Plus expenses, of course." I thought I heard him mutter, *like for a cleaning service*, but I ignored it.

"Hmmm. Five K plus." My eyes wandered to the ceiling. A small red light, indiscernible by Art, stared down at me. Good. The remote A/V camera was working. My oldest son hadn't disabled it yet this week.

"Sounds like a pittance, Art." I dropped my eyes to his face. "Sounds like an opening offer. A pretty insulting one."

"We could go as high as ten. Plus."

"What's in it for Mr. Dunphy?"

He held the printout at arm's length and puffed out his chest. For a moment, I was afraid he might emulate the flying rat and deposit his own billet-doux. "We're prepared to give Mr. Dunphy, once he signs all releases, the sum of $24,000."

I tapped the monitor. "These cases, Art, also list the judgments, or settlements, if you prefer. Twenty-four is a drop in the bucket." I punched in another website and pointed to the screen. "You guys stand to make millions. The cartoon alone will spawn a juvie movie mega-hit. I'll tell Mr. Dunphy, of course, but in my opinion that offer needs to be a lot sweeter."

He replaced the printout in the briefcase and snapped the locks. "I'll take that back to the principal. You'll hear from me."

I reported the offer to Walter, fended off his premature gratitude, and returned to deconstructing the traditional cozy.

I looked up. "I think your offer is pretty good." Delahanty let out his breath. "I'll take this to Mr. Dunphy tonight. Let's talk tomorrow, say, ten-ish?"

"Bring Mr. Dunphy to the publisher's office," he countered. "He can sign the releases and while they're being notarized and copied, we can celebrate. Punch and donut holes all right?"

"Faboo, Art. Now let me get to work."

As soon as he left, I ate a cookie and inspiration struck. Unfortunately, it wasn't for my book. I called my younger daughter, who immediately started squealing excitement. After a few more calls, I carefully leaned back and smiled. For once, the chair didn't squeak.

***

Friday dawned bright and clear. The ozone index was lower, the pollen count was down, and pigeon droppings were, well, dropping. Walter stuffed a donut hole in his mouth and scribbled his signature on the last page. I brushed off powdered sugar before handing it to Delahanty. The publisher sat a mile away behind his desk and beamed at us. At least, it looked like beaming. It was hard to tell. The red glow from his eyes hindered my vision.

I swigged punch as Art handed over one check with Walter's name and six figures on it. I swallowed and said, "If it were done when 'tis done, 'twere well it were done quickly."

Walter and Art looked at me. "What the heck does that mean?" Wally asked. A hundred thousand dollars had shifted his voice several octaves lower. Or maybe it was the beef.

I put down my plastic cup, met the publisher's glare, and said, "It means let's hustle to the bank, Wally, and cash that check."

"Afraid it's no good, Miss Gore?" Art sneered. "Or anxious for your cut?"

"Saving this poor man's ranch from you, Snidely Whiplash, is the only reward I need." Not my best exit line, but close.

I bustled Walter to the bank, saw the check transformed into cash, helped him open a money market account, then scooted back to the office. The faint voice of my muse could be heard above the racketing trains and belching buses.

***

Two weeks later, my door burst open. I quickly swung my feet off my desk. I had worn a skirt that day and didn't want anyone looking up my old address.

Delahanty started yelling before my feet hit the floor.

"We had a deal! He signed the releases! You helped him cash the check!"

"Why, Mr. Delahanty! You're so attractive when you scream."

He pounded on my desk, sending papers and puffs of dust flying. "I'll have you in court so fast your head will spin! Did you really think you could get away with it?"

"Get away with what?" I asked demurely.

"Wally, with your nefarious help, cut a deal with a cookie manufacturer. All kinds of cookies. Plain, frosted, filled, chock full o' nuts, you name it. All chocolate! All shaped like underpants!"

I shrugged. "So? Wally likes cookies. And please remember, he doesn't like to be called Wally."

"We *own* that character! We *own* all rights!"

I pulled Walter's file from the blessedly silent drawer. Several pigeons cooed on the windowsill. Darn. Had to get something else to shoo them away. Maybe I could find a cat.

"Says here, Edacity has the rights to the character and all publications, whether print, animated, digital, Web, or live action, in all languages in all mediums, whether now known or to be developed."

"Right! So how can he sell his character to a cookie company?"

I snapped the file shut. "He didn't."

"Did too!"

I handed a copy of Walter's newest contract to Art. "Show me where he sold the character. Or the town where the character lives. Or any pertinent detail of the character or the book."

"Underpants!" he screamed. "He sold the underpants!"

As his voice crescendoed, the pigeons flapped away in terror, leaving behind a badly soiled sill.

"The character doesn't wear underpants," I pointed out.

"That's right! That's the whole shtick! And the cookies are shaped like little Y-fronts!"

"You can't copyright a shape in literature. You ought to know that," I scolded.

"But everyone will associate the cookies with the character."

"Prove it. The character's name isn't on the cookies or the box. The book title won't be on anything. There's nothing to associate the cookies with the book. And even though my daughter and other children love the idea, Walter can't control what the kids might think."

"His endorsement is on it! The box, the cookies, the promotional literature! Slathered all over! And you put him up to it! I'm suing you, Wally, the Union, the cookie maker, the box manufacturer, the lawyer who drafted this contract—"

"I've told you for the last time." Art's mouth snapped shut at my tone. "He doesn't like to be called Wally. And I'm telling you for the first and last time. You didn't get food rights. *Your* contract language and *your* releases are specific and detailed. But you neglected to include food rights."

"It was contemplated by all parties that the rights—"

"Contemplation, shmontemplation." Boy, that was hard to say, but I managed without overtly spitting all over Art. "A judge will take one look at the four corners and rule that if you covered everything which you did cover, you also should have put in comestibles."

"We'll eat up that hundred thousand he banked and every penny he hopes to earn from that crummy contract. I'll tie him up in court till the day he dies."

"That's the way the cookie crumbles, Art. But I suggest you take a deep breath before running to the courthouse." I pointed to the ceiling.

Art stared up blindly, then noticed the tiny red light. He looked at me.

I nodded. "From your first step into this office up to this moment, a camera is recording every word, every threat." He looked around wildly.

"No, the camera isn't here, Art. It's at a security office." I crossed my fingers under my desk and hoped Art wasn't smart enough to figure out I couldn't afford a security firm.

"And it also has you," I continued, "on tape trying to bribe a Union official. Did you know that's a federal offense?"

His expression grew ugly. "You coerced Walter into holding out for more money. A grievance officer isn't supposed to do that. You pushed him into signing a cookie contract you knew was shaky at best. The Union will kick you out and the notorious publicity will keep every reputable publisher from touching you."

I spread out my hands. "I had Walter's full and informed consent for every step I took. Our contracts guy and the cookie lawyer cleared Wally's deal. Also, reputable publishers aren't really in your purview, Art. And like I said before, any publicity…"

He chewed his lip a while, then picked up his briefcase and slammed out.

The pigeons returned, twisting their heads back and forth before deciding the nasty loud man was gone, then started cooing again. I accessed my novel and scrolled down to where the village gossip had just had her neck wrung by an as-yet unknown, even to me, miscreant. Ah, bliss, thy name is writing.

Look for the Silver Lining

David Stuart Davies

A Johnny One Eye story

As a private investigator in wartime London, I can't be too choosy when it comes to the character of my clients. Times are hard enough without developing too many sensibilities about the riff-raff that cross my threshold. I need my spam and dried eggs to hold body and soul together just as much as the next man. So when I received an urgent summons from Harry Blackledge, I didn't think twice about slipping on my hat and coat and high-tailing it round to his office near White City. As far as I knew Blackledge was not a crook, but he was as shady as the biggest apple tree. He had more operations going on at the same time than a Harley Street surgeon, but I knew that his main interest was the dogs—greyhound racing. And indeed it was about the dogs that he'd requested my help. Or one dog in particular.

I was shown into his untidy office by a sharp-suited, sharp-faced minion who could have swapped features with a ferret any day and no one would have been the wiser.

Blackledge was on the telephone. He was a large man in his early forties with a ruddy damp complexion and bulging blue eyes, a candidate for a heart attack if ever I saw one. His pudgy fingers grasped the receiver tightly as he bellowed at the caller on the other end. "I don't care if your grandmother is ill. I don't care if she's got bubonic plague, get the matter sorted… or I'll sort you!"

He slammed the receiver down, his face ablaze with anger. For a moment, he didn't register my presence. When he did, his expression did not change.

"Who the hell are you?" he glowered.

"John Hawke, private detective. You wanted to see me."

"So I did." He took a run at a smile, but aimed short. His mouth turned into a weird grimace. "I've got a problem, Hawke. Silver Lining has gone missing."

"Silver Lining?"

"My champion greyhound. She's due to race on Saturday in the Frampton Cup at White City, and the damn animal's disappeared."

"She's gone walkies?"

"If I wanted a bloody comedian, I could have hired Max Miller. Look, some bastard has pinched the dog to stop her racing. They're out to ruin me. I have a packet on Silver. If she doesn't run, I will be seriously damaged. I want you to find her."

"What does she look like?" I found myself asking, as though I could tell one greyhound from the next.

Blackledge pulled a framed print from his desk drawer and handed it to me. It was easy to see why the dog had been named Silver Lining: it had a black coat with a distinctive gray streak running down its back.

"You've not contacted the police, I suppose," I said, handing the picture back.

Blackledge sneered. "You suppose right. I don't want the coppers crawling over my property. They might discover something to my disadvantage. Now, do you want the job or not?"

"You'd better tell me all about it," I said, extracting a Craven A from a very crushed packet.

"Not much to tell. The dog is kenneled with the rest of my hounds."

"Where is that?"

Blackledge narrowed his gobstopper eyes. It was obvious that he was not predisposed to reveal the whereabouts of his doggy domain, but realized with chagrin that he would have to if I was to investigate the matter. "I have a place on Warwick Road, Battersea," he said at length. When Charlie, my trainer, came to give the hounds their morning exercise today, Silver was missing. Her kennel was empty."

"Had it been broken into?"

"No. That was the strange thing about it. It was still locked."

"Looks like an inside job?"

"None of my employees would dare to double-cross me."

"Not even for money?"

"Money won't mend a broken back."

Nicely put, I thought. "Who would benefit most if the dog didn't run?"

"Why, that's easy. Titch Martindale. His mutt, Rainbow Lady, is second favorite."

In the same way I knew of Harry Blackledge, I knew of Titch Martindale. They were both from the same dodgy side of the street. In the whimsical way these types have of adopting inappropriate nicknames, Titch was actually a giant of a man, well over six feet and weighing around eighteen stone. He was certainly no titch, unless, of course, this appellation referred to a specific part of his anatomy.

"Have you challenged Titch about this?"

"No. What would be the point? He would simply deny it and laugh up his sleeve at the same time."

"I'd better take a look at your kennels and have a chat with the staff."

I could see that old Harry-boy wasn't too happy about letting me snoop around his secret premises, but he was sensible enough to realize that it was a necessary part of my investigation.

"I'll get Raymond to run you over there."

"Fine. How many people work at the kennels?"

"There's just old Charlie Pearson, my trainer, and his daughter Gloria. I'd trust both with my life."

***

It turned out that Raymond was Harry's son. However, he was far from being a chip off the old, rather unpleasant, Blackledge block. He was a young, fresh-faced lad, smartly dressed in a well-cut double-breasted suit and possessing a rather shy demeanor.

I engaged him in conversation as he drove me in a very smart sedan over to the Warwick Road kennels in Battersea. It seemed that he had hoped to join the army this year, but his father was not keen on the idea and had prevented him. "He wants me to stay in civvy street. I suppose he's just concerned that I might get hurt. Ever since my mother died two years ago, he has become very protective."

"Overprotective?" I ventured.

He smiled nervously. "You could say that. It's natural in fathers, I guess. The trouble is, he won't let me grow up. He won't let me take any responsibility or make any decisions on my own. I suppose he just doesn't want to accept that

I'm not his little boy any more. I've only just managed to get a place of my own, because he wanted me to stay at home. Was it the same with your dad?"

If only, I thought. "Not really," I said quietly. I didn't really want to open the file of John Hawke, the orphan who never knew his parents. It wouldn't help the lad, and it certainly wouldn't help me, so I decided to change the subject. "Have you any ideas who might have taken Silver Lining?"

He shook his head vigorously. "Can't say I have. It all seems strange."

"What can you tell me about Charlie Pearson and his daughter?"

"Oh, well, Charlie has worked for my dad forever. They knew each other from their school days. Apparently Charlie has always had a way with greyhounds. It's his passion in life."

"What about his daughter?"

At the mention of the girl, young Raymond's face colored. "Gloria," he said softly. "Why, she wouldn't harm a fly."

Eventually, the car turned down a cinder track and parked outside a low wooden building, situated within a stretch of wooden fencing with barbed wire trimming the top. I could see that it wouldn't take a master crook to prop a ladder up against the fencing and gain entry to the kennels.

Raymond unlocked the door of the premises and we entered, passing through the building to a stretch of ground which was set out like a small racing track. This was obviously where the hounds were put through their paces.

A tall gray-haired man wearing brown overalls approached us. "Hello, lad. Come to see our Gloria?"

Poor Raymond looked decidedly uncomfortable. "No, I've brought Mr. Hawke. He's investigating the disappearance of Silver Lining."

The man gave me a canny glance. "I wish you luck, cause I've no idea what's happened."

"When did you see the dog last?" I asked.

"Late last night. I live nearby, and I always come around ten o'clock to see if the dogs are all right, especially if there's an air raid on. The noise upsets them. All four hounds were fine. Then this morning, when I turns up with their feed and to give 'em a run, Silver was gone."

"Can you show me her kennel?"

"Certainly. Much good it may do you."

Leading the way, he took us to the far end of the track, to an old brick structure that from the outside resembled a restroom block. Inside, however, were four kennel runs, each with a padlocked iron gate. In three of the runs were dozing, indolent greyhounds who cast a dreamy disinterested eye in our direction as we stared in. One run was empty.

"As you see," said Charlie, tugging at the padlock, "it's still locked. I'm the only one with the key, and it's here on my belt. But nevertheless, the dog has bleeding well vanished."

I nodded, appreciating his succinct assessment of the situation. I examined the lock and the outside of the kennel very closely. It didn't look like the lock had been picked; there were no telltale scratches around the keyhole.

"Not got your magnifying glass with you today, Sherlock?" observed Charlie sarcastically.

"Can you open up?" I said evenly, ignoring the taunt.

"You want to go inside?"

I nodded.

For some reason, my trainer friend thought this was amusing, but nevertheless he opened up the kennel and I scrutinized the interior. There was some straw and the remains of Silver Lining's evening meal in a metal bowl. I picked up the bowl and sniffed it.

"I've got some sandwiches in the office if you're hungry," chimed in the comical trainer.

"Hungry dogs, greyhounds, aren't they?" I asked. "All that running, using up so much energy."

"Certainly are," replied Charlie. "Bite your hand off sometimes to get at their grub."

"And yet this dish of dog food is nearly full. It seems that Silver Lining has hardly touched it."

"What! Let me see." There was no whimsy in his behavior now.

I handed Charlie the metal dish and he examined the contents. "This isn't her usual mash. This is something else." He sniffed it. "Gah, this is not right."

Raymond, who had been standing back in the shadows, came forward. "What do you mean?"

"I mean it's been tampered with," snapped the trainer.

"The dog was probably drugged," I said. "It's easier to deal with a sleeping dog than with one who is ready to bark. Who prepares the feed?"

"You've got five minutes," he said, puffing on a large cigar. He was indeed a huge man, with wild red hair, startling blue eyes, and a pork sausage for a nose.

I told him who I was, and of the disappearance of Silver Lining, but not about the ransom note. He seemed genuinely surprised.

"There's no love lost between Harry Blackledge and me, but I think this is terrible." He paused and then, as though the penny had dropped, his demeanor and complexion changed. "Hang on a minute, mister, I hope you aren't suggesting that I had anything to do with the job. I can tell you, I've got no need to go half-inching his bleeding mutt. My Rainbow Lady will leave Silver Lining standing."

"I just wondered if you had any idea who might have wanted to snatch the dog. You have a reputation for keeping your ear to the ground, having your finger on the pulse."

Titch tossed me a sarcastic grin. "You're a sweet-talking fellow, aren't you?"

I returned the grin. "I try."

"Well, let me tell you, Mister Hawke, despite rumors to the contrary, on the whole the greyhound racing fraternity are straight. It's a sport, for Christ's sake. Where's the sport in nobbling your opponent? I know nothing."

Strangely, I believed him. I rose to go, but he held up his hand to delay me.

"Let me tell you this. Go back to Harry Blackledge and give him my deepest sympathies. I hope the dog turns up so it's able to run on Saturday. I want the satisfaction of seeing his face when my little beauty leaves Silver Lining standing in the traps."

When I returned to the car, Raymond was on the pavement outside, pacing up and down.

"Any joy?" he asked as I approached.

"Could be," I replied.

He looked surprised, and then expectant, as though I was about to divulge my thoughts. I ignored the invitation.

"Where to now?" he said at length.

"I've finished for the moment, Raymond. I need to do some thinking on my own. I do that best when I'm walking. Do you have your home number where I could contact you?"

Raymond looked hesitant, and then produced a card with his address and telephone number.

"Are you sure I can't drop you anywhere?"

"Certain. You go back and tell your dad that things are coming along fine."

I watched the shiny sedan disappear into the distance and lit a cigarette. I pulled a sheet of paper from my pocket and looked at it. I had a theory. It was built of twigs and cardboard and bits of straw and would probably fall down at the slightest puff of wind, but it was all I had and, rare for me, I believed in it. In order to strengthen its foundations, I needed to have a chat with Gloria.

I walked for a while until I caught sight of a taxi and flagged it down. In less than half an hour, I was back in the untidy office where Gloria spent her time. She had finished filing her nails. Now she was painting them.

I asked if I could chat with her for a while, and she seemed glad of the company. There didn't seem to be any pressing business to attend to, apart from applying the nail polish.

"Have you any ideas or suspicions about Silver Lining's disappearance?" I said, sitting back on a battered old armchair near the noisy little gas fire, which kept popping at irregular intervals.

Gloria rolled her pretty blue eyes. "Not a clue. It's a real mystery."

"It certainly is," I agreed with a wry smile. "But you like mysteries, don't you, like *Rebecca*? Good film, that. Did you guess the ending?"

Her face lit up at the mention of the movie. "Oh, no. I thought Maxim was a wife murderer, a sort of Bluebeard, y'know."

I grinned. "Where is it on? I wouldn't mind seeing it again."

"At the Astoria."

"You go with a friend."

"My boyfriend, yes."

"Raymond, d'you mean?"

She laughed. "No, not Raymond. With my feller, Rod. He's a boxer. A real hunk."

"Oh, I thought that you were seeing Raymond."

"We went dancing a couple of times, but it was nothing serious. On my part anyway. I think he was keen, but he's just a kid. No more than a lapdog for his dad. I go for real men like Rod."

"I think that Raymond still carries a torch for you."

"Well, he's wasting his time. He's a nice enough lad, but he's still in short pants as far as I'm concerned. I told him he'd have to prove to me he was a real man before I looked at him again."

Whatever else Gloria was, she was a straight talker.

Strangely, my interview had disheartened me, because it had only strengthened my theory. Certainly, if my hunch was right, I was very close to finding Silver Lining.

It was late afternoon by now and, before taking the investigation further, I popped into a bar to wet my whistle and have a little think. I played about with the pieces of the puzzle in my mind and, no matter how I arranged them, they still presented the same picture. Hey ho, I thought, as I drained my pint, let's get this over with.

I caught another cab to Kirton Close, a pleasant road not far from the offices of Harry Blackledge. It was where Raymond had his little *pied a terre*. The shiny sedan was outside. Extracting my trusty bit of wire from my wallet, I applied my skills to unlocking the trunk. After less than a minute, the black lid sprang open. I put my head inside and sniffed. The smell was unmistakable.

Raymond's house was a tidy little row house on the end, with a path down the side which led to a small garden at the rear. At the far end of the garden was a small hut. I approached it quietly and listened. There was no sound. I tapped gently on the door. Suddenly there was a shuffling noise, followed by a muted whimpering.

***

Raymond was surprised to see me on his doorstep. Surprised, and not a little apprehensive.

"Have you come for me to help you with your detective work?" he asked brightly.

"In a way," I said. "I've come for Silver Lining."

***

Raymond ran his fingers wildly through his hair. "It was a stupid idea that got out of hand. I didn't really mean to go this far. I… I just got carried away." It was a few moments later, and we were sitting in Raymond's neat sitting room. I offered him a cigarette, but he declined. "Tell me about it," I said, lighting up.

"I just wanted to prove… I just wanted to show that I could do something daring on my own," he said, his voice full of misery.

"Prove to who? To Gloria?"

He nodded. "To Gloria. To my dad. And I suppose to me, too. Gloria said I was like a little boy and my father treated me like one—always wrapping me up in cotton wool. I just wanted to show them what I was capable of. I know now I was stupid. I never thought through the consequences of what I did."

"Tell me about it."

"You mean…"

"How you did it."

For a moment, a smile flickered on his lips. "I wanted it to appear mysterious. I loosened some sections of the perimeter fence to the kennels, just enough to allow me and the dog through. Then, just before midnight, I slipped inside and got into the kennels. I'd been working on the mortar of the gate of Silver's run for a few days, so it was easy to slip the bricks out and loosen the gate away from its moorings. I didn't want to use a key. I thought it might throw suspicions on Charlie or Gloria and get them into trouble. Besides, it was more daring this way. I'd brought some drugged dog meat and put it in Silver's dish. That was another dramatic touch, really. I didn't let her eat it. She was used to me and came quietly without any fuss."

"And then you hid her in the trunk of the car and drove her home, and now she's in the garden shed."

Raymond nodded. "It was only then that I realized I hadn't planned what to do next."

"Sure. You can hardly tell your father. He'd probably burst a blood vessel, and I reckon Gloria isn't going to be too impressed with someone who steals his own father's greyhound, not when she's got Rod, the bulging boxer."

"Rod Merrison? Is she going out with him now?"

"'Fraid so."

Raymond's face melted into the glummest of expressions. "I am a fool. I guess they were right. I am like a little boy. And I made things worse by writing the ransom note. Well, I thought I ought to come out of this with something like £500. I intended to put the dog back. I wouldn't harm her for the world."

It took all my strength not to pat him on the back and ruffle his hair. "You have talent and initiative," I said. "I guess you just haven't pointed them in the right direction yet. I reckon you need to persuade your dad to let you join up. They can use lads like you in the forces. If he says no, enlist anyway. You're old enough."

He brightened a little. "I… I think you're right, but…" The shoulders sank once again, and the furrowed brow returned. "But what am I going to do about Silver Lining?"

"We're going to put her back later tonight."

"You… mean you're not going to spill on me? Tell my dad, the cops?"

I shrugged. "What would be the point? Let's just ladle the spilt milk back into the bottle, eh?"

A flurry of emotions raced across his features: surprise, relief, joy, gratitude, and then a kind of dismay. "How did you know it was me who'd snatched the dog? Was I that transparent?"

"Intuition, I guess, mixed with a few clues."

"Like what?" The young fellow was getting belligerent now.

"Like the ransom note was typed on the typewriter on your desk. It blocks out the spaces in the letters *e* and *a*."

Raymond's mouth dropped open. "You checked."

"It seemed appropriate. And then there was your obvious attraction to Gloria. I could see that you wanted to be 'a man' for her. Were you going to invite her round and show her what you'd done?"

I'd hit the nail on the head, and he grinned sheepishly. "You are a detective, aren't you?"

I reckon, in these grim roustabout days, praise doesn't come any higher.

Around eleven o'clock that night, we sneaked through the fence at the kennels with a dozing Silver Lining and returned her to her billet. She looked happy to be back, and she soon curled up for a good night's sleep.

***

Raymond drove me home to Priory Court, my home base, just off Tottenham Court Road. He thanked me profusely for helping him and we shook hands. "Off you go, Corporal Blackledge," I said cheerily. "You go and give the Germans what for."

Twenty minutes later, I rang his father. It was nearly one in the morning. A harsh, irritated, sleep-drugged voice rasped down the phone at me. "Who the hell is it? Do you know what time it is?"

"This is John Hawke, and it is 12:51 precisely."

"Is this some kind of joke? What the hell do you want?"

"Just to inform you that you'll receive two shocks in the morning. Silver Lining has been returned to the kennels safe and sound, and I shall be around to see you with my bill for services rendered."

"You found Silver Lining!" His voice went up an octave.

"Yes."

"This is on the level?"

"Yes."

"Why, that's bloody wonderful. Where was she? Who had her?"

"You don't really need to know, Mr. Blackledge. Just be satisfied that you've got the dog back and she's none the worse for her little holiday."

"You mean you're not going to tell me."

"No. We detectives have our code, you know."

There was a pause on the line, and then the voice came back softer and kinder. "She's really back, my little Silver?"

"She is. Good night, Mr. Blackledge. Sweet dreams," I said, replacing the receiver.

I poured myself a whiskey, turned off the lights, and drew the curtains back. I could see, far away across the rooftops, fingers of light searching the sky for enemy aircraft. It seemed that they were searching in vain. It was going to be a quiet night. I finished my whiskey and went to bed.

Dodie Golightly and the Ghost of Cock Lane

Paul Magrs

London, 1968

Dodie

The studio was somewhere between Smithfield and Holborn, in a strange, wonky lane hidden from the main road. Timothy Bold kept laughing because it was called "Cock Lane," but our Timothy's always had a puerile sense of humor. Cassie said it was a dark, wicked part of London: near the location of old Newgate Gaol. A place full of secrets and never-solved mysteries.

Dear Cassie—my loyal assistant—was only trying to cheer me up with this talk of macabre things. We were actually visiting the studios in Cock Lane for a very prosaic reason. Timothy had a friend at a London Radio station who was keen to interview me about my work. I had a new book out and so I thought, why not? Though I really loathe doing these publicity things. I'd rather be home back in Manchester dreaming up my next mystery.

So there we were, deep under Cock Lane, in a boxy, airless room with no natural light. Talking to a fellow called Keith who claimed to be a great fan of mine. He was hairy and burly in a nasty caftan and I didn't like the way he kept devouring me with his pinhole eyes.

It was only when Timothy came back from the toilets looking terrified that things perked up.

"There's a loudspeaker in the lavs," he said. "And you can hear what's being broadcast live. And I heard something! Something really weird…"

Keith was playing a lengthy piece of what he called progressive rock and had lit up a drug-flavored cigarette, so we had time to ask Timothy what on earth he was talking about. He looked really rattled, standing there in his cream turtleneck jumper and his purple flares.

"It was a… a… scratching noise… You could hear it, really distinctly, all the way through your interview with Keith, Dodie. And then… then there was this horrible, hollow laughter, too! I thought I was imagining it. But it went on and on… for about a minute. It was definitely there."

By my side, the evanescent Cassandra had perked up at this mention of something spooky. She loves anything like this, as well she might. "Ask him if it was a woman's laughter, or a man's!" she urged me. Poor Cassie. She's dependent upon me for making her thoughts and feelings known in the outside world. But generally I am happy to pass the poor dear's messages on.

"Cassie asks if it was a man or a woman laughing."

Keith the DJ frowned through his dirty-looking hair. "Who's Cassie?"

Timothy said, "Tell Cassie it was a woman. A crazy, bonkers, shrieking woman. That's what I heard."

The DJ sagged in his seat and sighed dismally. "So! She's at it again. We've had complaints, you know. Our listeners are hearing this quite a lot. Shrieking laughter. They think it's us being funny or avant-garde, but it isn't. Apparently there's a hideous scratching noise, coming over the airwaves. It's her. It's that bloody woman!"

His progressive rock record was coming to a turgid ending and he'd have to return to his program any second. Before we lost him, I asked, "Who? What woman?"

Keith's face went very dark. "It's Scratching Fanny. She was once very famous in these parts."

***

We're a great team, that's what we are.

Obviously, I'm the most effective in terms of solving actual mysteries, but that's to be expected. Cassandra is great moral support and, being dead, she's limited in what she can actually bring to the table. (For the longest time, the poor, dear thing didn't actually realize she was dead. She can be quite a ditz. Discovering her own moribund status came as quite a blow, but she's mostly over it now, I believe. She's a very buoyant, cheery type.) Timothy is a glamorous, hedonistic, rather famous, idiotic boy. We were at school together and I adore him, of course. But he really is an idiot, and he's usually the one who gets us embroiled in adventures and whatnot.

That afternoon—following my radio interview in Cock Lane—we separated: Timmy off to the King's Road boutiques to blow a wad of cash, as he delightfully put it; Cassandra to swoop and saunter around the ether, having an investigative rummage of her own, and myself to the British Library. I had a yen to do a spot of research on this Cock Lane phantom. With a couple of hours to kill under the august dome of the Reading Room, I could think of nothing more pressing than this business of Scratching Fanny. Yes, that is indeed what they called the ghost. It was back in the eighteenth century: everything was a good deal coarser in those days.

Later, in a King's Road coffee bar, I was sharing my insights with the others. "Samuel Johnson left the best account, as is to be expected."

Timmy slurped his frothy coffee from a smoked glass cup and gave every appearance of never having heard of Dr. Johnson.

"That summer of '17— the ghost of Cock Lane was the height of fashion," I explained. "The theatres, pubs and coffee houses would empty early, each evening, according to the good Doctor. The public flocked to one particular small, shabby wooden house hidden away on Cock Lane. And here there was a family whose lodgers had recently departed. One difficult, drunken woman had died of the scarlet fever—Mrs. Fanny Kemp—and apparently it was her ghost who had come back and was causing such a rumpus. Her slovenly widower had absconded, leaving their landlord and his young family to cope with the haunting and the hullaballoo and the sudden fame that a noisy apparition caused…"

Well, Cassie's eyes were aglow at the sound of all of this. She loved hearing anything about ghosts. It made her feel validated, I suppose.

Timothy's eyes were flitting around the coffee bar, checking out girls at the other tables. His attention span was appalling.

Cassie was staring at me. "Do you think this ghost of Mrs. Kemp could still be there? Still scratching away on Cock Lane?"

I'd looked at maps. I'd compared the tidy, perfect lines of the modern-day A-to-Z with the old, hand-drawn scrawl of the street maps of two hundred years ago. It seemed plain to me: the studio we had visited this morning was almost exactly on the spot of the house where Fanny Kemp had expired.

We sail around the rooftops and chimney stacks together, cooling ourselves in the streaming clouds and taking a lovely, calm aerial view of the twisting streets and their human congestion. Together we perch on the roof of the old church nearby. "And now you're haunting Cock Lane, too," I point out. "Like Fanny, you're unable to rest easy…"

"Sometimes I think I'll never leave this place," sobs young Elizabeth. "It's all so sad. We all died in Newgate, you know? Father, mother, me and my brother? We were carted off there for fraud."

"What?" There's a horrible stab of dread in my gut. "What happened?"

"For a little while we were the toast of the town. You can see the kerfuffle for yourself down there. Dad selling tickets so folk can sit up all night, watching me trying to sleep. Everyone listening to the scratching and screams… Well, soon the tide of opinion turned against us. They found us out, they said. We were evil fraudsters and connivers and flaunters of counterfeit spirits. They carted us off—not very far—to the old gaol and left us there to rot. And rot we did. I never saw my mum and dad or my brother again. I'm the only one who came back to relive those times, every night, again and again… And sometimes I think it will never stop. And that screaming and scratching will fill my head forever…"

Oh, that poor dear little girl. We'll try to sort it all out. Me and my friend Dodie. We come from the future! We come from two hundred years hence! But the little girl isn't very reassured, really. She sighs heavily and launches herself off the church rooftop, dwindling away through the fumy air. "Thank you for even listening," she tells me, and suddenly she's gone.

Dodie

It was a long night listening to Brontosaurus, whose tunes, I realized early on, were not very catchy. Their band's name was quite apt, I remarked to Timothy Bold. "Oh?" he said, distracted by chatting up their girlfriends. "Plodding and quite long," I told him, but he wasn't really listening.

Keith the DJ was there, rolling his funny cigarettes and nodding like he was having all kinds of profound thoughts. "Hey, man," he said to me. "Has your friend Cassie told you anything more about our haunting?"

Cassie hadn't reported back at this point, so I took the opportunity to ask our chunky friend what he himself knew about this phantom. "You already knew her name?"

"She's a legend here," he said. "Everyone who's recorded or broadcast from these studios has reported strange noises, one time or another. People usually think it's rats from the sewers getting into the basement. But it's not. We hear her voice sometimes, just like your Timothy did. There was one famous phone-in DJ who was so freaked out that he left and never came back. Gary's was a successful show, but he was really scared. She got into his head."

I asked our DJ friend if there would be any recordings in their archive of such visitations. As the droning, wibbling, dreadful music of Brontosaurus continued to maunder on behind the glass partition, my new friend looked shifty. "Our archive is chaotic. Just a room filled with boxes of old tape. But!" And here he looked rather cunning. "Some of us have made a point of keeping this Scratching Fanny material separate. It's important, somehow. Heavy and deep. I mean, it's communications from the other side, isn't it?"

I pursed my lips. "I rather think it is."

He beetled his eyebrows. "And you clearly believe in all this jazz, don't you? Because of your having a ghostly assistant of your own?"

"Precisely," I said, without a smidgen of embarrassment. A year into our investigating partnership, and Cassandra's phantom status was a mere matter of fact to me.

Keith went on. "I've often thought we ought to get someone in… to look into this business. I mean, it's disruptive and frightening sometimes… but it's something we need to understand, isn't it? There might be all kinds of wonderful stuff to be learned from a spirit like the one that's haunting us…"

I was more impressed by this sentiment of his than anything else I'd learned about our host so far. I asked if he could locate this special tape that he'd squirreled away. "The bootleg Fanny tape?" he asked grinning sheepishly, and scurried off to some unknown corner to find it.

I sat watching the band playing beyond the window in a fug of exotic smoke. Timothy Bold was canoodling with some of the girls on the beanbags in the control room. I caught his eye and waved him over. "Sorry about that, Dodie." He grinned at me. For all his messing around, he's a sweet boy. Quite innocent in some ways. He couldn't see that dolly birds like those were only interested in using his fame and glamour to further their own ambitions. He just thought all these people were fond of him on a personal level, and I could see him—one day soon—coming a cropper as a result of his naivete. I was keeping a keen eye on him and sometimes felt like his nanny.

"That ensemble looks marvelous on you," he told me, but I didn't have time for flattery: I knew I looked fabulous in my catsuit and poncho. At this very moment, Keith came bustling back in with several cans of tape. I explained quickly to Timmy what it was.

"Cool," he grinned. He'd become quite keen on psychic-research-type stuff since learning about Cassandra last winter. My dear assistant had piqued his interest in a way that wasn't quite the one she might have wanted, but any attention at all from Tim was okay by her. My two best friends were locked into a strange kind of off-on romance, with him more off than on, due to his not being about to see, hear, or sense her at all. It was bittersweet, really.

It took some moments for Keith to get the tapes threaded into an old reel-to-reel machine. By then Brontosaurus had mercifully terminated their endless number, and the last chords were still ringing in our ears as they entered the control booth to find us not at all interested in what they had just been playing. The gruff lady engineer Moira told them they could break for ten minutes, and they clustered round to see what we were up to.

"It's a ghost caught on tape," said Keith, and thunked down the heavy button that turned the spools.

All at once we heard the voice of Gary, the famous talk DJ who had reportedly left his job as a result of the haunting. He was jaunty and cajoling at first, as the conversation began.

"Look, this is kind of hard to believe… and who do you think you are, anyway? Interrupting my callers like that? Talking over everyone? How did you even get through? Sally on the switchboard says she didn't connect you…"

"I'm a bloody spirit, ain't I?" came a chilling, screeching voice.

One thing I was sure about, the very instant I heard it. That wasn't a voice coming down a phone line. That was coming through the ether, and no mistake. There's a particular sparkling, hollow quality to those dead voices. I shot a look at Timothy, and all the color had drained out of his dear face. This was exactly the voice he had heard in the lavatory earlier today, come back to wipe the smile off his face.

The Brontosaurus boys were amazed and agog.

"Are you saying you are a ghost?" asked the famous phone-in host. "Are you haunting us now? But, when did you live?"

The lights in the studio flickered and dimmed for a second, as if in response to the recording, as the woman's voice came back on. "I'm here now and I've always been here, as long as can be. Ever since he did me in, that bastard, and told everyone I'd died of scarlet fever."

"You were murdered?" asked the DJ. "Are you saying you're out for revenge?"

She laughed. "Too late for that, innit? He got away scot-free. I tried to get the message through, and my poor old landlord… he tried his best to get everyone listening to what I had to say. But people don't listen, really. They like the thrill and the scare of it all. But they ain't really listening. And they dragged that family away, jealous that they'd made a few bob from the haunting… They was getting above their station, so they chucked 'em all in Newgate in the end. Said they was lying. I guess I was to blame for that… They never really believed that poor little girl. Said the scratching and the shrieking was all her doing…"

The DJ piped up again, "Uh, I'm not really following your story. Try to be more clear if you want us to understand."

It was true that her voice was sounding rather slurred. She sounded like a drunk on the line, losing her thread and raving. "I'm Scratching Fanny!" she howled. "I was famous in these parts! Back in my day! Not while I was alive—oh no! No bastard came to see me then. But when I was dead—then they flocked! Then they couldn't get enough of me! All those mighty gentleman of Fleet Street and the coffee houses of Mayfair. They came elbowing into my bedroom then, didn't they? They wanted to listen to me then…"

The lights were dimming once more, and the voice on the tape was breaking up. "Fanny? Fanny?" called the DJ. "Are you there? Are you still there?"

But the conversation was over, and he was left with white noise. Keith clicked the tape off. "Twelve times she phoned in to his show. I think that time was the most coherent she ever got. Our friend Gary—the call-in host—got obsessed and freaked out, as I say. He said he started hearing her voice everywhere he went."

One of the Brontosaurus boys said, "It's really far out. Can we put it on our track? Like, subliminally winding through our track? That would be amazing."

Suddenly Keith looked annoyed. "No! We daren't make it public… This recording spreads bad karma. I'm thinking perhaps it was a mistake to play it aloud even briefly…" He glanced at the still-flickering lights in the bunker.

"I'm glad you played it for us," I told him. "It's very helpful."

Cassandra

I arrive back in the studio just in time to hear the end of that recording. It gives me the shivers in a way that meeting poor Elizabeth in the ghostly flesh never did.

Dodie takes me aside and I quickly tell her everything I have learned tonight.

"Oh, that poor girl!" my soft-hearted employer gasps. "She was forced to endure a violent haunting, and then the indignity of all of fashionable London crowding into her house and her room, and then they all turned against her. They doubted her so much they threw her in gaol. Until she died?"

I confirm this. "It's a ghastly story. But there's worse, too, Dodie. I hovered around a bit longer, sifting through the permeable layers of months and years… watching that taunting crowd visit the slum dwellings of Cock Lane. I think the worst thing was that they put her to the test."

Dodie frowns. "How?"

"They strapped poor Elizabeth down, hands and feet. So she couldn't budge an inch. It was cruel. They wanted to hear if the noise still came. They wanted to be sure that she wasn't doing it herself. They assumed she was just seeking attention, and enjoying all of this…"

Dodie shakes her head. "And the noises still came?"

"Of course. Fanny was real. But it didn't stop the so-called investigators stripping off the girl's night-things to see if she was concealing something underneath her stays. She was mortified. And there was, indeed, a small piece of wood that she kept encased in her undergarments, and they said she was a faker and a charlatan. They said she rapped and scratched on that piece of wood.

"Why did she have that wood under there? I wish I could have asked her, but the girl-ghost was gone by then. I watched as those men dragged her out of her room, triumphantly shouting and waving this small piece of wood in the air. They had found the true ghost! They had exposed her! And her parents fell back in shock, horrified that they had been taken in… and even worse—that they had taken so much money for a fraud…"

Dodie is very clever, of course. She snaps her fingers. "I've seen this before. Even in real hauntings, when outsiders come to look for evidence, the victims feel obliged to fake the effects, just to give everyone something to listen to. Just in case the ghost fails to show."

I nod. I've been thinking something similar. Besides, there was no way all that hullabaloo could have been caused by that little piece of wood she had strapped in her corsets. "But all those men felt silly, you see. Flocking there and getting scared. They felt embarrassed at quaking and getting excited. They decreed that a fraud had been committed. Money had been extorted. And so someone had to pay."

"And all the family were taken off to Newgate…"

I tell Dodie, "I've an idea. About how we might give poor Elizabeth… and maybe even Fanny herself… a little bit of peace."

Dodie grins at me. "Do tell, dear heart!"

I like it when she calls me that, I must say.

Dodie

The little church was still there, at the other end of Cock Lane. It was set back from the winding street, its roof partially fallen in and the small cemetery sunken, overgrown, neglected. The whole place had the appearance of being about to be swallowed up by the dark heart of ancient London. In short, ghastly.

An hour before dawn we ventured out of the studios, along Cock Lane, and broke our way into the crypt. I know: insane. But I had a scent. I had things I needed to follow up. We had a conclusion to come to.

And so we crept along the forgotten, twisted route of Cock Lane with the spires and towers of the City of London crowding above our heads and blocking the view of the sodium-lit skies.

Keith the DJ, Timothy Bold, the members of Brontosaurus, two of their lady friends, myself, and the mostly-invisible, ethereal form of Cassandra. In the darkness she looked just like the cool silver bubbliness of a gin and tonic, poured into the shape of a girl.

We got Brontosaurus to do the strong-arm stuff, though they were actually rather willowy boys. Their lead singer was a bit excited, hoping they might get a song out of this adventure.

The doors crumbled damply under their slight weight. The broken stones sepulchres feet seemed to be sinking and squelching with every step we took.

Keith shone his torch around the cramped cellar. "It looks as messy as our archive room" he breathed, and so it did. There were catafalques and sepulchers everywhere you turned. Tombs of all kinds were listing and slumping drunkenly, as if there had been an earthquake that had dislodged everyone from their slumbers. But there'd been no earthquake. Just time itself. Time dislodges us all in the end, I thought bleakly. The whole place had the feeling of a shop after a closing sale, with the last few unwanted items lying strewn and discarded in the dark.

Timothy Bold found the stone with Fanny's name on it. He's got a very keen eye, that boy.

"What do we do now?" he asked nervously, anxious about the grave mold and green slime he was getting on his pale slacks. "Some kind of ceremony or prayer to appease her soul?"

I shook my head. "No, we open her up, and we learn the truth."

They all looked pretty reluctant to indulge in a spot of grave-robbing. The Brontosaurus boys protested that they weren't sure about all that Van Helsing jazz. I was rather hoping we wouldn't have to stake anyone through the heart, but you never know. It's best to be prepared. I reflected that I could have asked the drummer for one of his drumsticks, which I might have sharpened to a ready point, just in case. But I really didn't think we were dealing with vampires here.

The boys and the two girls crowded round the tomb and heaved and pushed at the worn stone that covered her up. What a fancy grave, I thought, for some simple, common woman who screamed and ranted in an obscure corner of Cock Lane. She was infamous, though, I supposed. In her time, she had brought a crowd to her door.

The stone gave and there was the most horrible squeal as the tomb yawned open. My helpers gasped and panted and exerted themselves splendidly. Cassie peered over my shoulder as I trained my torch beam into the inky hole.

Fanny was glaring back at me.

Quite still. Completely dead. I jumped at first, and so did everyone else. But she wasn't budging an inch, thank goodness.

A haughty, hatchet-like countenance. Furious. Stymied.

And perfect. There wasn't a blemish on her face, and her hair and talons had continued to grow.

"Perfectly preserved…" Cassie sighed.

"Hmm, so it wasn't scarlet fever," I told them all. "If she'd died of the fever, this casket would contain liquefied remains. Fanny would have been reduced many years ago to a hideous, reeking broth."

Timmy blinked at me. "But she's perfect!"

"Arsenic," I told him. "She tried to tell everyone, didn't she? Her husband fed her that mixture of beer and gin and poison. He brought it to her bed every night and so he did her in. And that's why Fanny was screaming and scratching every night. That's why she haunted this street all this time. And that's what she wanted us to know."

We stared at her face. I wasn't sure if it was the dawn light coming through the transom windows, high up on the crypt walls, but maybe her rictus-like expression was softening? Maybe it was less furious and more resigned?

Brontosaurus took photos of themselves clustered around the tomb, but I didn't really approve of that. I urged them to cover her up again, and we left, just as a soft magenta light was creeping over the city.

"Those poor women," Dodie sighed, floating alongside me.

Timothy was sniffing the morning air. "Hang on… Can you smell bacon sandwiches?"

Sharon Leigh Takes Texas

Sandra Murphy

"I signed your skip jumper over to the sheriff's office. They'll wire the money. My share better be in my account in two days. I'm on day three of the payment grace period for the Mustang." I shifted around on the car seat as I passed a slow-moving RV. I shouldn't argue with a knucklehead, drive seventy miles an hour, and talk on the phone at the same time. "I swear to gawd, Jimmy Lee, I will not ever tart up like this again. Find somebody else to do your bounty hunting. Oh hell, these pantyhose just gave me a wedgie."

"Don't get your panties in a bunch." Jimmy Lee laughed. "Maybe it's time for some queen size pantythingers, you think? Don't fret, we like our gals big in Texas. Why'n't you come on down for a little visit, sugar?"

"If I do, you'll be sorry. And just so you know, I'm not wearing panties." Let him think about that for a while. You can't slam down a cell phone, but I got in the last word. He deserved it.

That little chat took place back in September, when Jimmy Lee talked me into doing "a little job" for him. Come Christmas, I still didn't have my money. The snow in the Midwest was heavier than ever, due to that global warming. Everybody talks about it, but nobody does much to fix it. The first day the roads were clear, I hopped into the Mustang, yep, still had it, and headed for Texas, home of Jimmy Lee, one of the biggest scoundrels God ever created. I'm Sharon Leigh, Jimmy's ex-wife. How I ever got talked into marrying that man, I'll never know. Liquor might have been involved. Sharon Leigh Lee. Must have been liquor and lots of it.

I've been here a couple of weeks now, got part of my money, a taste for tequila and tamales, and no reason to head north. I can do PI work most anywhere. Thing is, I have to work a number of hours with a local investigator to get my own license down here. That's a drawback and a half since Jimmy Lee is not only my ex, now he's my boss. Well, whoopee and sing hallelujah.

Tuesday, the office was boring as all-get-out. I was desperate enough to call time and temperature just to hear another voice when the phone rang. For a second, I wondered if time and temperature had called me.

"Lee and Leigh Private Investigative Services, what problem can we solve for you?" Stupid-ass slogan, but Jimmy Lee insists. I didn't point out that Private Investigative Services was often shortened to PIS.

An almost silent voice whispered, "I need to see you."

I whispered back, "Okay, why's that?"

"Go to the dumpster, throw out the trash."

"How will I know you? Should we have a secret signal?" Okay, I was just messing with her, but gawd, really? Cloak-and-dagger in this dinky town?

"How many people do you think will be out there?" Her voice got a little loud.

"Sorry, I'll be right…" She'd hung up, so I guess that plan worked for her.

I took the sports section from Jimmy Lee's desk and wadded each page up in a big ball to stuff in the trash bag. Truthfully, it was the most fun I'd had all day. I locked the front door and headed out back.

As I tossed newsprint tumbleweeds into the trash one by one, the whispering started from behind the dumpster. "Somebody's been in my house. My car. Reading my mail."

"You want me to find out if it's really happening?"

"*No!* I want you to make him quit!" Her voice headed for a scream, but skidded to a stop and reversed into a whisper. "My things have been moved, but nothing's missing. I sent my cat, Jorge, to stay with my sister. I was afraid whoever's doing this might hurt him."

"Alright, calm down. I'll come to your house, check for bugs, set little traps, and like that. We'll figure this out."

"If he's watching the house, he'll know. He might escalate."

"You've been watching *CSI*, haven't you?"

She paused. "*Criminal Minds*."

"Okay, what *would* you be comfortable with?"

"Go to the diner. In an hour. Act like we haven't seen each other since college. We'll build up to you coming by my place. The University of Missouri, they call it Mizzou. That's where I went. I had to come home after two years to take care of my momma."

"How will you recognize me?"

"You'll be the only one I don't know."

***

I got a peek as she stepped from behind the dumpster and melted into the shadows. Well, I looked up Mizzou, mascot a tiger named Truman, colors black and gold, about halfway between Kansas City and St. Louis according to Google Maps. Veterinary teaching hospital. Good rep. Go Tigers!

An hour later, I strolled into the diner and grabbed a table for two. Although it looked like I studied the menu, I really scanned the crowd. It was two o'clock, so the late lunchers were in a hurry to get back before their pay got docked.

A few minutes later, a thirtyish woman came in. Everybody said howdy-hi as she made her way between tables. She told an older woman a book she'd requested was in and on hold, come by any time. A librarian then.

People invited her to have a seat, but she waved her book and kept walking. A casual scan for a table turned into, "Oh my gosh, Sharon Leigh, is that you? It's me, Allie? From Mizzou?"

I followed her lead, jumped up, and yelled, "Allie! You look just the same as the last time I saw you!" That was the truth. I'd had that glimpse an hour ago, and yep, she looked just the same as then.

We did the obligatory hug and squee, dancing from one foot to the other as if we couldn't get over the coincidence of meeting again. She turned to face the other diners and announced, "Hey, y'all, this here's my friend, Sharon Leigh, from up in Missouri. Y'all be nice to her, hear?" A few hollered back, "Hey, Sharon Leigh."

"Why don't you skip your book and sit with me?" I lowered my voice. "Good enough?"

"Sure, I've got an hour for lunch today."

After our chef salads arrived (dressing on the side, ranch for me, honey mustard for her), she mumbled around mixed greens and hard-boiled eggs to tell me she thought someone was following her, had been for weeks. She'd never spotted anyone, couldn't prove somebody'd been in the house, but she knew, just knew, they had.

Conversation got derailed a few times as people passed on the way to the restrooms or when Velma, the server, dropped by with refills of sweet tea or extra napkins and more crackers. I'm partial to club crackers, but the cellophane evidence of just how many I ate vanished as the silent busboy whisked the wrappers away. Allie and I did forty-five minute's worth of the Q&A dance before she had to leave.

She laid cash on the table. I stayed to finish my tea. And maybe a side order of bacon for dessert. The smell of it put me in dire need of a fried fix. About halfway down the aisle, she turned and said, "Hey, Sharon Leigh, where are my manners? Why don't you come by my place later? I'll get out my yearbook and we can make fun of the hairdos we had for picture day, remember?" I nodded, she said the address and left. No one followed her.

***

Seven o'clock found me in front of a small house, not the tiny kind, but not family-sized either. I was surprised Texas houses didn't have basements. Where do people hide when tornados hit? After the deadbolt clicked and the chain guard rattled, Allie peeked out. "Cute place you've got here," I said. She held a note where I could see it. "Bugs, cameras?" I nodded.

"Come on in. It was my momma's. Remember? I had to leave school to take care of her? Well, she passed about a year later."

"You must have loved her a lot." I strolled around the room, checking books on the shelves and knickknacks on end tables. No cameras that I could see.

"She was a difficult woman. Being sick made it worse," she said. "I don't miss her much. Mostly, I relish the quiet. Hey, you want some coffee or a Coke?"

I said sure to a Coke, but didn't know what to say when she asked what kind. Texans, a strange bunch compared to Midwesterners. I guess they think the same of us, what with one level of our houses being underground and us having six different names for a soft drink. I snooped while she got glasses and ice and floated endless chatter my way from the kitchen. I uh-huhhed and no-wayed in appropriate places. After a bit of searching, I got out the gizmo that detects eavesdropping equipment and wandered through the living room and into the eat-in kitchen.

"Mind if I use your bathroom?" At her nod, I went through the other rooms and checked them too.

"I didn't see any cameras or bugs, used this thing to be sure." I waved the gizmo in her direction. "How long has this been going on?"

"Three weeks at least." Allie twisted a napkin into confetti. "I started lining things up in drawers and putting a thread next to them. If it was moved, I knew he'd been here."

"Could it be the cat?" I snatched another cookie, chocolate chunk, from the plate she'd brought to the table with the uhh, Cokes. I'm the victim of a pushy sweet tooth.

"Jorge's fifteen. He used to jump." Allie smiled at the memory. "One day, he missed the windowsill. Now he meows to be picked up for the bed or couch. He never got the hang of opening drawers."

I made a note, Jorge innocent. "Husbands or boyfriends?"

"My boyfriend and I broke up when I went to Mizzou. Long-distance didn't work. He's married with three kids now, preacher over to the Presbyterian church." She drank the last of her Coke. "I've dated some, but it's slim pickings in my age group. Momma took up so much time, dates fizzled out, and haven't livened up since. I've got work and Jorge. Single's not a bad thing."

"No affairs with married or otherwise taken men?" Could be a jealous woman.

"Most of them, I wouldn't take if they were served up on a platter. A Texas woman doesn't like another gal rustling her man, even if she's not all that fond of him herself. It's not proper. Plus, they all have guns." She reached for another cookie, but the plate was empty. "How about I fire up the grill and make us some burgers? You want jalapenos on yours?"

After we ate, I told her to get her clothes ready for the next day. I set a few traps but didn't tell her what kind, just to test her theory—and her sanity.

Around nine, I headed to the motel. It didn't offer much in the way of amenities or have a homey feel. It was just…dreary. I'd have to fit house-hunting into my schedule, along with laundry and compiling my list of 101 ways to make tacos.

The next morning Jimmy Lee came in as I scanned the paper to find an apartment. There wasn't anything in print. Huh, maybe Craigslist or LinkedIn. He looked at my notes.

"Stay with me." He grinned and that damn dimple carved a spot into his left cheek. That might have been one of the things that got me to marry him. "Two bedrooms. No hanky, no panky, unless you want." Damn, both dimples were teasing me. "I got a hot tub. No need for a swimsuit."

Time to change the subject, before *I* got hot. "I found us a case. Librarian's being stalked, or at least thinks so. Seems odd in a town this size, she can't be sure."

"Remember that arson job? Firefighter had a crush on you and left presents on your car. When you saw him, though, he acted so proper, we didn't have a clue until you caught him in the act."

"Yeah, kinda sweet, but creepy. He met a paramedic at a crime scene, a quadruple homicide. They make a nice couple." I tossed the newspaper aside. "After work, I'll stop by Allie's. Maybe we'll get lucky."

The day dragged on slower than a thirsty man crawling through the desert, just like yesterday and the day before. I got a lot of crossword puzzles done and hardly had to cheat at all. Going by Allie's house didn't work out like I'd planned. I texted her as I walked to the car and hopped in, sat a lot lower than usual, a surprise to my backside. I thought I had a flat tire. I was wrong, of course.

All four tires were flat.

I guess Allie was right. He did escalate.

I called Stan the Garage Man to replace my slashed tires. Jimmy Lee drove me the few blocks to Allie's. She was in tears when we got there, holding a college yearbook, or what was left of it. Scrawled in red was a note that said, "There is no Sharon Leigh," which I guess summed it up. My job just got harder. He knew who and what I was. Damn.

Jimmy Lee stayed with Allie while I went to the motel for my stuff. I'd sleep over, just in case. It didn't hurt that the towels would be fluffy, something motel towels had never experienced.

If Allie was like me that night, she jumped at every sound. I double-checked for cameras and listening devices, relocked windows and doors, and dozed. The next morning, I escorted her to work, met her for lunch, and drove her home. Bouncing between Netflix movies, we went over where she'd been and who she'd seen. Nothing.

"Maybe I ought to take that transfer." Allie looked depressed.

"Transfer? What transfer?"

"A month ago, I got a letter about a promotion at another branch. I'd have to move, wouldn't know anybody. It's a lot of trouble for a little more money." Allie looked around the living room. "This place wouldn't be big enough for a family, so I couldn't count on a quick sale. At least it's paid for. The position's still open. If we don't figure this out, I could still go."

"What about an alarm for the house? You okay with that?" I reached for more popcorn.

"Lordy, I forgot! I have an alarm. Why didn't I think of it? There's been no reason to set it since before momma went. The few times I did, she forgot, so I just quit." Allie looked near tears. "How stupid is that, to just forget?"

"You've had a lot going on, don't worry about it. Show me where it is and we'll go from there."

We put out the story that I didn't know how long I'd be around, so I'd stay with Allie. We varied lunch spots, which wasn't easy, considering the size of the town. Sometimes her friends joined us. We covered Whataburger, three Tex-Mex joints, the bowling alley (she'd been on a league), and two nicer restaurants, the kind with cloth napkins.

"You always put lipstick on before we come in to eat. As soon as you order, you blot it off." I had to laugh at her.

"Gags me to see lipstick smears on my food," Allie said. "I bring paper napkins so I don't mess up cloth ones. Stop laughing!"

I picked up her napkin. "You don't scrub lipstick off. You end up with this perfect open mouth imprint." I turned it to face her. "Sell this to a rubber stamp company for 'sealed with a kiss.' Or maybe a porn site would be interested. Why not just go without?"

"I like to look nice. I don't know how it started, but it's a habit now." She got the giggles then and laughed until the table rocked and iced tea threatened to send a lemony wave over the rim of the glass. Our server arrived, so we tried to behave.

"You're weird," I told her. I looked up at our server. "I'll have the beef fajita special with a cup of chili." I was so confused when he asked if I wanted lime wedges that I nodded. What am I supposed to do with limes?

"I'll have tortilla soup and the three peppers mini quiche. Bring a chocolate lava cake first, please." She looked at me. "I love that ooey-gooey inside stuff. They make it with caramel here."

Our orders soon arrived, the aroma of roasted chili peppers and dark chocolate tickling my nose before the plates landed on the table. After the server left, I whispered to Allie. "Why are there lime wedges sitting on my chili?"

She just rolled her eyes and told me to figure it out. Personally, I believe lime wedges should only sit on the rim of a margarita glass.

As I leaned forward, I bumped my fork, and it landed on the floor with a metallic clatter. In a flash, the busboy was there to replace it. Mom always told me to keep my elbows off the table. You can't take me anywhere nice.

I used my new fork to snag a bite of the lava cake before Allie could pull it away and no kidding, it was fabulous. I dropped her back at the library and headed to the office to go over my notes and take a few Tums to put out the chili fire. There had to be a pattern that would point us to the stalker. Cases like this were akin to *Where's Waldo*, but with added danger.

Although we'd locked up and set the alarm, at the house, things were worse. Allie went to her bedroom to change and let out a scream that could be heard from here to Oklahoma. I skidded to a stop in the doorway. Every pair of panties and every bra she owned were laid out on the bed, slashed and shredded. In the middle of it was a red-splashed white rose. No coppery smell, although it was still wet.

We called 911, which brought one uniformed officer, a crime scene tech, and a ten-galloned detective whose attitude toward women I failed to appreciate after he called me Missy and patted my shoulder with one meaty hand as he hitched up his pants with the other.

The tech didn't find fingerprints, footprints, or strands of hair. Small-town budgets don't usually run to DNA analysis anyway. The "blood" on the rose turned out to be corn syrup and red #5, according to the sniff and taste test performed by Detective Martin. The rose was cheap silk, no tracing it through a florist.

The next morning, Jimmy Lee and I arrived at the office at the same time. "Let me run this by you. Allie and I've been eating out quite a bit. I noticed something odd, to me at least. I've got a suspect." I didn't get the feeling he was the one. "But I'm missing something."

"I could check him out while you're with Allie. I'm always wandering around, so I won't be obvious."

I was of two minds on that. Jimmy Lee tends to take over everything he touches. On the other hand, there was only so much I could do by myself. "It's still my case, right?"

"You got control issues, sugar. Sure, it can be your case, it wouldn't do for me to stay with Allie. Besides, you gals getting close to some perv stalker, well, it would be dangerous. You leave that to me, honeybunch."

He might as well have patted me on the head. It was on, baby, it was *on.* I smiled a kill-him-with-kindness smile and said, "The busboy at the Hungry Steer, never says a word, glides past the table with the speed of a vampire and before I register he's there, plates are cleared, bread basket's full, fresh napkins appear, and water's topped off. I swear I've seen him before, but where?"

"That'd be Mikey, I bet. He works part-time at two or three places. Easy for him to eavesdrop on conversations, I'd bet." Jimmy Lee looked at his watch. "Time for my lunch. I'll bring you something back." He was out the door before I could say "Get me the lava cake." Lime or no lime, chili and fajitas only go so far.

I worked crossword puzzles until Jimmy Lee got back two hours later—with lava cake. My enthusiasm was for the cake, not him, no matter how he took it.

We talked about who'd joined Allie and me for lunch. One friend, Beth, just happened to drop by three times as we discussed the stalker. When Allie went to the restroom, Beth mentioned that Allie had gotten a scholarship to Mizzou and then didn't even use it all. "Other people" needed it just as much and would have appreciated it more. It sounded bitchy at the time. Now it was bitchy and suspicious.

"How's Mikey strike you as a primo suspect?" I wiped caramel from my lips. Well, licked it off. "He's just always *there*."

"It's hard to pin down. He has three part-time jobs. He would have been available when all the ruckus took place. Y'all better watch yourselves."

"I can take care of myself. I took self-defense classes." I leaned over to toss the cake container in the trash. As I sat up, an arm snaked around my neck and started to squeeze. I gasped for air and clawed, trying to get loose. My knee banged into the desk. The rollers on the chair kept me from getting my feet under me, but I was able to do considerable damage with an elbow to his stomach. Once he bent over, I managed to flip him, not gracefully, but still put him on the floor in a heap.

"Damn you, Jimmy Lee! What the hell? Don't you *ever* do something like that again, you hear me?" My voice was raspy. I still wasn't getting enough air.

"Taking a class and being able to use what you learned when somebody comes at you unexpected-like, that's two different things, sugar." He wheezed a bit as he tried to stand. "Whoever this is, they're getting serious. Dead serious. You okay?"

"No, I'm not okay. I just had a crazy man try to choke me after he brought me cake. I'm going, I don't know, I'm going somewhere you aren't. Find somebody else to work with. I'm done." I backed to the door as I spoke, timing my exit for maximum effect. I pushed it open, rushed out and crashed right into the mail carrier.

The door bounced back on me, hard. I knocked letters and ads out of his hand and almost tipped him over. "Sorry, I didn't see the door opening," he said. He picked up the spilled mail. "Are you hurt?"

"My fault. I was having a hissy fit and not watching where I was going." I touched my cheek where it had met the door. "Is there a fine for accosting a federal employee? Through rain, sleet, snow, and angry women, the mail must go through?"

He laughed. "No, but it sounds like a good idea. How about I buy you a sweet tea? It's about a hunnert degrees out here and time for my union break. The diner's my next stop."

Tea calmed me down. Velma did a double-take when she saw my cheek. I guess it was turning colors. She didn't mention it. When Paul, the mail guy, asked what my hissy fit was about, I blamed the crossword puzzle. If he didn't believe me, he didn't press the issue. I blotted my lipstick like I'd seen Allie do, to keep the imprint off the glass. She's right, Sultry Sunset isn't appetizing.

"You're staying with Allie, right?" Surprised me that he knew. "Small town. I thought, you know, if you're staying, maybe you need to fill out a change of address form."

"I haven't made up my mind." Time to change the subject. "So what's with those little bobbing-bird machines I keep seeing all over the place?"

"Those are oil wells." He laughed. "Everybody leases their land to the oil companies and they get paid for every barrel that's pumped. Easier than cattle. No muss, no fuss, just a check in the mail. That's all going to change, though."

"If people are making money, why mess with it?" I'll never figure Texans out. First Cokes that aren't real Cokes, then limes in my chili, bobbing-bird sculptures sucking oil from the ground, and no basements.

"Fracking. Forcing the oil out of the ground with water, instead of drilling. Some folks are for it, some against." He stood. "Time to get back to my appointed rounds, even though there's just the damn heat to deal with, not rain, sleet, or snow. I'll see you around, Sharon Leigh. Let me know if you change your mind about that change of address form."

I sat a while, thought hard and drew circles with the condensation from my tea glass. Velma brought a refill and an extra glass of ice. "You seeing Paul?" She didn't make eye contact.

"Huh? No, I stomped out of the office and about ran him over. Mad at Jimmy Lee, the bastard. Why?"

"Just wondered. I've never known him to date, is all. Here's more napkins, that glass is all sweaty. Use the extra ice on your cheek. You want pie?"

I didn't even think of pie until she mentioned it. Cherry sounded good. It's a fruit and that's healthy. I'm doubly healthy at the moment.

***

"Does anybody have a key to your house and the alarm code? You don't hide one under a rock or inside a fake dog poop, do you?"

"Fake dog poop? You call me weird?" It was good to see Allie laugh. "Fran, across the street, she does."

"How old is Fran? She ever use the key?"

"She's gotta be eighty or more. She takes in packages for me and brings them over. Momma gave her a key and the code years ago. I let her keep it in case there was an emergency so somebody could get in and rescue Jorge." Allie turned the blender on high to mix a pitcher of margaritas, putting limes on their God-given mission in life.

Something was nibbling at the edge of my mind, but I only got crumbs of an idea. In the meantime, I was the designated cook, so I dumped salsa from a jar into a bowl and opened the bag of tortilla chips. No use dirtying a second bowl. My part of dinner was done.

***

The next morning there was a big heart carved into the electric blue hood of the Mustang. Damn, that was original paint. We called it in, got the same patrolman, the same tech, and the same chauvinistic detective as before. "You got yourself a secret admirer." Detective Martin took off his hat and scratched his head. "'Course, didn't do the car any favors, you know?" Sometimes it's a privilege to watch the police in action. This wasn't one of those times.

Allie went on to work. Across the street, a curtain twitched. I waved, real friendly-like, and walked over. Fran's curiosity overcame any hesitation about letting a stranger in. After all, I was staying with Allie.

"It was just a scratch on my car. Must have happened during the night. Did you hear anything?" I bit into a sugar cookie. I would have said no, but they were fresh out of the oven. Can't be rude where homemade is concerned.

"I sleep sound after I take my pill at nine o'clock." Fran was a tiny woman, kind of tilted forward and slow to move because of an arthritic knee, but good for her age, which she said was eighty-seven. "You know Allie from school? She shouldn't have come home to take care of her momma, that nasty old bitch. I thought she faked being sick, but then she keeled over dead."

Cookie crumbs landed on my t-shirt as my mouth fell open mid-bite.

"Old ladies shouldn't curse? Sometimes you gotta use the right words, proper or not." She pushed the cookie plate toward me.

"Allie said you had a key to her house. If I lock myself out, can I borrow yours?" I took one more cookie, just to be polite.

"Sure, honey, that'd be all right. See those glass paperweights? Lift up that pear-shaped one. There's her key. You get it any time you need it. My spare key is under the third flowerpot. Everybody knows, in case I fall."

"I'd better go," I said. "Don't want to be late. Thanks for the snack, I haven't had anything so good in a long time." I conveniently forgot about the cherry pie and lava cake. I left with a paper bag full of cookies, thanks to Fran.

I stood by my car and looked at the key Allie had given me. It didn't look anything like the key Fran had.

***

At the office, Jimmy Lee was telling some bimbo how to answer the phone. "Just say the slogan like I wrote it down." He pretended not to see me.

I walked over, grabbed the paper, tore it up, and said, "Get the hell out of my chair." She looked at Jimmy Lee. "Don't look at him. I told you, get out. And stay out."

She grabbed her purse. "She's way meaner than you said." I took what some might interpret as a threatening step toward her. She scuttled for the door and didn't look back.

"I thought you quit." He started with some self-serving apology, but I cut him off.

"I know who's been stalking Allie." I laid it all out for him.

"There's no proof." Jimmy Lee paced. "I can hide in the house after you and Allie leave."

"The plan is for you to be the distraction so I can sneak back in." I could tell he didn't like that. Tough. "My case, remember? Besides, you owe me. You just had some…person making butt prints on my chair. Here's what we'll do."

***

The next day, Allie went to work. I stopped by the diner for breakfast. It's the most important meal of the day. After, I went into the office by the front door and left out the back. It only took a few minutes to work my way behind the buildings and come out at Allie's back gate.

I figured I had until mid-morning before anything would happen. About eleven o'clock, I heard the key in the front door. There was our culprit, right on time.

"Hello, Paul. Going to leave another surprise for Allie or me?" I leaned against the doorway, holding Fran's glass pear in my hand. "You stole the key from Fran, didn't you?"

He looked around. "Anybody here with you?" I shook my head. "That's either brave or stupid, don't you think? How'd you figure it was me?"

"When we had tea at the diner, I blotted my lipstick on a napkin. After you left, the napkin was missing. I'd bet you have a whole collection with Allie's lipstick on them."

"Allie left those kissy lip prints as a message to me. It was easy to pass the table and pick one up. Nobody notices the mailman. I'm, like, invisible. I gave Allie's packages to Fran and she brought them over," he said. He looked pleased with himself. "One day her arthritis was acting up, so I told her I'd set Allie's package inside the door. I switched my old garage key for Allie's house key. Fran never noticed."

"But why start spying on her? Threatening her?"

"If she takes that transfer, everything I've done will be wasted. She has to see that I can take care of her, protect her."

"You opened her mail?" I stood a little straighter. It shouldn't have been a surprise.

"It's easy if you know how. I missed her so much when she went to college. I gave her momma pills to make her sick, so Allie'd come home. And it worked.

She came back to me." He pulled a knife from his mail bag and just stood there, turning it from side to side, watching light reflect off the blade. "I can't let her leave again."

"Her mother died, for Pete's sake!"

"Only because the stupid cow made fun of me. I wrote a poem, but before I could give it to Allie, her momma took it and she laughed at it. I got even with her though. I made her some tea and put extra pills in it. She didn't laugh then. Then you showed up, telling lies. You're ruining everything, just like her momma."

He'd moved closer as he talked. I didn't worry until he smiled. It's a sight I never want to see again. "Did you get all that, Detective Martin? Cell phone, Paul. He can hear everything. Put the knife down."

Paul screamed and lunged, knife pointed at my chest. I brought my right arm up, took aim, and hit him right between the eyes. He went down like his bones had melted in the Texas heat.

Jimmy Lee burst in the back door, followed by Detective Martin and the patrolman. I never did get his name. Jimmy ran to me as the cops called for an ambulance. "What did you do to him?"

"Beaned him with a glass paperweight. It's pear-shaped." I think the adrenaline wore off about then. "I hope it didn't break. It's Fran's. I didn't tell her I borrowed it."

Detective Martin looked up. "Missy, this here's Texas. You shoulda just shot him."

As I walked to the front door, I stepped on Paul's outstretched hand with a satisfying crunch. Gawd, I love me some cowboy boots.

***

Turns out there were dozens of lip-printed napkins in Paul's apartment, all dated and sealed in plastic. I didn't want to think about what he might have done with them. The napkin with my Sultry Sunset lip prints on it was pinned to the oak table with a steak knife.

So here I am, still in Texas. I've got new friends, a taste for tequila and tamales, and no reason to head north. I can do PI work from most anywhere. I'm still working on that list of 101 ways to make tacos.

It looks like I'll need that change of address form after all.

Resolution

Keith Brooke

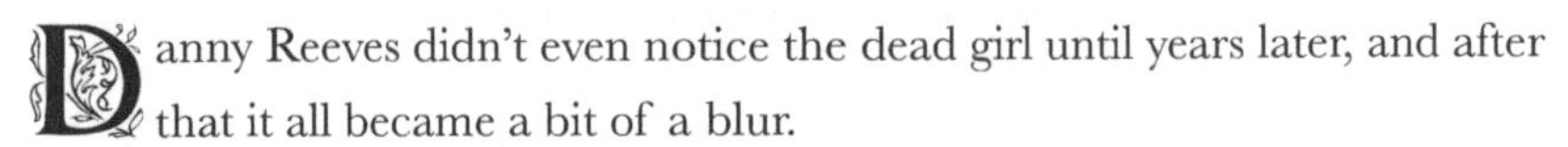

Danny Reeves didn't even notice the dead girl until years later, and after that it all became a bit of a blur.

How had he not seen her until now? He couldn't believe it, but now that he had…

He remembered bursting out of the flat, the door banging. Not knowing if he'd locked up and not caring. Running through town like a madman.

He remembered almost falling face first on the steps up to the police station's entrance. The stares. All the faces in the waiting room turning toward him. He'd been shouting, he realized. That was why they were staring. They must think he was mad.

"Detective Inspector Carver. I need to see Donald Carver. It's important."

The copper behind the plexiglass screen paused long enough for his gaze to wander very pointedly over Danny's features. They all thought he was mad, and now this officer was working out how to handle the situation.

Danny forced himself to take a deep breath, calming himself at least a little.

"It really is important," he said, keeping his voice lower, steadier. "It's the girl. I've found her. The dead girl."

***

The interview room was about as anonymous as it was possible for a room to be. Gray walls, minimal plastic and metal furniture, a clock on the wall. The table was secured to the floor, between Danny and the officer who'd introduced herself as Detective Sergeant Annie Malik. She was short and broad-shouldered and she was just as suspicious of him as the desk officer had been.

"A dead girl, you say?"

Danny nodded. He reached for the shoulder bag he'd dropped beside his chair, and the officer visibly flinched even though the bag had already been searched.

He opened a manila folder and pulled out a twelve by eight color print. A beach scene, viewed from a vantage point high on the promenade. A summer day, people in swimsuits on the beach, children paddling and playing with inflatables in the waves. Near the camera, a young couple, the guy in jeans and shirtless, the girl tucked into the fold of his arm. The lines of their bodies led the eye artfully into the broader scene, clearly a careful composition.

"What am I looking at?"

"A photograph." He didn't mean to sound facetious, it just came out that way. Malik was not impressed.

"I can see that. Why are you showing it to me?"

"She's there. In the picture. I didn't see her at first, but she is."

"Who? I still don't understand what you're trying to show me." She pointed at the girl nestled under the boyfriend's arms. "Her? Is that who you mean? She doesn't look too distressed. Or someone else? I can see families, kids playing. People strolling. Nothing out of the ordinary."

"It's not always what's in the picture. It's what's missing."

"If I wanted an art lecture, I'd sign up for the Open University. So tell me, what has my untrained eye missed?"

Danny pointed. A child. A blonde girl in a spotted dress, about four or five years old. "That child. Like I say: it's what's *not* there. No parents. Nobody with her. A child so young, all alone… I'm sure it's her. Katie Sellers. The missing girl. DI Carver knows all about it. Why isn't he here?"

"DI Carver retired seven years ago. He lives in Tenerife now."

Malik paused then, clearly making connections. She looked again at the photograph, and Danny could see she was taking in the clothes, the hairstyles, the cars just visible in the distance on the left.

"It's an old picture," she said slowly. "Katie Sellers. That was, what, fifteen years ago?"

Danny nodded. "Didn't I say? I'm sure I said. I took this picture. It's been haunting me for years. I've done some work on it. I've only just seen it, though."

"Seen what?"

"*Her*. Katie."

Malik glanced down at the picture again. "It's just a blurry photo. Yes, there's a child, but it's hard to really see anything. It's hardly the basis for an ID."

"But it's so much clearer than it used to be. I'm sure it's her."

"Clearer? What do you mean?"

"I'm a photographer," Danny explained. "Back then I was a student, out taking pictures for a college project. The quintessential English seaside and all that. You're right. It's not a great photo. Blurry—my shutter speed was too slow. But it's much clearer than it was. Back then DI Carver had copies of my pictures, but they weren't any use."

"So why's it any different now?"

"There are things you can do now that weren't possible back then. Once I'd scanned the old Kodachrome slide again this week, I ran it through some image-processing software. The program uses AI algorithms that learn from millions of comparable photographs so that it can interpolate the missing pixels where the original was blurry, restoring details that weren't originally captured. Intelligently sharpening and restoring beyond anything that was possible even a couple of years ago."

"You mean adding stuff that wasn't in the original image?"

"That's right. But it's data that *would* have been there if the equipment had been able to capture it. You can see so much more in this photo now. You can see *her*. Katie."

Malik sat back in her plastic chair. "So let me get this straight. You've come here with a not-very-good photograph of a scene where a girl might have been abducted fifteen years ago, with information added to the photo by experimental software–"

"It's not experimental. It's commercially available."

"It's still making shit up."

Danny opened his mouth to speak, but stopped himself. Her tone had been sharp, like a slap. He wasn't sure how much he could take of this. Her. The police station. The interview room. It was opening up too many damaging memories…

"It's her," he said softly, and Malik looked at him as if she'd realized something had changed. The air of defeat about him, the slump of his shoulders. "I thought it might help," he said. "It shows she was there."

"Thank you, Mr. Reeves." Kindness in her voice, almost as damaging as the sharp tone of moments before. "I know you're trying to help. But this is an old case, and it's not clear what your… *enhanced* image adds. May I keep it, though? Thanks. I'll look at the case file, talk to a couple of people. But now…"

"I know. I didn't think…"

"Here's my card. My number. In case anything else comes up."

He took the card, but he didn't believe she meant it. She was just going through the motions and hoping he wasn't a crank who would call her ten times a day from this point on.

Later, standing outside in the sun. The weather was unseasonably warm, much like that day fifteen years ago.

He was in the park, only a few minutes' walk from the promenade where he'd taken that photo.

He didn't know how he'd got here.

So much of the day was a blur. Absences and blanks.

The girl, Katie Sellers. He'd referred to her as the missing girl, but everyone knew she must be dead. No trace of her in fifteen years. Until now. His photograph. Surely that must tell them something new?

He'd felt close to exploding in there. Cracking up.

He'd never been good with pressure.

Not since that week, fifteen years ago. The series of events that had shaped his life ever since.

He found himself wandering along the promenade, finding the precise spot where he'd stood to take that picture. He remembered being pleased with the composition, believing he'd captured something insightful in the arrangement of the young couple against the seaside backdrop. And being disappointed when the slides had come back from the lab, the focus just a little bit off.

Nowadays, when everything was digital and autofocus, results were instant, and any mistakes like that could be rectified on the spot, but fifteen years ago the old technology had still been central to any photography student's work.

He went home. He wouldn't gain anything by standing out here like a madman.

***

That evening he sat reading in the living room that doubled as his work space, one end of the room taken over by desk and computer, and storage for all his gear.

A heavy, repeated thumping on the door of his ground-floor flat made him jump, his heart racing, his breath catching in his throat.

Before he'd even reached the door, he heard her shouting. DS Malik.

"Daniel Reeves? It's DS Malik. Please open the door."

He did so, and immediately she had a foot inside before she said, "Mind if we come in?"

He had to step back. He had no choice, or she'd have barreled into him. The DS was followed into the flat by two uniformed officers.

"What… What's happening? What have you found?"

Malik turned, fixing him with a stare that would have intimidated the most hardened criminal. "You," she said. "We've found *you*." And then she turned and walked through into the living room where Danny had been sitting quietly moments before.

"Mind if we look around?" she asked.

They already were. While Malik flicked through the papers and prints spread across Danny's desk, one of the uniformed men was opening cupboards.

"Please be careful," said Danny. "That kit's expensive." Then: "What do you mean, you've found *me*?"

Malik fixed him with that look again, and he felt himself shrinking inside. Too many bad memories being stirred.

"I did a little digging," she said. "I was curious. When I saw you earlier I didn't realize how close you'd been to the original investigation."

Why had he done this? Opened it all up again.

"You were a witness at the scene where Katie Sellers was last seen, although your statement said you didn't actually see anything. You came forward with photographs that didn't help. You hassled the parents for pictures and interviews until Katie's father lodged a complaint with us. You started hanging around the station and press briefings, asking questions, wasting police time."

"I was a…a photography student with an interest in photojournalism." He was starting to stutter. He hated himself at times like this. "I was looking for a story, a…a break."

"There's a well-known pattern," Malik told him. "It's where the guilty party inserts himself into the investigation—claims to be a witness, or helps with searches, or whatever. They get off on it. It's part of the thrill. It's all there in the case file: you were an almost textbook example of someone inserting himself into a police investigation."

"I was young and pushy," said Danny. "I wanted to make a name for myself." The only thing he'd been guilty of, though, was crass insensitivity, shoving his lens in the faces of the police and traumatized relatives of the missing girl.

Then he paused, his brain finally starting to catch up. "But…but why are you here? What's going on?"

"I'm curious," said Malik. How had she come to be standing so close to him, squaring up to him like this? "You did this fifteen years ago. You badgered DI Carver with your photos and your questions, to the extent that we have more notes in the file about you than we do about anyone else outside the family. But why now? Why did you march into the station this afternoon and start it up all over again? What are you trying to stir up? Or, worse, what else might you have done that we're not yet aware of? A cynic might think this is your way of taunting us with something, maybe something we don't yet know about."

He'd only been trying to help. He'd seen the girl. They should have wanted to know something like that.

He said nothing. He didn't trust his stuttering voice. And he knew he would only make things worse. Just as he had fifteen years ago.

He couldn't even remember the point back then when he'd realized he'd gone from witness to suspect. But he remembered very clearly the day he'd been waiting outside the station and two uniformed men had seized him and half-dragged him inside. He remembered what had seemed like hours of intensive questioning, and the night at the station. The humiliation and fear.

And the walk down the steps the next day, released without charge. The looks, the chattering clicks of camera shutters. And the interminable limbo as the case dragged on, as Katie failed to be found, the cloud of suspicion hanging over him.

These things shape you. They change who you are and what you might become.

They make you into what Danny Reeves had become.

"Are you going to arrest me?" he said, his voice little more than a whisper. "And if so, on what grounds?"

"Just give me something," said Malik. "Anything. Consider this a calling card. One that's a little more substantial than the one I gave you earlier. I'm aware of you now, Reeves. I know who you are. And I'll be watching."

Moments later they were gone.

Danny looked around the flat—for a sign, for anything that would confirm this had all just happened and he hadn't imagined the whole thing. Then he rushed through to the bathroom to be sick.

***

He tried to get on with normal life, whatever that was.

The next day he showed up for his shift at college, despite the anxiety bubbling away beneath the surface of everything he did. He had a part-time job behind the scenes, helping run the Art Department's photo labs and maintain the equipment. He could have got away with calling in sick, but he knew that hiding from the world never did any good. That was why he still lived in this town, fifteen years on, despite the whispers and slander of that time.

That evening, he called up the scans of the old slides in Adobe Lightroom and studied them again. He zoomed in on the enhanced features of the little girl. She was the spitting image of the pictures the police had released of Katie Sellers. How could DS Malik not see that?

Methodically, he dragged the magnified view across every face in the picture, as if he might suddenly see something in an expression that he had missed before.

He had other scans from that day, but only three that showed the girl, and none that showed her as clearly as this one.

He lost track of time, and it was midnight before he realized how much his eyes and head ached, and he forced himself to stop.

The next morning he'd planned a sunrise shoot at the beach, but when his alarm went off the weather apps didn't look promising, so he allowed himself to sleep in.

When he eventually rose, the headache had shifted, and he decided to head down to Rose's Cafe for a full English breakfast, and when he opened his front door, it was just as DS Malik had her fist raised to knock.

Both of them jumped back, startled.

"I–"

"Sorry, I..." Malik smiled awkwardly, then started again. "I was just about to knock."

She really did like to state the obvious. Danny said nothing.

What could she want now? Was she hoping to intimidate him into something? He struggled to work out his feelings, lying somewhere between anger and abject fear.

"Sorry," she said again. There was something different about her manner today. "Mr. Reeves," she said. Polite. Cautious. "Do you have a minute?"

Was she doing some bizarre kind of good-cop-bad-cop thing all on her own?

"Do I have a choice?"

"Yes." Again, something in her tone made him pause.

"What is it?" he asked. Then he stepped back to let her in.

She stopped in the cramped hallway. "I spoke to my DI yesterday. Stephen Welham. He worked on the Sellers case. He remembers you. He asked me to go over the case notes again and see if I can come up with anything."

"A cold case."

Malik nodded. "I've never worked on anything this old before. I don't know what he expects. There's really nothing to go on, not even any evidence of a crime."

"The girl went missing."

"I know. But we don't know how, or why. It could have been a tragic accident, her body washed out to sea. I've been looking to see if there might be any ties with other cases from over the years, but with so little to go on..."

"Why are you telling me this?" It was weird, the abrupt shift from hostility to this.

"DI Welham asked if you might be able to help."

"Help with your inquiries?" He wasn't able to keep the sneer from his voice.

"Not like that. I told him what you'd done with the photograph. He was interested. There are other photos in the case file. He wondered if you might be able to do the same with them. Enhance them, whatever it is you do."

A short time later, they sat at Danny's big work table, a wide area where he could spread out prints and equipment as needed. Now they had two mugs of steaming tea, and Malik had spread out the contents of a folder across the surface.

Danny positioned a bright work lamp and leaned over the images. Some of them were pictures he was sure he'd seen from the newspapers—the parents at a press conference with the police officers working the case. He recognized the heavily mustached features of DI Carver, sitting next to the parents at the press conference, and there were other photos from that gathering. He remembered it well, the anguished atmosphere as the estranged parents took turns to plead for their daughter's safety. He'd taken some powerful images that day, which he could add to this selection for analysis.

There was also a photofit composite image and an artist's impression of a suspect. "Who's this?" Danny asked. "Why did they do a photofit of this man?"

"I can't disclose the details," said Malik. "Sorry. But you don't need to know any of that; we just want you to do your magic with the photos and see if anything useful is revealed."

Danny sensed that Malik was treading a very careful path. She clearly didn't like disclosing even this much to someone who could cause her all kinds of problems if he chose to. Unprofessional conduct. Inappropriate disclosure of confidential details of a case.

It still broke his heart that people didn't trust him.

The other pictures were ones he hadn't seen before. Mostly six-by-fours of the same beach scene he'd photographed that day.

"There was an appeal," Malik explained, as if Danny would have forgotten. "Anyone who'd taken photographs at the beach that day."

He spread those photos out more evenly, checking each in turn. Smiling faces. Innocent fun. Kids in swimsuits. Grandparents with cones from Mr. Whippy.

Then one that stopped him in his tracks. He recognized this one. A pixelated picture of mother and daughter. Mrs. Sellers and Katie. This one had been in the newspapers. The last picture together.

"Who took this?" He knew Rachel Sellers had been alone with her daughter that day at the beach.

Malik hesitated, as if weighing up how much to disclose, then said, "Just a passing stranger." She prodded at the photofit. "This guy. DI Welham wondered if he might show up in any of the other pictures once you'd enhanced them. See if he shows up anywhere—at the beach, or even at the press conference."

"Inserting himself into the investigation." That came out far more sarcastically than he'd intended.

"It happens," said Malik. "That press event was open to the public, a general appeal for information. The guilty party—if there actually was one—might easily have attended, either for thrills or just to keep up to speed with the investigation."

Danny looked again at the array of pictures. So many people, most of them indistinct in the background. Now he understood Malik's request. If he could make those figures recognizable, maybe they could be matched to the photofit or to any other known suspects.

And it wasn't just the suspect, it was Katie, too. If the little girl had shown up in *his* photograph, then maybe she would show up in others, and if she did, maybe she would not be alone.

"Can you do anything with these?"

Danny didn't answer, too preoccupied. He'd already picked up the mother and daughter photograph and was studying the blurry people in the background under a magnifier. Was one of these the culprit, just lurking, waiting for his chance? Danny turned to his flatbed scanner, put the picture in face down and closed the lid.

"It's a slow process," he said. "I'm not saying that to get rid of you. You can stay as long as you like. The scanning's quick, but the processing takes forever, even on a fast computer like this. The software runs millions of operations on every scanned pixel and its relationship with the pixels around it. It's not exactly magic, but with the right image it can recover a hell of a lot of obscured information."

"I appreciate this," said Malik. She looked away, then back at him. "Particularly after… well…"

Danny shrugged. He understood that she might feel awkward, but this was normal for him. Suspicion was a constant in his life.

"I only ever wanted to help," he said.

Malik said nothing, just watched as Danny set the first scan going and the preview appeared on one of the wide screens on the side desk.

"Is it okay if I leave those with you?" She indicated the array of pictures on the viewing table. "Will you keep them safe? This isn't exactly conventional."

"You must use outside consultants all the time."

"I guess."

"But usually ones you trust."

At least she had the decency to look awkward at that.

***

Danny worked through the night. It wasn't deliberate, he just got caught up in what he was doing. Scanning the prints one by one. Loading them into Lightroom for cropping, and for basic exposure and color balance tweaks. Then putting the scans through the Topaz AI image-processing software, the stage that took the longest as every element of the image was analyzed, assessed, refined.

He did the mother and daughter picture first, then studied it closely as he set the next one processing.

The refined image on screen was so much clearer than the print before him. So much more poignant because of that: he could see the expressions more clearly, the carefree laugh of the small girl, the tired, perhaps a little wary, smile of the mother.

He knew the focus of Malik's interest was the man who'd taken that picture, although Danny suspected he was just another innocent caught up in the tragedy—an act of kindness, an offer to take a photo of mother and daughter at the seaside, and now that unwitting stranger was unknowingly the focus of a police investigation.

Danny studied the people in the background. So much sharper now. Several of them must certainly be identifiable to anyone who knew them. On his second screen, he called up his own enhanced photo of the beach that day, comparing figures, faces, but he couldn't be sure that anyone other than Katie appeared in both images.

The next scan was someone's snapshot of the beach scene. Again, he repeated the process, studying the enhanced image closely, trying to spot anyone who appeared in the others.

He knew this wasn't really part of the task. The police would do all this analysis later; all they wanted from Danny was the enhanced images. They'd have a far better idea of what they were looking for.

Another image. More faces. This time he noticed a young couple who also featured in the background of the mother and daughter picture. It meant nothing, of course, but was part of the process of building up a view of who had been where on that day.

It was well into the early hours before he'd scanned all the images of the beach. His mind was spinning with permutations. Faces that appeared in more than one image, until he had a sense of comings and goings, almost more vivid than his own memories of being there on that day.

He couldn't see the photofit man, though. The dark, cropped hair, the square face, the dark eyes under heavy brows—they were the kind of features that would be distinctive even in a bad photo.

Did that mean the man had kept a low profile, or simply that he'd only been at the beach briefly?

He made another cafetière of coffee and kept going.

The remaining images were from the investigation itself. The press briefing. Some pictures of lines of police and the general public searching the park behind the promenade.

Danny even found himself in some of the images. A lanky kid taking pictures at the press conference, and then standing aside at the search, taking pictures, rather than actually helping. He wasn't proud that he'd been so selfish back then. That he'd seen a missing child as an opportunity rather than the tragedy it was.

He stared at the pictures until his vision blurred.

The enhanced scans had come out well, but it was beyond him to get anything useful from them. Maybe Malik would manage.

He was reaching for the monitor to power it down when he saw it.

The face.

The connection.

His eyes jumped back and forth between the two images. The press conference photo and his own picture of the couple by the promenade with little Katie Sellers in the backdrop.

You'd never have seen it in the original. The figure standing near Katie but not quite with her was a blur, features lost in the shade of the promenade. The enhancement process had recovered detail from the shadows, and sharpened what had been blurred. Had made the face recognizable.

But it wasn't the man from the photofit.

***

The faces all turned to him. The suspicious, assessing gaze of the officer behind the plexiglass security screen.

"DS Malik. I need to talk to her. Tell her it's urgent. It's Danny Reeves. I need to see her right now."

A short time later he was in the interview room again, tipping glossy prints out of a folder onto the table between him and Annie Malik.

"This one, see? Him." He jabbed a finger at the man standing near to Katie. "He's with her. He's approaching her."

Malik looked at the picture and then back up at Danny. "Last time you interpreted this picture very differently. You said the girl was clearly on her own. You said that was the key thing: that she was a small child on her own, and that was what was wrong."

"But she's not!"

"Don't you think you might be over-interpreting?" She was trying to be kind, softening her clearly skeptical tone. "When your mind wanted to see her as alone, that's what you saw. And now you're saying she's being approached. That's not what I see. I see a child, who may or may not be Katie Sellers, and there are several people within a few yards of her. It's not clear from that whether anyone is approaching her or not."

"But don't you see who that is?"

Malik stared again. "Tall. Mid-brown hair. Heavy build. That doesn't really narrow it down."

"It's her father. Jonathan Sellers." Danny pushed a photo from the press conference toward her. DI Carver, the mother, Rachel Sellers, and her estranged husband, Jonathan. A solicitor and local councilor, Jonathan Sellers was a pillar of the community. He'd been separated from his wife at the time, fighting for custody of Katie.

He'd have been the obvious suspect if he'd actually been in town at the time Katie disappeared.

"I've read the case files," said Malik. "He had a cast-iron alibi."

"Except he didn't. He was *here*." Danny jabbed his finger at the picture again. "Right here. His alibi must have been faked. So why did he lie?"

"But he *didn't*," said Malik. "He was away that day, playing golf with Stephen Welham—who is now my DI. You don't get a much better alibi than that. Look again. What do you see? A tall man. Mid-brown hair. Heavy build. It could be just about anyone."

Danny stared. How could they take someone's word over the evidence before their eyes?

"You're doing what the AI software does," said Malik. "Your mind is filling in the gaps, adding data that wasn't there—but you're not necessarily capturing what was actually there, you're capturing what you *think* should have been there."

"Making shit up."

"No, not making it up. Just trying too hard."

He stared again. Saw a tall man. Mid-brown hair. Heavy build. A man who may or may not have been approaching the small girl, who might not even have been Katie Sellers.

Malik shuffled the photos, looking at each of the big prints in turn. "I can't believe these are the same pictures," she said. "They're so much clearer. I can't believe you got this out of them."

She was trying to be nice.

"I hope they'll be useful," he said. "Maybe you'll see something."

"They're great."

He looked down, unable to hold her look.

She was right. He was over-interpreting. Overthinking things, as he always did.

"Thank you so much for your time and expertise."

Which had all been for nothing. All they had now was a set of sharper images that still didn't show either the photofit man or anything else that added to what they already knew.

"Let me know if you need anything more," he said, and stood.

Fifteen years, and he still was unable to put this all behind him.

He left the station and walked slowly home. The unseasonal warmth had gone and there was a chill in the air, and somehow that only seemed right.

***

He tried not to dwell on it. Tried to focus on other things. On anything other than the case.

Malik had been right.

He'd been overthinking. His mind had been filling in gaps, until he saw what he'd wanted to see.

Later, he went to the computer and stared at the thumbnail images in Lightroom. He opened his own picture of the seaside scene full size, the image that had started it all. The young couple, the beach backdrop, the little girl who may or may not have been Katie Sellers.

That man, the tall one with mid-brown hair and heavy build… Malik was right about that, too. He might have been approaching the girl, yes, but equally he might have been oblivious to her. Just a juxtaposition frozen in the photograph.

How had he been so convinced the man had been approaching Katie?

He'd been overthinking. Wanting it too hard, just as Malik had suggested.

It was time to file everything away, try to find some way to restart his life.

He reached for the computer, but his hands didn't get as far as the keyboard, because that was when he spotted something.

He paused, his throat tightening.

Stared, just to be sure it wasn't his imagination playing tricks.

He wasn't. He was sure.

After all this time, he had the answer.

***

This was a part of town he rarely visited. Grand houses set back from the road, flashy cars in the driveways. This was where the other half lived.

He didn't know how to handle this. All the way here, his thoughts had been rushing madly, but now…

He'd wanted to take control, but now he realized he couldn't do this alone.

He called Malik.

"I'm standing outside Jonathan Sellers' house. I found something. Proof."

"What are you doing there, Danny? Why didn't you come to me?"

Because none of them ever trusted him. He didn't say that.

"What are you planning to do?" she asked into the silence.

"I don't know. I was going to confront him with it, but–"

"Don't. Listen, Danny. Give me…three minutes. I'm in my car. I can be with you quickly. Three minutes, Danny? Can you do that?"

He cut off the call and stared at the house. It had been easy enough to find the address of such a prominent man. But what had he hoped to achieve, coming here on his own?

***

Jonathan Sellers was unmistakable even fifteen years on, even though the mid-brown hair had turned to silver and the heavy features had shrunken, as if retreating.

"We're making a few inquiries into your daughter's disappearance," Malik said, after introducing herself.

The man's jaw sagged. "What? Is there something new? Have you…?"

His act was convincing. He'd had fifteen years in the role, after all.

"I know it's a long time ago, Mr. Sellers, but would you please confirm your movements on that day?"

"Me? What…?" Sellers straightened. "I assume you've read the statements," he said. "You know where I was. So why this? Why now?" He was trying to intimidate Malik, but Danny knew that was not an easy thing to do.

Malik reached into her bag and produced one of the prints Danny had given her. "Would you confirm that this is you in this photograph?"

Sellers stared. "Of course it is. What's this about?"

The photograph showed DI Carver sitting with Rachel and Jonathan Sellers at the press conference, a picture that had featured widely in press coverage of Katie's disappearance. In the picture, Sellers was wearing a white shirt and a dark tie as he talked animatedly to the audience.

"And would you confirm that this is you in *this* photograph?"

She showed him Danny's enhanced picture of the seaside scene, pointing at the still-indistinct figure of a man standing close to Katie.

"What? This is ridiculous. That could be anybody."

Now it was Danny's turn. He thrust another photograph in Sellers' direction. "And is it you in this one?"

"Yes, of course it is. You know it is."

This picture was an informal one Danny had taken as the press conference wound down. Jonathan Sellers—tall, mid-brown hair, his heavy frame hunched over as he talked to one of the police officers.

But in this picture, Sellers had pulled on a scuffed brown leather jacket with a distinctive tear in one cuff that made it hang loose at the left wrist.

"And this one?"

The search of the park, volunteers and police lined up as they worked their way from one side to another. Jonathan Sellers had taken part in that, too, and—yes!—he'd worn what appeared to be a favorite brown leather jacket again.

"Yes, yes, it is."

"Now look again at this picture," said Malik.

The beach scene. The tall figure, his features indistinct but his scuffed leather jacket showing clearly…the jacket with a tear so that it hung loose at the left wrist.

"You were there," said Danny.

"You said you were playing golf, but that was a lie," said Malik. "And Stephen Welham helped with the lie for some reason. But it was a lie, wasn't it? You were there. At the beach. When Katie went missing."

Sellers stared…at Malik, at Danny, and then at the photograph of the seaside scene, perhaps the last photograph ever taken of his daughter.

His shoulders slumped.

"Maybe you did play golf with your policeman friend," said Danny. "Maybe you left earlier than you claimed and he wasn't sure, but was just happy to agree with whatever you'd said, because you were a friend and why would you lie? But afterwards you went to the beach. Why? What were you trying to do?"

"I know you," said Sellers. "That pushy student."

He wasn't denying anything. He almost seemed relieved now. He looked down for a long time, then up again, meeting Danny's look.

"Welham was drunk by the end of that day. Why wouldn't he agree with what I said?"

Danny stared. Finally hearing the words that would absolve him of the tangled-up feelings of guilt and responsibility that had blighted his life for fifteen years. He wondered if that was why DI Welham had encouraged Malik to dig into the old case now: nagging doubts and memories, guilt…

"What happened to Katie?"

"I didn't plan it…"

He could barely hear Sellers' words, they were so softly spoken.

"I only wanted to talk with Rachel. Try to work things out. But I saw Katie, on her own. Rachel had let her wander off, as she often did. Rachel was always flaky, easily distracted. I saw Katie, and all I wanted to do was protect her from that woman."

The photo. It had encapsulated that moment: Sellers approaching his isolated daughter.

"Katie saw me and she literally jumped up into my arms and I caught her and suddenly I knew I could never let her go. Rachel didn't deserve her."

"What happened to her?"

Bizarrely, Danny found himself clinging to a sliver of hope for the girl, even now, but what Sellers said next quashed that.

"It was an accident."

Four simple words that said so much more.

"I carried her to my car. Drove her home. But as I drove she started crying for Rachel, and when I pulled up into the driveway she started to scream, as if I'd done something awful to her. If anyone had heard her…seen her like that, I knew I'd never see her again."

Sellers was crying now, his words punctuated with great big gasping, heaving sobs.

"I… I only wanted her to be quiet. It was an accident."

Danny closed his eyes, struggling not to see it. The small girl screaming in the car, the panicking man who suddenly knew he had no way out. A hand over the girl's face to smother the cries. A hand held in place just a little too long.

The details might be different, but that didn't really matter. It was like the image of the beach, the before and after as the details were filled in, sharpened, resolved.

The details didn't matter, he realized. It was the story they told that did.

He realized Malik was studying him, trying to read him.

She reached out then, put a hand on his arm. "You okay?"

He nodded. "Yes. Yes, I think I am."

He didn't know what came next, it was all a blur. The rush of cars arriving. The blue lights. The police officers pushing him aside.

He remembered turning away, and an officer trying to stop him, and then Malik saying it was all right, let him go.

Walking home, the details resolved, and finally ready to start the rest of his life.

Around the World in Five Serial Murders

Yvonne Eve Walus

First Murder, Kiruna, Lapland

When I tell people I'm a criminal profiler, their second thought is always *FBI*, which couldn't be farther from the truth. Their first thought is, of course: *say what?*

They have a point: it's difficult to be a woman in this job. "You won't have the stomach," the university dean declared when I signed up for a forensic post-grad qualification. "You won't have the physical strength for the obstacle course," the law enforcement academy decided when I applied. "We don't have vacancies," was the police force's excuse when they didn't hire me. What they meant was, "You don't have the imagination to get into the mind of a serial killer."

Thinking like a serial killer (and I'm not being sexist here when I say they're almost all male) is difficult enough for any so-called normal person, but for a woman to try to get inside such a man's head—that's inconceivable.

Which is why here I am at twenty-eight, with a degree in criminal psychology, a five-year-old son, and no steady job. Granted, my son is not a result of the world's discrimination toward female perp profilers. He's the result of my discrimination toward abortion, and my single status is the result of my discrimination toward charming holiday romance partners who turn into violent arseholes back home. Suffice it to say, Jack's dad is now out of the picture on a permanent basis.

Anyway. To make a living, I follow rich guys whose wives worry about being upgraded to a newer model. To fuel my passion, I follow international murder news reports, siphoning and shaping Big Data into patterns and anomalies.

The Lapland murder was the first in the pattern, yet it caught my attention right off the bat. Everything about it shouted *anomaly*: location, victim, the setup of the murder scene.

The location was a Lapland hotel, a distinctive structure made of ice. Or, as the hotel's website helpfully informed me, the walls were constructed with "snice," which is a mixture of snow and ice. Every piece of furniture in the room was pure frozen water: tables and chairs and, of course, the bed. The website contained more detail about the building process and what kept the hotel from melting in the summer months, but what caught my eye were the room names. Each hotel suite had ice sculptures that contributed to its theme. The murder had taken place in the House of Cards suite, so named because the walls were decorated with gigantic Aces of Spades, Jacks of Clubs, and Threes of Diamonds.

There, on the slab of ice that served as a bed, lay the body of a red-haired woman, her face painted white, her lipstick exaggerated into a red heart. The Queen of Hearts. It was discovered on the morning of 26 December.

The murder didn't make a big splash in the post-Christmas English media, and I only stumbled upon it thanks to my very well-trained AI search bots. Couldn't find any photos from the murder scene online, but fortunately all the articles in the local papers (thank you, Google Translate) were as gory and detailed as any Jo Nesbø thriller: the reindeer hides on the ice bed, the icicle in the victim's heart, the pack of cards on the floor.

More than anything in the world, I wanted to visit the scene of the crime—take a dog sleigh ride to the hotel, see the room, talk to the local cops. My budget constrained me to a Skype exchange with a fellow true crime enthusiast from Rovaniemi. Or at least he said he was from Rovaniemi. Who knows anything about anybody they meet online nowadays?

Anyway, Rovaniemi is the capital city of Lapland and the official home of Santa Claus, over three hundred kilometers away from the Ice Hotel.

"The cops won't tell you anything," he said. Not Santa Claus—the true crime enthusiast from Lapland, the only person in my online forum who seemed remotely interested in this murder. "They're worried about the effect on the tourist industry. The press is cooperating by"—he hesitated, searching for the right English word—"downplaying the event."

He didn't have more for me, except to put me in touch with the local *poliisipäällikkö*, police chief in charge. After a lengthy video conference, in which I did things my mom taught me never to do online, I learned a few vital pieces of information not disclosed to the public. Sometimes it's good to be a woman in this business, after all.

So, the victim remained unidentified, a Jane Doe or whatever they call them in Lapland. According to the ice hotel's guest register, the room had been unoccupied that night. Being the Christmas period in a remote tourist attraction, the hotel had been nearly empty. All the other guests (all four of them, and all of them women travelling together) had been interviewed. Nobody had seen anything or anybody unusual.

Icicles were plentiful in the area after the recent unseasonal warming and then a subsequent drop in temperature, and no, nobody had been insane enough to go looking for its original hanging place, especially seeing that it had been inserted into the wound post-mortem. The actual murder weapon may have been an ice pick. Not of the *Basic Instinct* kind, more like an ice chisel used by sculptors.

There was no forensic evidence to speak of. The temperature in the room was below freezing point, so victim and perp alike would have been wearing gloves, leaving no fingerprints and no bits of skin under the fingernails. No stray hairs or fabric threads. No signs of sexual interference.

The pack of cards found in the victim's room was brand new and not part of the hotel supplies. It was also incomplete: it lacked the Queen of Hearts.

"Clearly the work of a madman," the police chief concluded. "I know all the local troublemakers, and I can tell you, none of them have the imagination."

There it was again, that word. *Imagination*. People had no idea how twisted some minds could get.

In this case, though, I agreed. This was not a local yokel at play.

Frustrated. Disempowered. Immobilized. I felt all those emotions and many more. My mind loves puzzles, and it hates not having enough data to solve one.

New Year's Eve found me at home in front of the TV, my son asleep next to me on the sofa, waiting for the clocks country-wide to strike midnight. I didn't feel right watching my usual diet of serial killer shows with a preschooler curled up into my side, so I chose a nature documentary, which turned out to be nearly as disturbing.

being part of the pack. No, they still hadn't identified the murder weapon, but it wasn't the stalactite.

"You mean, the stalagmite?" I interrupted. "That's what the newspaper said."

Nikolay shrugged. "Newspapers. They probably don't know the difference. It was a stalactite. Grew downwards. Like that icicle."

Because of the public nature of the mine chamber and the number of tourists visiting the mine every day, there was forensic evidence aplenty, though none useful. Again, no sexual interference of any sort.

The victim remained nameless.

I did the only thing I could: spent all my thinking time between jobs, during boring stakeouts, while washing dishes and tossing sleeplessly in bed contemplating the two cases, examining the similarities, considering the fetishes. We had female victims, stabbings, decks of cards.

We had nothing.

Time spent with my son was off-limits to the investigation, though. When Jack and I played checkers, watched *The Princess Bride* for the tenth time, read bedtime stories, or walked our dog on the beach, my mind was solely focused on being a mom.

Compartmentalize—I could do it as well as any man. Love my son—I could do that as well as any woman loved her child. Solve the puzzle—I sure hoped I could do that way better than anybody else. Especially as nobody else seemed to be working on it.

Third Murder, Naxos, Greece

It was April the 12th before the killer struck again, this time in Greece, which confirmed my theory that he was moving down the map. A Naxos harbor drinking hole called the Queen of Clubs was the murder scene, down a steep half-flight of rocky stairs into what was generously called the wine cellar. A range of photos on a vacationer's blog ("take a look, we were in this bar only last week, and now someone's been murdered here") showed me that the basement was more of a pantry, with a vat of olives, a few bottles of wine on the racks, and bunches of herbs hanging off the ceiling. The only place the body could have fitted was on the sandy floor.

Definitely part of the pattern. First the Queen of Hearts, then the Queen of Diamonds, now the Queen of Clubs.

As expected, the victim was an unidentified woman, the cause of death stabbing through the heart with a replica of a Greek *kopis*. I looked it up. A *kopis* was an ancient Greek short sword, single-edge, used both for cutting and for thrusting.

The news article mentioned a pack of cards found clutched in the woman's hand as a teaser.

I emailed Nikolay. He had no contacts in the Greek police and couldn't afford to take any more time off to travel to Naxos. He said he was sorry. Not nearly as sorry as I was, I told him.

Back on the home front, one of my clients got impatient after my three-day invigilation of her husband revealed no extramarital affairs. She suggested I should speed things along and use my female charms to entrap him.

"He's going overseas tomorrow," she told me. "A conference in Europe. Greece, I think. Or maybe Turkey. I wasn't really listening. One of the islands, anyway."

My ears pricked up at the mention of Greece-I-think-or-maybe-Turkey, despite my moral objection to her plan of action. She'd buy me a business-class plane ticket, I'd get her husband's attention in the airport lounge, check into the same hotel.

"You don't need to sleep with him if you don't feel like it," she continued. "I certainly don't. Just get the intent recorded on your phone. In his job, he has to be squeaky clean. Any whiff of a scandal, and he's out on his arse."

"How will that help you? If he's unemployed?"

She looked at me like I was a half-wit. "Naturally, I wouldn't take the recording to his board of directors. I'd play it for him and make sure I get a fair divorce settlement."

Somehow, I had a hunch our opinions differed on what was considered a fair divorce settlement, especially if blackmail were involved.

The trip to Greece-Turkey sounded exactly like what my serial killer investigation needed. Unfortunately, I despise blackmailers only a little less than I despise serial killers, so it was a no-deal.

No good deed goes unpunished. My refusal cost me the spousal invigilation contract as well.

Fourth Murder, Cape Town, South Africa

Less than a month later, I read the following in the *Cape Times*:

Cape Town—An unidentified woman was stabbed to death in a luxurious hotel in the Oranjezicht area on 9 May. Police have appealed to anyone with information about the killing to come forward.

According to Sergeant Noloyiso Mpayipheli, the murder is believed to have happened between ten p.m. and midnight. The body was discovered in the Queen of Spades hotel games room by a staff member at closing time.

"Police attended to the scene and upon their arrival they found a body of a woman with a stab wound to her chest," Mpayipheli said.

Nobody has been arrested yet for the murder. It is unclear whether the woman was a local or a tourist; however, it is confirmed that she was not a guest at the hotel.

A spokesperson for Community Safety, Yvette de Jong, said crime is reaching rampant proportions in the Western Cape, with more than ten cases of murder reported every day last year.

Sergeant Mpayipheli said the circumstances were being investigated and an autopsy would determine the cause of death.

Anyone who has any information about the murder can anonymously contact the Oranjezicht police station, or Crime Stop on 0860010111, or SMS Crime Line on 32211.

I hadn't needed my internet-trawling bots. I found the article myself. I knew what I was looking for: the Queen of Spades.

The order of the suits bothered me. As a bridge player, I'm used to the clubs-diamonds-hearts-spades sequence. That's also the most common poker sequence, although some poker variations change it to alternate the red and black, ending up with diamonds, then clubs, then hearts, then spades. But hearts at the bottom and spades on top? I knew of only one game that used such a convention: the Russian Preference. Of course, the sequence might just be due to the rarity of appropriately named venues, and the north-to-south trajectory. What did I know?

Right. What did I know about the serial killer's modus operandi so far? The cause of death was always a single stab wound to the chest. Now, if you know anything about the human anatomy, you understand how difficult it is to access the heart. It hides behind the breastbone, partially protected by the ribs as well as the tough intercostal connective tissue between them. To strike the heart with one stab on four occasions requires medical training, or military training, or many hours on YouTube and a medically-correct dummy to practice on. It also requires above-average strength of the upper body. There are much easier ways to kill a person. Even if you insist on stabbing as your method, almost any target would have been better: the major vessels above the breastbone, the throat, the eyes, the kidneys, even.

Who could kill with a single stab to the heart? A surgeon. A butcher maybe, like Jack the Ripper. Who else? A Green Beret, a Navy SEAL, a former KGB spy, a Mossad agent.

The dates didn't seem important: 26 December (Boxing Day), 8 March (International Women's Day), 12 April, 9 May. I ran them through Google anyway. 9 May turned out to be Victory Day, celebrating the fall of Berlin to the Russian army and the end of World War II in Europe.

The staging of the body: yes, it meant something for sure. I just didn't know what.

What else? Most serial killings are about control and power and sexual pleasure, even, whether or not any sexual assault has actually taken place. This perp didn't go for sexual activity.

In the name of due diligence, I also analyzed the victims. In my profession, we often use victimology to discover the motives of the killer—profiling the victims to profile the killer, so to speak. I compared the photographs of the murdered women. No obvious physical similarities, although all the victims were of European descent. There were no further points of intersection. The hair, for example, ranged from sandy to black via red, and there was nothing in the faces to suggest a fetish for high cheekbones or beauty spots.

This time, I didn't reach out to Nikolay. I didn't have to. All it took was a phone call to my twin sister to please come over and babysit Jack for the afternoon (when he was younger, I sometimes wondered whether he could even tell us apart, and to this day I'm not entirely certain of the answer) while I drove up to Cape Town and spoke to Sergeant Mpayipheli.

Sergeant Mpayipheli turned out to be an extremely busy woman, with the Queen of Spades murder low on her list of priorities. Small wonder, what with ten murder cases reported in the area every day. Having perused my PI license and confirmed I wouldn't be charging for my time, she was happy to hand over the thin case file.

"We have a computer backup," she told me. "But with load shedding, we find paper more reliable."

I nodded. South Africa's electricity demand exceeded our supply. The solution was to schedule regular power cuts on parts of the network in order to avoid excessive load on the generation plants. Most companies and government institutions were backpedaling on their conversion to digital paperwork.

The report from the detective first on the scene, who happened to be Sergeant Mpayipheli, described the position of the body (on her back, on the billiards table), with the pool cue protruding from the chest. There was a lot of blood—this was the first significant difference between this case and the previous ones. At first, I wondered whether the cold temperatures in the ice hotel, the salt mine, and the wine cellar could have contributed to the victims bleeding out more slowly, but a quick Google search didn't support my theory. More likely, the newspapers suppressed that fact to shelter their readers. I fired off an email to Nikolay asking him to check with his contacts in Lapland and Poland.

"Where is the autopsy report?" I asked the sergeant.

"The pathology team hasn't sent anything yet. It's only been two days. Maybe next week."

"Fingerprints on the pool cue?"

"If the report's not there, forensics are still busy processing."

Slowly, very slowly, I counted to ten in my head. Then, just as slowly, I counted back from ten. When I reached one again, I was still fuming at the inefficiencies of the system, so I kept going. Zero. Minus one. Minus two. I was at minus forty-one before I trusted my voice to convey only polite neutrality. "From the photos I see, there were several decks of playing cards in the room. What happened to them?"

Sergeant Mpayipheli looked up from another manila folder, her expression distracted. "Sorry?"

"What items were taken into evidence?"

She closed her eyes briefly, remembering. "The pool cue. Trace evidence of hairs and fibers. We didn't take the pool table, just photos of the blood."

"Not the decks of playing cards?"

"No. What for? I'm sure we took prints off them."

"Can I get access to the crime scene?"

I expected the sergeant to say no. Instead, she shrugged. "We've turned it over to the hotel management for cleaning. They wanted to reopen the games room as soon as possible. Understandably so. Their guests pay top dollar. Nobody wants crime scene tape to spoil their stay."

Armed with a written authorization from Sergeant Mpayipheli, I drove to the Mount Nelson Hotel, careful not to exceed the speed limit by more than ten percent. Okay, full disclosure: twenty.

When I reached the hotel's marble arch gate, I slowed down. Crawling at five kilometers an hour along the palm-tree-studded drive leading to the main building, I couldn't help but wonder what sort of people could afford to stay here. Foreign tourists. Drug lords. Russian oligarchs.

Something clicked inside my brain. Russian oligarchs. Russian special forces, the Russian Preference. I pressed the accelerator, impatient to see the hotel's guest records. I found several Russian families and one Russian businessman, travelling solo. The receptionist provided me with security footage corresponding to the day and time the Russian businessman checked in. I reviewed it three times, then made a copy for myself.

Before I left the hotel, I let myself into the Queen of Spades games room and went through the decks of cards. One of them was indeed missing the Queen of Spades. But it didn't matter anymore.

From the Mount Nelson, I drove to the morgue. The pathologist was just writing up the Queen of Spades case. Even though I showed her my authorization note, she didn't let me take the report to Sergeant Mpayipheli. She did let me read it, though. I skimmed the pages, looking for two pieces of information. One was that the victim had been drugged and unconscious at the time of death, the sleeping pills mixed into an alcoholic cocktail. The second was the murder weapon.

"Something sharp and narrow," the pathologist said. "Not a knife. A screwdriver maybe."

"An ice pick?"

"I guess. Certainly possible in theory. I've never seen one at the shops, though."

Dinner was waiting for me when I got home. Three cheers to my awesome twin! We ate together, then she bathed Jack and sang him to sleep.

"Tell me," she said when she returned to my living room, a gin and tonic in each hand.

We Googled the dates together.

April 12 : Yuri Gagarin in space, the first human and also a Russian.

March 8: the Russian Revolution.

December 26: the date the Soviet Union was dissolved.

And May 9, of course, the Russian defeat of the Nazis.

I Skyped with Nikolay later that night. "I've changed my mind," I told him. "Let's meet face to face. I'll come to Lapland."

"I'm travelling this week," he replied. "Meet you in Singapore. I'll book your ticket."

Fifth Murder, Singapore

My ticket was Singapore Air, first class. At the airport, with a heart only slightly heavy with regret, I changed it to two business seats. They wouldn't let me downgrade any further.

Business class on Singapore Air was better than I imagined first class to be. Separate cubicles, seats that extended into full beds, beef fillet cooked to perfection served with truffle sauce.

Despite the luxurious surroundings, I couldn't sleep. I missed Jack, even though I knew he was safe with my mother for a few nights.

A limousine took me from Changi Airport to the Raffles Hotel. Nervous and tired, buzzing with caffeine, I barely took in the white pebbles at the entrance, the turbans on the doormen, the lobby full of air and light.

Someone touched my elbow before I reached the check-in desk. I didn't turn around. "Nikolay," I said.

"It's a pleasure to meet you at last, Luca."

"The pleasure is all mine." It wasn't a lie.

The pressure on my elbow increased. "I'll show you to your room. The paperwork is all taken care of."

"Not just yet, all right? I'd like to try that famous Singapore Sling first."

Nikolay consulted his watch. “The bar is still closed, but we can get room service.”

He steered me out of the entrance again, and to the left. “Yours is one of the courtyard suites,” he said. “The limo driver took care of your bags already.”

I bet he did, I thought.

We crossed a very green, very thick lawn and Nikolay unlocked one of the doors. “After you,” he said, releasing my elbow.

I stepped over the threshold, turned, and landed a punch straight into his nose. Uppercut. He swayed but didn’t fall, which suited me just fine. I didn’t want to drag him any more than was needed.

Leia appeared in the doorway and shoved Nikolay between his shoulder blades. He stumbled deeper into the room, recovered his balance, turned to face her.

And froze. For a fraction of a second, his brain couldn’t comprehend why he was seeing double. It gave me time to grab the syringe and plunge the needle into his neck. I’d carried it through customs with all the medical certificates for type I diabetes, but it wasn’t insulin in the chamber.

I pumped the poison without regret. It was either Nikolay or me, I knew that much. Inside the room, I’d already spotted a deck of playing cards and a curly sword. Probably a *kris*. No doubt my Singapore Sling would have come with an additional ingredient, just like for the other victims.

The paralysis of the limbs was instantaneous. He could still talk well enough to ask, “How did you figure it out?”

I didn’t tell him.

We didn’t bother setting the scene. Nikolay’s body lay where he fell. I wondered whether to remove a card from the deck, a joker perhaps, but in the end, I decided it was a waste of time and energy.

I glanced at Leia and I knew we were thinking the same thing. Unlike with Jack’s monster of a father, this time we didn’t need to get rid of the body.

A Little Tennessee Williams Drama

O'Neil De Noux

For Debb

There's a story that Tallulah Bankhead used to host parties naked.

That evening, when she greeted us at her apartment door, she wore a long silver dress and gave us that deep-throated, Alabama drawl, "Dahlin'. Dahlin', ouu, *dahlin'*."

The "ouu" was for me. She patted my chest and gave me a wicked grin.

This was the woman who was the first choice to play Scarlett O'Hara, only she photographed poorly in Technicolor. Every southerner knew stories about Tallulah. She had to be in her mid-forties now, still a pretty woman but not wild enough to host a part in her birthday suit anymore. She had a wide face that seemed long at the same time. Probably due to her pointy chin.

"You must be Lucien," Tallulah said in her husky voice. "Tennessee told me you looked like a young Cary Grant. And he was right." She brushed her hair back. "Tennessee's not here yet. He's next door finishing his latest opus." She turned to my date and extended a hand. "And who is this ravishing beauty?"

"Miss Bankhead, this is Carolina Leigh."

"As in Robert E.?"

"No, ma'am," Carolina said. "As in Vivien Leigh."

Tallulah had to look up at my five-foot-nine date. "Carolina Leigh. How perfectly southern. But you don't sound southern."

"I'm from Milwaukee."

"No wonder you are here, dahlin'. Who the hell wants to be in Wisconsin? Wherever did you find this lovely Yankee, Lucien?"

Miss Carolina Leigh brushed her long black hair from a face made up for a movie star shoot, her full mouth accentuating sculptured lips with its slight

Admirers moved around Tallulah and the playwright, who hadn't spotted me yet. Smartly dressed people, older than me and dripping jewelry, even the men. I knew my friend Tennessee's work, had seen *The Glass Menagerie*. I remember the newspaper proclaimed Tennessee a new, important "New Orleans-based" author. Of course, if you weren't born and raised in New Orleans, you really weren't from the city. You were "New Orleans-based."

We finished our drinks and I was easing through the people for refills when a small man rose from an armchair in front of me. That face. *Oh, Lord.*

"Excuse me," said Peter Lorre, weaselly Joel Cairo from *The Maltese Falcon* and the slimy thief in *Casablanca*. "Anybody ever tell you you look like an American version of Rudolph Valentino?"

"No." I turned away and turned back. "Liked you in *Arsenic and Old Lace,* Mister Moto."

I moved to the wet bar for another Falstaff and ginger ale.

Carolina met me halfway back, holding up several business cards. "I've met two Hollywood producers, a screenwriter, an actor, and two agents."

"They promise you anything?"

"The casting couch." She caught me with a mouthful and winked at me as she took a sip of ginger ale.

Tennessee Williams came straight to us, raised his highball glass and said, "Bourbon makes the world warm and golden." He took my hand. "Lucien, introduce me to this raven-haired beauty." He leaned close enough for me to smell his liquor breath. He wasn't drunk. Yet. "I do appreciate a pretty woman with a sharp mind. Do you have a sharp mind?"

Carolina nodded slowly as she sipped her drink.

Tennessee touched my arm. "I may not indulge myself with feminine beauties the way my friend here does, but I adore women at a deeper level." He turned to me. "I just finished the first draft of…a masterpiece. Set right here in New Orleans."

His gaze moved back to Carolina.

"Have you kissed him yet, my dear Carolina?"

"What makes you think I want to kiss him?"

"The way you look at him when he's not looking."

Carolina took the offensive, putting a hand on Tennessee's shoulder, and looked down as she toyed with her shoe. Nice, smooth move.

Tennessee leaned close to me and said, "If she throws herself at you, I'm sure you're wily enough to keep it quiet." He backed away, raising a finger to his lips. "Let everyone wonder."

He almost tripped over an ottoman and pointed at Carolina. "If you do want to talk, talk to *me*. I am always gathering material."

We stepped back to the open French doors and the cool breeze smelling of rain, Carolina pressed against my side. Voices rose and fell, Peter Lorre's nasal voice, Tallulah's twang, Tennessee's drawl. A couple guys with Midwest accents stepped close enough for us to hear them.

"One hit. That's it," Clark said, tapping the pencil-thin moustache.

A pretty boy with a thick mane of blonde curls said, "Flawed people limping about."

Ferd stepped up, said, "Macbeth is full of flawed people and Richard III limps all over the stage."

"You can't compare him to Shakespeare," said Clark.

Pretty Boy lowered his voice but not enough. "He'll never top *Menagerie*. I heard his mama told him the story."

Ferd grinned. "One never knows."

The three eased away to the wet bar and I turned to Carolina.

"Amused or bored?"

"This is interesting."

The breeze increased and I reached up to brush a strand of her hair from her eyes, then my gaze moved to those glistening lips. We finished our drinks, her shoulder pressed against mine. She caught me smiling.

"What?"

"Ginger ale. Keeping your wits about you."

She drew a finger up to my throat.

"With you, I think I have to."

We let our eyes do some talking for a few minutes. I saw a hint of excitement in those green eyes, as well as a little worry. I opened my mouth to say something clever when Tennessee's unmistakable voice cried, "It's gone!"

Tennessee stood just inside the apartment door with Tallulah, cigarette raised, and Peter Lorre. Tennessee looked as if someone had just yanked his curly hair into an Albert Einstein hairstyle.

"I tell you, it's gone." Tennessee's eyes darted about. "Someone stole my play!"

Tallulah patted his shoulder. "Now. Now. Tell me what happened, dahlin'."

He shoved her hand away and his eyes narrowed.

"Someone went next door and took my play off my desk. It's gone." His eyes panned the room. People talked over each other, I could make out nothing now.

I moved to Tennessee and Tallulah, the frazzled playwright explaining he'd just stepped next door for cigarettes and saw his play was gone.

"It was right there on the desk, sitting neat and square, and now it's gone."

"Did you lock your apartment door?" I asked.

"No. The building door is locked downstairs." Tennessee looked around. "Someone in here stole it."

Tallulah had buzzed us in.

"Did you make a carbon?" Tallulah asked as others came close.

"No. It was the first draft."

"I know how awful that is," said Tallulah. "Can't imagine rewriting something as intricate as a play."

Tennessee took her arm. "It has all the subtleties not in my notes." He looked at me. "I had the cadence, the characters talking to one another, and put it down that way. The little nuances of speech." He pulled at his hair. "Right now, my mind is a blank."

His eyes darted around and he took two steps, flopped into an easy chair.

"Who would steal a play?" Tallulah said loud enough for all to hear.

"Another playwright," said Tennessee. He leaned over, head between his knees. "All he has to do is send it to the copyright office and it's his." He looked up, saw me. "I haven't had a chance to copyright it."

"You should have your notes." This came from Peter Lorre as he closed in from the front door.

"Notes? Notes?" Tennessee stood, faced the short actor. "Shows how little you know about writing, Mr. Lorre. Notes are scribbles on paper. Dialogue flows."

Peter Lorre laughed that same maniacal laugh he used in *The Maltese Falcon* before Sam Spade slapped him. He stepped up to Tennessee, put a hand on his shoulder, and said, "Stop worrying, my friend. I saw who stole your play."

Tennessee jumped up. "What?" He looked over his shoulder at me and I moved close.

Lorre clapped his hands. "Let's make a game of this. Mr. Moto is about to solve your mystery." His Hungarian accented-voice shifted slightly, acquiring a Japanese lilt. "There are no other investigators here."

Carolina grabbed my elbow as she followed.

"Lucien!" Tennessee rushed over. "You have got to help me."

Carolina announced to everyone, "Lucien Caye here is a private eye."

Peter Lorre's grin broadened and I don't know what caused me to do what I did next, but I stepped up to Lorre and lowered my voice. "I want to know about this."

He laughed. "Didn't Mr. Spade say that to Brigid O'Shaughnessy before the police came?"

I let my head tilt to the side, raised a hand, and knuckled his chest, not too softly.

"Miss Bankhead. You have a phone?"

"Of course, dahlin'."

"Call the police. The Third Precinct isn't far."

"There's no need for that." Mr. Moto's voice was back. "You really a private investigator?"

I opened my suit coat, showed him my .38 Smith and Wesson.

Lorre ducked past me and did a jig, saying, "I was at the door and saw the thief leave and come back with something under his arm. I tiptoed after him." Lorre did a little tiptoe.

"Did anyone else see?"

No one admitted seeing anything.

"I saw where he put the manuscript." Lorre tiptoed to Tennessee and looked back at me. "It's out on the patio, behind the large red pot with the huge fern."

I turned to Tallulah. "Don't let anyone leave. I'm serious." I grabbed Peter Lorre by the elbow. "Show me."

He led me through the kitchen to the balcony running to the rear of the building and down to the brick patio. A large oak and two magnolia trees dominated the entire back yard with potted plants at the four corners. One plant sat in a red pot, a fern, and behind it I found a stack of paper clipped together. Typed on the front page was "ASND. FIRST DRAFT."

I brought it and Peter Lorre back to Tennessee, who snatched the manuscript, flipped through it, then held it to his chest, glaring at Lorre.

"Okay, hotshot." I grabbed the little man's arm again. "If it wasn't you, who did it?"

Lorre pulled away from me, straightened his shirt, and said, "Our renowned H. H. Clark." He smiled at Mr. Pencil-Thin, who jumped back, shaking his head.

"Or," Lorre said, "it was the celebrated Ferd." Mr. Heavy-Set Balding Ferd Chesterfield. Named for a cigarette.

"Or was it the young Adonis, wannabe-actor Ruffin Adams?" He looked at the pretty-boy blonde.

Ruffin Adams growled and said, "I didn't do it."

H. H. Clark said, "Neither did I."

Ferd Chesterfield said, "Clark did it."

Clark jumped back, then laughed.

The three sat on the sofa, next to one another with their arms folded, Clark still laughing at Ferd, and I wondered if this was some sort of bad act. Peter Lorre moved in front of them, seemed to be thinking hard, and then looked at me with that creepy smile.

"Mr. Moto will say, with certainty—only *one* of those statements is true."

Peter Lorre sat on an arm of the sofa.

"All right, Lazlo." Tallulah Bankhead came over and towered over Lorre. "This isn't a game."

"Who is Lazlo?" Carolina asked. She stood next to me now.

"This weasel isn't Mr. Moto, and Peter Lorre is his stage name. His real name is Lazlo Lowenstein." Tallulah gave the little man a hard stare. "And I think *you* did it."

"My dear Tallulah. Think. I was with you since Tennessee came in. Until the thief came back in and I told you'd I'd be right back. You saw who I followed?"

"No." Tallulah looked at me now. "The little stinker's right."

I watched an older couple moving to the door and I reached over, grabbed Lorre's arm.

"Well, you saw something. You knew where it was."

"I saw who did it and you have the solution. You heard the statements and only one is true. If you *are* a private eye, you should be able to figure it out."

"Smartass playing a game, huh?"

"A brain game."

I looked at the three on the sofa. "One of these three, right?"

"Positively. And you have your clues, Mister Investigator. Only one of those statements is true."

Clark started to stand up and I shoved him back down.

"Let me think a second," I said.

"I'm leaving," Ferd Chesterfield said and started to get up. I shoved him down harder and asked Miss Bankhead to go lock the front door. "This won't take long."

Peter Lorre laughed again. "I told you. Just figure it out."

"This isn't a game." Tennessee said.

"Oh, but life is a game, is it not?"

The three on the sofa all looked guilty.

"Okay." I pointed to H. H. Clark. He said, "I didn't do it."

I pointed to Ruffin Adams. He said, "I didn't do it."

I pointed to Ferd Chesterfield. He said, "Clark did it."

"Bravo." Peter Lorre applauded. "Such a memory. Only one of those statements is true."

Tallulah huffed and a couple of her guests grumbled. The men on the sofa looked hard at me.

A goddamn logic game. I felt Carolina's hand on my arm.

"Okay" I said. "If Chesterfield stole the play, then Clark's declaration was true, so was Ruffin's. That makes two true statements, so Chesterfield did not do it. If, on the other hand, Clark was the burglar, then what Ruffin and Chesterfield said was true, so it wasn't Clark. That leaves Ruffin. If he's the thief, then only one statement is true. Only Clark's." Cold smile as I move close. "Ruffin is the burglar."

Lorre explodes. "Yes. Yes. Bravo! I saw him sneak out the front door, then back in with something under his coat, and then go through to the patio, only to return immediately, and you found the play in the patio. Excellent work."

Tennessee stood next to me, asked Ruffin why he did it. Got no answer.

"Tell me why and I won't press charges."

I grabbed Lorre's arm again. "Were you in on this?"

"Oh, my goodness, no. I do love a good logic puzzle. Don't you?"

"I've never liked you." I said. "In every movie. I never liked you."

Lorre smiled and kissed my cheek.

"My dear. That is the best compliment I've had in a long time." He pulled back, looked at me. "You're not supposed to like Cairo or Ugarte. An actor who gets you to dislike him, even hate him, must have genuine talent. You see, I'm a thoroughly nice fellow in real life."

Tallulah stepped up, shaking her head. "I have to admit, dahlin', Lazlo is a nice fellow. Or was, before he ruined my party."

"I did not ruin your party." Lorre pointed at Ruffin. "He did."

I grabbed Ruffin by the collar, yanked him up, asked Tennessee, "You want me to give him the bum's rush or call the police?"

Tennessee looked at the man who'd stolen his play. "Tell me why and we'll drop the matter."

The pretty boy looked at his feet, let out a long breath. "I got tired of people fawning over people like you."

"What does that mean?" Tennessee stuck out his chin.

Could the jerk mean Tennessee was a touch effeminate?

Ruffin snarled, dug a shoe into the carpet. "You're not even from New Orleans, man."

The playwright shook his head and told me to give him the bum's rush. I took the punk outside and shoved him along, until he shuffled away along Saint Peter Street.

Tennessee Williams waited until I came back to grab my hand and squeeze. "Thank you."

I tapped the manuscript he still had pressed to his chest.

"Can you tell us anything about it?"

Tennessee beamed, lowered his voice. "It is about a woman named Stella and her brutish husband Stanley and a fading Southern belle named Blanche who has always depended on the kindness of strangers. It's about carnality. About love and sex and violence. You know. The great American trio. Set right here in this steamy city that draws passion from everyone, does it not?"

"ASND?"

"It's the title. A title that can only be New Orleans." Tennessee leaned against my ear. "Don't tell anyone right now. ASND. *A Streetcar Named Desire*."

Tallulah Bankhead stood in the center of her living room with arms spread out, said, "You have to admit, dahlin', dahlin', dahlin', I do throw a dramatic party."

Tennessee Williams narrowed his eyes, did not seem amused.

Me either.

When I took Miss Carolina Leigh home later, we kissed outside her front door, a feathery kiss that sent a chill through me.

"What does ASND mean?"

"It's a secret for now."

Those full lips pressed against mine, and the second kiss lingered until she pulled back.

"You sure I cannot tempt you into telling me?"

I shook my head. "I promised my friend."

Her left leg moved between mine and remained there.

"I think I can tempt it out of you."

I shook my head again.

"You can tempt me into a lot of mischief, ma'am, but I don't break a promise."

She leaned back, gave me a long look, and chewed her lower lip a moment before reaching back to open her door.

"You have potential, Mister Lucien Caye."

She gave me a sexy smile and went inside.

I waited three minutes, in case she changed her mind, took in a deep breath, and headed home.

Potential?

Not a bad night. Miss Carolina Leigh and those kisses and I did solve a little Tennessee Williams mystery, didn't I?

A Streetcar Named Desire. That had potential written all over it.

The Single-Handed Soldier

Jane Finnis

I knew he was a soldier as soon as he walked into the bar. He wore a patched blue cloak and was without armor or weapons, but he had the look of a legionary, tall and strong and confident. He strode across the room, and only when he came close did I notice there was something wrong with his left arm. He held it dead still by his side, hidden under his cloak.

I like soldiers. Of course I do. I'm a Roman settler in a frontier province, with barbarians across the border just waiting to invade. We need the army to keep Britannia safe and peaceful. Besides, I'm an innkeeper, and soldiers like their drink. So I smiled and said, "Welcome to the Oak Tree. You've picked a cold day to be on the road. What'll it be?"

He smiled back. "A jug of red, please. I need something to warm me up. It's bitter enough to freeze the wings off a bronze eagle, and I've walked fifteen miles today."

"Fifteen miles! Then you've earned this." I put his jug of wine on the bar, and poured out a beaker. "But you'll be used to longer marches than that, in the legion."

He made a face. "Don't remind me. Twenty miles a day, carrying my pack, wearing full armor, and some pig of a centurion yelling at me to go faster. Days like that, I used to wish I'd joined the cavalry." He glanced down at his left arm. "I miss some things about army life, but not those endless marches. Well…" he raised his wine mug. "Here's to your pretty green eyes, my dear."

So he was an *ex*-soldier. Presumably he'd been discharged because of his arm. It must have been a serious wound. I watched as he shrugged out of his thick cloak, pulled up a stool and sat down, put some coins on the bar, tossed back his mug of wine and poured himself a refill. He never moved his left arm once. I couldn't see how it was wounded because it had a fawn cloth cover over it.

He glanced round the barroom. There were hardly any customers: a group of farmworkers were drinking beer and playing dice at a corner table, a couple of army messengers were eating a hasty snack on their way to the coast. The fire burned brightly, and someone had put a vase of autumn flowers on the bar.

"This looks a nice place," he said. "Pleasant atmosphere, good wine."

"Thank you. People say we run the best inn in northern Britannia. Other people, I mean, not just me."

He laughed. "Is the innkeeper about? I'd appreciate a word with him, if he's not too busy."

"I'm the innkeeper. Aurelia Marcella, at your service."

Some people are surprised to find a woman in charge, but this customer took it in his stride.

"I'm pleased to meet you. I'm Sergius Fronto, former legionary, now jack-of-all-trades."

Sergius Fronto… I knew the name, but it took me a few heartbeats to place it. Then I remembered. "Are you the man they call the Single-Handed Soldier?"

"That's me. I lost my left arm in the service. The one I've got now is made of wood."

"You're doubly welcome, then." I meant it. This man was a hero, a legend almost. He'd saved the lives of several of his comrades in an ambush north of the frontier, even fighting on one-handed after his arm was hacked off by a barbarian. "So, Sergius Fronto, what can I do for you?"

"I'm hoping you might find a spot of work for an old soldier who's down on his luck. I'm between jobs just now, and it'll be December soon. No time to be on your own, sleeping rough."

That struck an odd note. Everyone knows legionaries get a good payout when they leave the service. If he was on the road looking for work, he must have lost his money, or squandered it. I should be cautious about employing him, but I couldn't help liking him. And he was a hero, after all.

"What have you been doing since you left the army?"

"Oh, this and that, you know. I'm good with horses, and I can be pretty useful at making and mending things. Don't let this bit of timber put you off. As I often say, I may only have one hand, but I can turn it to anything." He grinned at his own terrible joke.

There was a sudden commotion from the group of dice-players in the corner. They'd been drinking since before noon, and were now drunk enough to become quarrelsome. There were raised voices and accusations of cheating, and I reckoned they'd be fighting soon. I said quietly to one of the barmaids, "Fetch a couple of the stable hands in here, will you? I think it's time those four left."

"I'll sort them out, if you want." Fronto got up and strolled across to the natives. They looked up in surprise when he loomed over their table, and briefly stopped arguing. He said into the silence, "No violence please, lads. If you can't behave, it's time you were on your way home."

"And who might you be, telling us what to do?" The biggest of them half-rose and swung a wild punch, which Fronto easily dodged.

"I'm a friend of the innkeeper." With his good hand, he gripped the big man's arm hard enough to make him wince. "And she wants you out of here if you can't behave properly. Are you going quietly, or do I have to teach you manners? It's your decision."

They glowered and muttered, but they left. I'll admit I was impressed, and his next jug of wine was on the house. By the end of the day I'd agreed to find him some work in exchange for his keep, at least until the weather improved and he could move on.

He proved useful at odd jobs and local errands, managing remarkably well with his single hand. He was at his best in the bar, entertaining the customers with tales and jokes, and our midday trade picked up as word got around about the hero working at the Oak Tree. The men admired him, the woman adored him.

He was completely matter-of-fact about his false arm, making everyone groan with dreadful puns on the subject. ("Shall I give you a hand with that?" was one of his favorites.) His only embarrassment involved taking a bath, which he wouldn't do when there was anyone else in the bathhouse, even a slave. Everybody respected his privacy.

There was only one puzzling thing which made me slightly cautious about him. He was full of war stories, some hilarious and some grim, but nobody could get him to tell how he lost his arm. I ask you, did you ever meet a soldier who was reluctant to talk about his exploits? No, neither did I. And Fronto's legendary last fight was certainly worth the telling. But he always changed the subject if it was mentioned, and would even leave the barroom if customers got too persistent in their requests for details.

It bothered me a little at first. But then I thought, it's his business after all, and if he doesn't want to speak about it, where's the harm? I stopped worrying, and by the time the general's wife came to stay in December, he was more or less part of the furniture.

Now I know I brag about the Oak Tree, but this was the first time we'd had a general's wife as a guest. Plenty of other army types, yes, but high-ranking officers' ladies are normally much too grand for us, and stay in private villas with acquaintances along their route.

So I was delighted to welcome Lady Caelia, even though she arrived two days before the Saturnalia holiday, and I'd been looking forward to a quiet time without overnight guests. She was gray-haired, with a nose like a beak and an air of formidable authority. She explained that she was on her way to Eburacum, and had planned to make her next stop with acquaintances further along the main road. But her entourage—three bodyguards and a maid—had all developed serious stomach upsets, having eaten oysters at midday. They did look like death warmed over, and were, as she put it, "as useless as wax javelins." She'd been forced to break her journey at the Oak Tree.

The lady herself, who said she never ate oysters, was in excellent health, and she gave her instructions crisply. "We'll need breakfast early in the morning. I intend to reach Eburacum tomorrow come what may, to be there for the holiday. I've told my people to go straight to their beds so they are fit to leave at dawn. And they won't need anything to eat. They can have a little well-watered wine, nothing else."

"You'd like a full dinner yourself, my lady?"

"Certainly. What have you got to offer?"

"Chicken with leeks and carrots, followed by spiced plums. And some excellent Gaulish red wine to wash it down."

"Good. Now just one more thing. Among my baggage there's a large leather saddlebag, which I'd like stored in a locked room, please, with a guard posted outside all night. It contains something extremely valuable."

The bag was bulky and heavy—full of gold, perhaps? If so, it must be a consul's ransom. I locked it in one of our outside storerooms, and asked Fronto to stand sentry for the night. He agreed readily, commenting that it was the sort of easy job he could do with one hand tied behind his back.

When I reported back to Caelia and told her about Fronto, her face lit up, and she smiled.

"The Single-Handed Soldier? Really? What's he doing here?"

"He's been travelling about doing odd jobs since he left the army. He's staying with us till the better weather."

"He served under my husband. I used to know him quite well." Her eyes had a faraway gleam. "An extremely brave soldier, and rather a dashing one, though a bit of a rogue. If he's looking after my baggage, I'm content. My husband gave me strict instructions to keep it protected at all times. He was supposed to deliver it himself, but he broke his leg in a riding accident last month, and the task has fallen to me. It's a Saturnalia gift from Caesar for the garrison commander at Eburacum, who happens to be a kinsman of ours."

"Am I allowed to ask what the gift is?" I was born curious, and she could only say no.

She smiled again. "It's a marble bust of the Emperor Domitian himself."

"How very—ah—generous."

"Indeed. The commander will think it's more precious even than gold...if he knows what's good for him. And in fact, there *is* some gold in the saddlebag also, but only a small amount, which is mine." Her smile broadened. "But how extraordinary that Fronto will be guarding it! When I've finished my meal, I think I'll pay him a visit. Just to check the security arrangements."

Naturally I accompanied her—you can't let grand ladies wander about in the dark alone, can you? As we went outside, I wondered just how well Caelia had known the dashing Sergius Fronto in the old days. There was something about her smile... But when we got to the locked room, the tall figure on guard wasn't Fronto, but my handyman Taurus.

Caelia was annoyed. "Why isn't Fronto here? Where is he?"

Taurus explained that Fronto had gone to fetch a heavier cloak, because the night was turning even colder. "I think we'll have snow," he said. "Those clouds..."

"Never mind. Tell him I'll expect to see him in the morning."

Later, before going to bed, I went out to check that Fronto had returned. He made a suitably fearsome figure, wearing a thick sheepskin cloak and carrying a huge cudgel.

"Lady Caelia came specially to see you," I said. "She was sorry to miss you."

"Taurus told me." He lowered his voice. "To be honest, I'd rather we didn't meet."

"Oh? She says she knew you well, when you served under her husband."

"We… It was a few years ago now." He didn't meet my eye.

"Fronto, is there something you're not telling me?"

"Let's just say sometimes a gentleman should know when to be discreet. I'll avoid her if I can. What's in the bag, did she say?"

"A valuable present from Caesar. More precious than gold, apparently."

"I'll look after it, never fear. Sleep well now."

But none of us slept for long. In the night a thunderstorm blew up, and it woke me. Jupiter, the king of the gods, must have been holding a triumph, or throwing a tantrum, or both; there was almost continuous lightning, and peal on peal of thunder. Our buildings were solid enough, but the din was bound to be upsetting our horses. Reluctantly I left my warm bed, pulled on a heavy cloak and boots, and went outside to check.

I was amazed to find that it was snowing. I'd never known snow and thunder together, and the strange effect of the blue lightning on the white flakes made me want to stop and stare, but I couldn't linger. I could hear, even above the storm, that the horses were scared, stamping and calling to each other.

As I reached the stableyard, I saw something that stopped me dead in my tracks. A light where there should have been darkness…flames showing through the window of one of the tack rooms. Fire. My worst nightmare!

It had started well away from the horses' stalls, but if it spread, the whole wooden building could go up like a torch. The animals were close to panic, and they weren't the only ones.

I yelled out "Fire! Help here! Fire!" But my voice was lost in the driving storm. For a few heartbeats I stood paralyzed with indecision. I needed to rouse help, and I needed to get the horses out of the building fast, and I couldn't do both at once.

A flash of lightning showed me a tall cloaked figure hurrying round the corner into the yard.

"Fronto, thank the gods! You've seen the fire?"

"I smelled the smoke. I've woken the stable hands. I'll fetch more help, we'll need it."

"Yes, wake everyone. I'll start leading the animals out."

We soon had plenty of willing helpers, and Fronto himself was a tower of strength. He seemed to be everywhere at once, organizing and encouraging. Having led the horses out of danger into the big paddock, we made a human chain to bring buckets of water from the well, and by dawn we had the flames under control. By then the snow and the thunder had stopped too. We'd lost a good half of the stable block, and quite a lot of hay and equipment, but no people or animals had been hurt.

As things settled down I went looking for Fronto to thank him. If he hadn't been there to help…I wondered fleetingly how he'd managed to be on the scene so quickly. Never mind, he *had* managed, and I was extremely grateful.

He wasn't at his post outside the storeroom, and the door was locked. Could he be inside? I called his name a couple of times, but there was no answer. I was slightly irritated. Whatever his reservations about meeting Caelia, he shouldn't have left this room unguarded.

Caelia herself came to stand beside me at the door, and didn't waste time on greetings. "Where's Fronto? I thought he was supposed to be on guard here."

"He has been, but perhaps he's gone to change his clothes. We had a fire last night."

"Yes, they told me. I'm sorry to hear it. We're ready to leave now, so I'd like my saddlebag, please."

"Of course." I produced my own key and unlocked the door.

The room was empty. There was no Fronto, and no saddlebag.

I stood staring, shocked into silence, until Caelia said sternly, "So much for your promises of protection. Caesar's gift is gone. My money is gone. Stolen, presumably. By Sergius Fronto."

"No, it can't be. Someone must have broken in here in the night when he was fighting the fire."

She looked skeptical. "The door was still locked, and there's no indication that anyone has entered the room by force." She was right. But still…

"Who had a key? Apart from yourself and Fronto?"

"Nobody."

"So it must have been Fronto."

"I suppose so. But I'd never have believed…"

"Quite. However, what we believe is irrelevant. The facts speak for themselves. What do you propose to do to recover the bag?"

My mind raced. I should have paid more attention when Fronto said he didn't want to meet Caelia. I'd let myself believe there was a past romantic connection, but perhaps it was something more sinister. Could he have a grudge against her? Was he paying her out by stealing from her?

At least it was easy to see what we must do. "He can't have got far. He was about the place at first light, I can vouch for that. Luckily it hasn't snowed since then, so wherever he's gone, he'll have left footprints. We'll send every available man out searching. Your guards too, please."

It didn't take long. All the men had to do was find tracks heading away from our buildings and follow them. One set led to Fronto, crouching in a thicket in the woods about a mile away. Caelia's chief guard brought him back into the stableyard, and I was relieved to see that he brought the saddlebag too. "He'd left this along the way," the guard said. "Must have got too heavy for him."

My relief was short-lived. While a servant went to fetch Caelia, who had gone back inside for warmth, I unfastened the saddlebag. It contained a large cloth-wrapped bundle, Caesar's present presumably, but no gold. The money was still missing.

Caelia's voice rang out as she strode across the yard. "And who, pray, is this? Because it certainly isn't Sergius Fronto."

I gaped at her. "Not Fronto? But of course it is."

"Don't argue with me. I know Fronto. This man seems to have suffered the same disability, but he isn't Fronto." She addressed the captive. "You're an impostor, aren't you? You've no right to the name or the reputation of the Single-Handed Soldier."

I couldn't believe what I was hearing, and his reaction surprised me even more. He might have been angry if she was wrong, or ashamed if she was right. Instead, he merely smiled at her.

"No, my lady, I'm not Fronto. You of all people would know that."

"Then who are you?"

"Helvius Maximus. Fronto was my comrade and my best friend."

"Helvius Maximus… Ah, yes, I remember you now. You were in that final ambush with him?"

"I was. He saved my life. We left the legion together."

My astonishment was quickly followed by anger and disappointment. I'd liked this man, I'd trusted him, yet he was not only a thief, but a fraud as well.

"So then, Helvius Maximus," Caelia continued relentlessly, "what have you done with my gold?"

"I don't know about any gold. I took that bag of yours because I thought it must be valuable, but then it was too heavy to carry far, and I left it. I never looked inside."

"I don't believe you." She turned to her guards. "He must be carrying the coins. Search him."

They stripped him and thoroughly examined his clothes and boots, but they found nothing suspicious. I watched him, mildly curious. Naked men are no great wonder, but this one had jealously guarded his privacy. Now here was his false left arm exposed to full view, fawn cloth cover stretching from shoulder to hand. A clever piece of wood, I thought, fitting snugly by his side, so lifelike in shape. It couldn't be solid, surely, it would be too heavy for him to carry all the time.

Then I knew. If that wooden arm was hollow, it would make a perfect hiding place. I looked round the yard and spotted Taurus carrying a bundle of tools. I beckoned him over, took his long saw, and pointed it at the soldier. "I've realized where those gold pieces are hidden. They're tucked away inside that wooden arm of yours. Get them out now… or I will."

"No! It's solid, this arm is, I swear it. Solid timber."

"We'll see, shall we?" I stepped up close to him, and told his captors to keep tight hold of him. "I'll saw through this. It won't take long."

"No, please!" His face had gone ashen pale. "Don't take my arm away. Please!"

I placed the blade squarely across the cloth cover, just above the elbow. I began to saw at the arm, and it wasn't easy, because the teeth caught in the cloth, as they do in rough tree bark. But I persisted. Back and forth went the blade, once…twice…

"All right!" he shouted. "You win. Take that thing away, and I'll show you."

I lowered the saw and stepped back.

With his right hand he fumbled under his left armpit, loosening the straps there. He pulled sharply, and I thought the whole arm would come away, but instead he peeled back the thick cloth cover, stripping it right down the arm and over the wrist and hand. As he did so, a rain of gold coins cascaded out from all along the inner arm, where they'd been concealed beneath the cloth.

And under that cover was a perfectly ordinary flesh-and-blood arm. I found it far more shocking than the wooden one I was expecting.

Caelia was the first to recover her voice. "Well, that's something, I suppose. Gather those coins up and let's go inside."

I sat everyone down in the bar, and one of the maids brought warmed wine, and a spare blanket for Fronto, I mean Helvius. He was shivering with cold, and drank gratefully, and it was strange watching him warming his two hands round his beaker. His left arm was paler-skinned and thinner than his right one, and as I looked at it, my anger returned. But before I could tell him what I thought of him, Caelia took charge.

"So, Helvius, you admit you're a fraud and a thief?"

He shrugged. "I can hardly deny it, can I?"

"Where is Fronto now?" Caelia asked.

He sighed. "He's dead. I'm sorry. I miss him."

"I'm sorry too." She paused and wiped a hand across her face, as if to tidy a loose strand of hair, except there wasn't a hair out of place. "How did it happen?"

He sipped some wine. "We stayed together after we left the army, we even tried to settle down. We had a farm for a while, but we didn't take to it. We didn't want to be stuck in one place for the rest of our lives. We went travelling, picking up casual work. All over the place we went. It was a good life, and it suited us." He shook his head sadly. "But last year he took fever and died. We were in the far west, where nobody knew us. So I buried him there, and then I—well, I became Fronto."

"But why?" I asked. "Why give up the use of your arm when you didn't have to?"

"That's easy," Caelia answered. "My husband arranged a special military pension for Fronto, as a reward for his bravery. You couldn't tell the army about his death, could you, Helvius? Otherwise the money would have dried up. You despicable little worm, stealing from a dead hero."

"We were friends, he wouldn't have minded. And it wasn't just the pension, you know. I saw the way old Fronto was treated. Wherever we went, he got the best of everything. Free drinks, free food, and the women—he could take his pick. Everyone tries to help a wounded soldier."

I could vouch for that. I felt a fool for having been taken in, and yet, in spite of everything, I couldn't dislike the man entirely. He'd worked honestly for me, and last night he'd saved my horses.

Helvius sighed again. "I reckoned the chances of meeting someone who'd known either Fronto or me were pretty remote. Seems I was wrong."

"Wrong in all respects," Caelia said severely. "You're a thief, and you'll be punished as one. You've stolen a pension from the army, and the reputation of a hero. And you'd have taken Caesar's gift and my gold, if it hadn't been for the fire."

He nodded. "I wanted to disappear before morning, because once you saw me, my game would be up and no mistake. I was about to ride away last night under cover of the storm, but then the fire started, and I couldn't." He looked, of all things, embarrassed, and took a long swallow of wine to hide it. "I couldn't do that to Fronto."

"What do you mean?" I asked.

"Maybe I've not been completely honest. Fronto wouldn't have minded that. But running away, that's something different. That's dishonorable. *He* didn't desert his friends when they were in trouble, and I couldn't either, when I was pretending to be him."

"But if it hadn't been for the fire?" Caelia asked.

"Oh, then I'd have got clean away. The snow would have covered my tracks, and you'd never have found me. After all, you'd be looking for a one-armed man." He finished his wine and held out his mug for a refill. Automatically I poured it. "But I missed my chance. I couldn't take a horse in broad daylight. I started walking, which meant I had to dump the bag after all, and only take the coin." He looked at Caelia. "I'm sorry, my lady. I was wrong to steal. And wrong to take Fronto's pension."

"It's too late to be sorry." She wasn't mollified; indeed, she seemed angrier than ever. "You know the punishment for what you've done. You're for the arena, and you'll deserve it. And as for you, Aurelia Marcella," she rounded furiously on me, "you'll be punished too. You've employed a criminal…"

"But I didn't know!" I protested.

"…and failed in your duty to guard Caesar's property, and mine. You'll be reported to the authorities, and very likely thrown out of the Oak Tree and replaced with someone more reliable."

Thrown out? I was as innocent as she in all this. She was being completely unfair. But she was powerful enough to carry out her threat, and we both knew it.

She banged down her beaker. "I'm disappointed in you, Helvius. Truly disappointed."

Disappointed… as the word hung in the air, I saw what was really causing her fury. It wasn't the theft, or even the chicanery of an old soldier. She was disappointed because she'd been hoping to see Fronto, maybe to rekindle some old memories. So she had indeed known him well, better than a general's lady would normally know a legionary. And she'd presumably managed to keep it a secret from her husband. What would happen now if the affair reached his ears? Fronto was beyond his anger. But not Caelia.

What I said next was reckless, a gamble. But if she was going to take away the Oak Tree, I had precious little to lose.

"It was generous of your husband to grant Fronto a pension. I mean, in view of all the rumors. But of course the general would never get to hear those."

Caelia snapped, "Rumors? What rumors? What do you mean?"

"About Fronto's romantic escapades. There were all sorts of stories… Mind you, I don't know how much of it was true. Do you, Helvius?"

He was quick to see where I was driving. "Quite a lot of it, I can tell you. A lively lad was our Fronto. And it wasn't just the common camp-women who fell for him. Some very grand ladies too. There's a few husbands who'd be pretty annoyed if they heard what their wives got up to. But then again, what a man don't know can't hurt him."

There was a pause, then Caelia said softly, "Are you threatening me, Helvius Maximus?"

He was a picture of wide-eyed innocence. "I'd never dare threaten someone like you, my lady. Wife to such a powerful man as the general."

"Good. Because I can do whatever I like with you, as well you know."

"Sure you can. And if it has to be, then I'm glad it'll be Helvius Maximus in disgrace, not Fronto."

I was touched by his words, even while I knew that this was exactly what the rascal intended. I remembered all the things I liked about him, and how he'd helped save my horses, and the thought of him dying in some arena, nailed to a cross or torn apart by wild animals, was more than I could bear. "Lady Caelia…"

"Well?"

"He should be punished, certainly. But he behaved honorably last night. He risked his life. I don't believe he deserves to die now. And he was Fronto's friend. Isn't there some other solution?"

She was silent a long while, then she sighed. "Perhaps you're right. Very well. Helvius, I'll give you two choices. Death in the arena, or life in the army. If you reenlist as a legionary, I'll consider you've paid your debts."

"Reenlist? Willingly, my lady. Now that Fronto's gone, I'd like that. Thank you."

"And as for you, Aurelia Marcella: do you swear that you didn't know this man was an impostor?"

"I swear it, by all the gods. How could I know? I was never lucky enough to meet the real Fronto."

I'd struck the right note. She sniffed, and once again raised her hand to sweep a nonexistent strand of hair out of her eye. "Alright. I shan't report you this time. But if I hear of any more trouble here, or if I discover that either of you have been spreading these ridiculous rumors you spoke of…"

Helvius grinned. "What rumors?"

I said, "The only rumors I'll be spreading are about the heroic war record of Sergius Fronto, and how we were lucky enough to have him working here for a short while, just before his very sad death. I'm sure we're all familiar with those, aren't we?"

Caelia got up and said quite gently, "I must leave now. Helvius, you'll accompany me to the garrison at Eburacum. You can reenlist there."

"Thank you, my lady. And Aurelia, thank you too. I won't let you down. No more single-handed soldiering for me."

"Then good luck go with you, Helvius."

They rode away, and I decided we would begin our Saturnalia celebrations a day early. I needed a jug or two to get over the fright Caelia had given me. And I wanted everyone to drink a toast to the Single-Handed Soldier.

"Yeah," Lani said. She was sick to her stomach now. It was hard, thinking of the past, of Jeremy, or his fist overhead, blocking out the light from the chandelier in their shared living room like the moon eclipsing the sun.

"His mother killed him. It was too bad," she said. "I liked her. She liked me too. Even after I finally worked up the courage to leave Jeremy, she'd call and check on me. That's why she..." Therapy wasn't immediately helpful when it came to dealing with these feelings. Lani had known that walking in, but still, this was rough. Like *physical* therapy, except instead of cracking joints and stretching tendons, it was her memories getting worked.

"How did you feel about the trio of exes originally believed to have been the killers?" the therapist asked.

"I admire them," Lani said. "They're strong women. Jeremy was a monster. They reached out to one another, found solidarity and sisterhood."

"But they didn't reach out to you."

"They were planning to murder him. They thought...they knew..."

"That you have an unerring moral compass and would turn them in for conspiracy to commit murder."

"I'd already been in the papers," Lani said. "Because of Maureen, and the Williamsport College serial killer."

"And the third case." That merest hint of a question again. Just enough to invite a response. The therapist ran her thumb across the screen of her phone again. Was she reading the news reports?

"Officer Scsavnicki," Lani said. "Daniel. You know about this. This is a state-mandated therapy session. Do we have to rehash everything? It's..." Lani paused. "Triggering."

Lani noticed the therapist raising an eyebrow. It could mean anything, but did it? *Triggering* was a word used by people mostly younger than Lani, and more casually. And Lani didn't just solve the mystery of who had killed Daniel Scsavnicki; she used the officer's own gun to defend herself against the murderer.

Who had also been a cop.

It's hard to shoot a police officer and get away with it. Even a crooked one who was himself a cop-killer. Even in self-defense.

Her first, and only, time using a gun. Triggering.

"I'm not exactly Jessica Fletcher here," Lani said to fill the void of silence.

"Heck, you're not even a novelist or an otherwise idle playboy. They make it look easy on TV and in novels," the therapist said. "But it's not easy, is it? Solving three murders. Ending one life. Finding yourself in danger."

"*Putting* myself in danger," said Lani. "More than just finding myself in danger. I'd never done anything like it before Maureen was killed."

"Yes, and you did it with no training. No support. You're neither a police officer nor a PI. How does it feel now? Do you feel as though you're putting yourself in danger?"

Another scan of the room. Lani hoped she wasn't making it too obvious. The therapist's shoes (sensible). Her nails (unpainted, well-clipped). The ventilation (seemingly idle). That aspidistra (still plastic, still weird).

"I mean to say," the therapist said, "are you experiencing the same feelings now that you did when you first realized you were in danger? Say, back at your alma mater, or when confronting your ex's mom..."

Lani inhaled. No unusual smells, just her own sudden burst of sweat. She tried to recall if anything had seemed out of place that morning; did any car hang in her rearview mirror for longer than necessary? Did the insurance form she'd filled out in the equally nondescript waiting room leave her vulnerable to doxing, SWATting, or even just coming home to a man with a gun waiting, naked, in her living room, her carpets already coated in plastic tarps?

"Lani. Lani Weiland," the therapist said. Lani felt her face burn. She had drifted again. But when she had drifted in the past, it had always been for a reason, because something was out of place, something she couldn't let go of until she figured out what was going on.

"Why do you have a plastic aspidistra?" Lani demanded.

"Are you into horticulture?" the therapist asked.

"I have many eccentric hobbies."

"Just like so many amateur sleuths..."

"But why would you have a plastic aspidistra?" Lani asked again. "They're too hardy to die—they thrived in stuffy Victorian homes; they can withstand massive neglect, care little for temperature extremes, and barely need watering."

"Doesn't mean I want to have a real one in this office, though," the therapist said. "I have a black thumb."

Lani clutched the sides of her chair's seat to keep from rising to her feet. "I was...imprecise." If it came to it, Lani could jump up, spin on her heel, and fling the chair right at the therapist. That calmed her. "I mean, why would *anyone* have a plastic aspidistra? Why would such an item be manufactured? They're not a popular houseplant in the US, or even in this century, anywhere. You can't find a real one at most nurseries anymore, so why would there be a plastic one anywhere, much less here?"

"Why do you think there might be one?" the therapist asked. "Why do you think this is more important than the symptoms you've been experiencing?"

"This is one of my symptoms," Lani snapped. "I see anomalies everywhere. And connections too. Connections between anomalies; anomalous connections. Orwell wrote a novel called *Keep the Aspidistra Flying*, about middle-class respectability and advertising. Then he wrote *Nineteen Eighty-Four*, about an omnipresent surveillance state—"

"I'm familiar with George Orwell," the therapist said. She put her phone down, finally.

"The point is the connection. How do we keep to middle-class respectability without going overboard with either greed or oppression? The world is *limned* with crime and deviance."

"Limned," said the therapist, a bit hesitant now.

"Too inarticulate for law," Lani decided. "To be limned with something is to be suffused with it. Usually it means with a bright color, like a golden thread stitched into some garment, but…"

"Crime is dark, not light," the therapist said, brightly. Perhaps, Lani thought, the therapist was pleased to believe that Lani thought her intelligent enough for medical school, even if she had ended up a mere psychologist.

"It's light to me. It's like finding an abandoned flashlight under a bush, still on and sending a beam through the leaves and branches," Lani said. The therapist made to open her mouth, but Lani snapped. "Yes, like with Maureen, my college roommate. Or like your phone buzzing to life with a notification from an app you've forgotten you even had. Yes, like with Jeremy…or like a gun going off in the dark and for one terrible moment the whole room is lit, like with—"

"I understand," the therapist said. She was very much keeping her gaze on Lani, and trying not to look at the aspidistra.

"Do you? *You're* a suspect now. Do you understand that? You're up to something."

"I understand that one aspect of post-trauma is hypervigilance…" the therapist began.

"I'm not paranoid," Lani said. "I'm observant."

"It's just a fake plastic fern."

"Aspidistra," Lani said. "Did you have it made? I am sure there are no mass-produced plants. Did someone give it to you?"

"You said I was a suspect—you've adopted some cop lingo, Ms. Weiland," said the therapist. "What do you suspect me of? Close ties to the bespoke plastics industry?"

"I suspect that you're testing me, to see how good I am," Lani said. "How good at detection I am. Whether I'm all I'm cracked up be" Lani's lips twitched. "There are a couple little Freudian bits in there, eh? How *good* I am; I'm *cracked up*."

"It's not unusual for a client to read up on psychology, to 'psych out' the therapist. You're intellectualizing."

"I think you're a bit too straightforward to be a therapist," Lani said. "You work for the government, sure, but there's something else going on here."

"I'm a psychologist, not a psychiatrist," said the therapist. "I can't diagnose you."

"But if you could...paranoia? Maybe even paranoid schizophrenia?" Lani said. "Histrionic personality disorder? Generalized anxiety disorder?"

"If the state wanted a diagnosis—"

"Ah."

Lani thought. *The state*. That was a little different from a serial killer, or an angry mother, or a crooked cop. The state was inexplicable. It was different from the sum of its parts, different from the personal feelings of its representatives. It cared nothing for love, or vengeance, or psychological compulsions. The state made a show of caring for justice, for middle-class values even, but for the most part, the state seemed to care for its own existence and expansion. The state was interested in maintaining its own monopoly on violence. The state, yeah...

"If the state wanted a diagnosis, it would find a way to get one, and lock me up. I could lawyer up, appeal to the media."

The therapist said nothing.

"The aspidistra is a test," Lani said. "Not your test, the state's test. Would I notice it? Would I say something? Would I just wig out? Am I just someone with trauma and a hypervigilant streak, or can I really...detect?"

The therapist peered at Lani, moved her lips without speaking. Then it all came out. "No questions, remember? And that seems like a roundabout way to recruit detectives, don't you think? You're…" she glanced at her phone, tapped the screen, and read from it. "Forty-three years old now. No athletic background. You don't even have a driver's license. You wouldn't last a day in the academy."

Lani nodded. "Exactly! This isn't some test for policing. Not mainstream policing, anyway."

"Mainstream policing," the therapist repeated. Not a trace of a question in that, but perhaps a hint of cynicism.

"You've been nudging me, here and there, to reach some specific conclusion."

"Is that your job?"

"No, I'm an amateur," Lani said, her tongue acid. "I get what you're hinting at. You're *not* a therapist, or not much of one. Maybe a lawyer after all, probably a cop, or at least an employee of the police department and not the courts."

The therapist said nothing.

"Confess," Lani said.

"Me?"

"Yes, you."

"What do you want to hear, Ms. Weiland? That you're so special, so observant, that the police department is testing you? To make sure your crime-solving wasn't just some fluke? To see if you could be an off-the-record secret detective for the department? Someone we call in when there's a case we can't untangle, or one that's too politically sensitive or tied up in legal red tape to deal with?" the therapist said. "Maybe we're not even the police. We're the FBI. The NSA. Some organization you've never even heard of, with agents embedded in every level of law enforcement, observing and recruiting savants such as yourself." She exhaled pointedly.

Lani waited for a moment. The trick was box-breathing, something Daniel Scsavnicki had taught her about interrogating hostile but non-violent suspects. Just to retain the initiative when challenged. Inhale slowly, mentally counting to four. Hold the breath for four. Exhale for four. Then speak.

"You said *we*," Lani said.

"Well, then, I suppose the offer is yours to accept or decline, Ms. Weiland," the therapist said.

Lani's heart thumped, blood filled her ears. *Yes, yes, I say, yes…* She'd always wanted to fight for justice, to right wrongs, to help people. To fight evil.
But then something in Lani's veins felt thick, like a poison. More betrayals, more danger, the possibility of another gun pressed against her sternum by a giggling man, a thick forearm around her throat, a sniveling "please don't" she'd sworn she'd never say but found herself mouthing while the woman she had once called "Mom" stood over her, knife in hand. Her heart didn't slow down at all, but it beat at a different, darker tone. Enthusiasm buried in a tar pit of fear.

"But…" Lani said. "The trauma. I do have PTSD, I think. I spend so much time just in bed, crying and crying, my eyes squeezed shut so I won't see anything and start drawing connections. Will you help me?"

"No questions," the therapist said.

"But, can I receive treatment for it?" Lani asked.

"Oh, dear," the therapist sighed. "If we treated you for that, you wouldn't be useful to us at all."

Rosy Is Red

Sally Spedding

Monday 23 November 1985, 9:00 a.m.

Just think, right now in sunny Sydney, some lucky dude was trotting along to Bondi with his board under his arm. Or, as it would still be the weekend there, reclining on his airbed by the pool with an ice-cold 40 in his hand.

Damn.

His desk phone…

More trouble.

***

After the call, Sam Cottrell stared out of his Apex Private Detective Agency's office window ten floors above Shoreditch, east London, where even the pigeons had given up waiting for the tea trolley's first visit. Diagonal, rust-colored rain from some desert or other battered the vast sheet of glass in front of his desk, and if he shut his eyes, he could imagine he was back home at Killiemore in the depths of winter. A scared kid waiting for yet more lightning to strike. And even though he'd built up this business from a basement in Tottenham five years ago, he was still scared. Ever since last Thursday, when he'd smelled that distinctive, male body odor and felt hot breath on the back of his neck, he'd wanted to be anywhere but here.

***

A tap on his door.

He swiveled too fast away from his Amstrad and the chair spun him around an extra circuit. Not very clever. From now on he must make sure both he and his desk faced what could be a lucrative new assignment door. Bad feng shui otherwise, so the tea lady had opined. And she knew a thing or two.

"Only me, the Mongoose," came a young woman's voice, and Sam let out a ridiculous sigh of relief. Seconds later, there she was, Jenny Mason, his original partner in crime—with rain-glazed skin, brown hair almost black from being wet, showing the shape of her clever head. With her cell phone clamped to her ear, she gestured to him that the call was almost over.

"No worries," he said, returning to his screen, adding to his preparatory notes for a client meeting.

He'd nicknamed her the Mongoose after she'd solved their first tricky case. She'd admitted being flattered by it. Better than Snake Killer anyway, but right now, given what was happening in his life, that might be more appropriate.

"The hospital's just phoned," she said, frowning, returning her phone to its pouch belted around her shapely waist. "Mom's struggling. They're giving her oxygen all the time now." She checked her watch. Squeezed her eyes shut, then opened them again. He'd never seen her cry and didn't want to. Since leaving the Met after too many years of sexist crap, she'd become the main brick in his wall. Invincible, and with useful contacts.

Sam got up and, without reserve, gave her a hug. Her musky scent and the weather she'd brought in filled his nose. "I'm so bloody sorry," he said. "Anything I can do?"

"Thanks, but I'll be fine. St. George's hospital's really good, so I've heard."

"Look, I've had a call too. I'll be over at Temple Gates if you need me."

"Where the hell's that?"

He gave her the full address, printed off his page of notes before picking up his phone from the desk's top drawer, and his bulging briefcase from beside it. "If your Mom's alright, I'll see you there. If not, no stress…"

However, when he looked up, about to warn her of his very own personal stalker, she'd vanished, save for the faint whiff of her perfume making him feel seriously alone. Also aware that locking the office meant possible loss of income. Most inquiries to Apex began with an in-person visit, and each one taken on kept the wolf from the door.

***

Sam hurried past his poster collection, showing Sydney Harbor Bridge, the Cape Byron lighthouse, and Ayers Rock in all its forbidding beauty, into the lift and down to Albion Street. Selfishly he hoped the Mongoose's mother would hang on. Both women had grown much closer since Mr. Mason, newly retired, had died in a pileup on the M25 last Christmas. If his widow went too, the personable and diligent ex-cop and crime fiction fan, who'd kept business coming in and his accountant off his back, might just jump ship…

Sam ran to his Volvo across the flooded car park, instinctively glancing back at the office block, where even the filthy rain couldn't disguise what was standing at the canteen window directly above his office.

His dirty secret, following his every move.

No….

***

Given the weather conditions, he drove way too fast along Stratford Road with Arctic Monkeys filling his space, blocking out what he mustn't remember and the fact that she wasn't sitting next to him. He had a job to do. The puzzling matter of the vicious death of a broodmare at Temple Gates, the Coleridge-Burton family seat in Essex. Also a prestigious stud farm and racing stables established shortly after the last war. Its well-bred thoroughbreds regularly picked up the biggest prize money, both on the flat and over fences.

So far, nothing was tailing him.

Past Ilford, and its premature army of inflated Santas crawling up house walls and drainpipes, before he turned on to the A113 northeast where gunmetal clouds shifted and separated, letting in some blue. But even this couldn't dispel the darkest cloud that was Calum, his older brother, let out of the Scrubs at 08.00 hours last Thursday morning. His threatening closeness behind him one hour later had made him seem more like three feet taller than the four inches he actually was. Estuary, not Irish, in his voice. Harder than nails.

"Ye've got till Christmas Eve to settle yer debt," he'd snarled. "Got it? Or else I'll be wrapping ye up nice and tight with tinsel and the works for the fuzz to open…"

Settle yer debt…

Exactly what he'd said.

***

Just past the sign for Weald Bassett, Sam dropped a gear up Temple Hill as those three ominous words fluttered in his mind like the bats in Killiemore

Cottage, where both boys and their mother had spent too much of their lives. Where trigger-happy Calum would take a pop at anything that moved.

And twelve years ago, he had.

***

Another sad item on Sam's wish list loomed into view as he drove up the hill toward his destination. A place like this with what seemed like half of Essex for its grounds.

Bejesus. Could a house be much bigger or a driveway much wider? He asked himself. And look at those cedars, whose strange, layered limbs spread motionless and black against the brightening sky where an aircraft and its vapor trail was heading west.

The perfect image for a true crime book cover, he thought. Then thought of what awaited him, and who needed fiction? He also asked himself if he'd want a tree like that as a permanent feature outside a main window.

No way.

***

He cast around for the best place to park, also checking the expanse of weed-free gravel for any recent horse trailer's wheel imprints, or those of a loaded vehicle in a hurry, but as far as he could tell, the embedded chippings lay undisturbed.

Curiouser and curiouser, given that his latest client had said this was the only way to and from the stables. The crime scene.

He then turned his attention beyond it to the mock Palladian pile hogging the sky, tempted for a moment to record on camera its position in relation to other possible factors. But manners dictated the proprietor must give permission first. This was a case that wouldn't be involving the fuzz just yet. He mustn't spoil what had, only a week ago, been an accidental and very useful meeting with the stud's owner and trainer, Felix Coleridge-Burton, at the local point-to-point race.

The man had never trusted the police since a bent newly-promoted chief inspector was found snooping by the gallops and had funded a villa in the Algarve on his tipster proceeds. So, a flatfoot with excellent references and a feisty, good-looking sidekick who'd ditched the force had been Coleridge-Burton's first port of call…

Sam switched off the engine and checked himself in his rearview mirror. Although he looked every one of his twenty-nine years, his latest haircut, stubble-free cheeks, and good clothes helped present the image he wanted.

***

Just then, a tall, skinny guy in dark green livery that included a peaked cap appeared from a booth built as solidly as the house itself, but half-hidden by deliberately untrimmed hawthorn bushes. Having slapped a visitor sticker on the Volvo's windscreen, he gestured to Sam to continue walking round to the rear of the house, from where a line of horses could be seen moving like a surreal brown chain across the gallops.

"No perky Miss Mason with you today?" asked the guy in a Yorkshire accent before checking Sam's ID. He'd obviously heard of her from his boss.

"Family stuff. She may be along later."

"We certainly hope so. We need all the brains we can get."

Reeking of Lynx and a recently stubbed-out cig, this guy, who'd given his name and previous life as Graham Sturt, ex-SAS in Belfast, led him past an annex of garaging, storage units for the stables, and the stableyard itself. Or rather, the stable acre.

Sam glanced around, mentally totting up what this and its well-bred, four-legged occupants were worth. He estimated at least fifty million, given the Group One winners housed here, plus broodmares and stallions from Europe and beyond. Then he sniffed hay and molasses mingling with leather and invisible dung. These delivered another surge of memories best forgotten. At this point, Sturt held out a white-gloved hand, stained around the wrist. "Your phone please, sir. It's security."

This must be a joke. He *was* security. Here to investigate the theft of an almost full-term colt from a top broodmare. A crime which must, for the moment, be kept under wraps.

Sam hesitated, and in that pause, the offending phone rang.

"Excuse me," he said, turning away to listen. "It's Miss Mason."

She seemed tense, brittle. Not like her at all.

"To be honest, Sam, I'm not coping very well," she began on a poor line. "For a start, it took me over half an hour to find Mom. Right next to the morgue, if you please…"

He guessed the worst.

"How is she?"

"Gone. Ten minutes ago. Got to hang around and do all the necessaries. Is that okay?"

Aware of the uniform listening in, Sam couldn't say what he really wanted. "Don't be so bloody daft," came out instead. "'Course it is."

"Where are you?"

"Temple Gates, like I said." He glanced at his watch. "I'll be back in the office by two. Hang on in there and let people help you. Promise?"

No reply, and all the while, that impatient, white-gloved hand was waiting.

***

An anemic sun cast the inside of loose box number 32 the color of that thin honey his Gran used to make before she lost her only daughter and before she herself passed away. For a moment, Sam had to search for the stricken mare, half-buried in the bloodied straw in the unlit corner. Then his hastily-eaten breakfast began to travel upwards into his throat. The neatly severed umbilical cord trailed into the sunlight. Her lips were pulled back over her teeth as if she'd died in agony.

Suddenly that partial sunlight vanished. Felix Coleridge-Burton was standing in the doorway behind him. The trim, buttoned-up owner-trainer stood in silence while Sam made rapid shorthand notes on the grim scene. Judging by the mare's eyes, her blood's color, plus the multitude of flies already settled on the open wound, the time of death could have been early that same morning. Five, six, or seven o'clock, most likely, and being well into November, darkness would have been an asset to her violator. Singular or plural, too soon to tell.

"You said your vet's already taken a look. Is he around?" Sam asked, once he'd finished writing.

The middle-aged owner-trainer shook his head. "It's a she. Our best Derby prospect has suffered a burst blood vessel. She's tied up with that for a while…"

"And her opinion on this?"

"Speechless. For the first time in her life."

Sam bent down to stroke the mare's rigid head. "What's this poor bugger's name? You never said."

"Rosy Dream. A lovely, lovely girl…"

The guy was choked alright. Who wouldn't be? Here was a bright chestnut with a fine winter coat, four white socks and a straight blaze, reminding him of the filly foal he'd cared for as a teenager. Saved for by sticking at a paper route for three years in all weathers. Sunny, he'd called her, over whose head Calum had fired a shot for a laugh. Until the barbed wire fence stopped her panicked escape…

He found himself looking for traces of old scars; other possible violations. There were none.

"She was a stunner," he said out loud.

"So's the stallion. Pas de Deux by Sadlers Wells. Damned thing is, if his missing foal survives this trauma, he really could hit the big time."

"Surely he'd be recognized?"

Coleridge-Burton let out a sour laugh. "You clearly don't know how far the unscrupulous will go to disguise an animal. But if the foal's not registered with Weatherbys…"

"Go on."

"Worthless."

Sam stood up and pulled out his new camera. "Be interesting to see who crawls out of the woodwork."

"Indeed."

"May I take some shots of Rosy?"

A frown, a doubtful pause. After all, both men were still strangers.

"Only if they become my property when this is all over."

"No worries."

Using flash, Sam took four photos, focusing on the gaping wound in the poor creature's belly, then turned around. "To me, sir, this caesarean looks like an expert job. Someone, or more than one, knew what they were doing. There's no evidence of her being restrained or stunned. Or needle marks either. Was there any chloroform residue when you found her?"

"No, but there wouldn't be. Harry Barr, my Head Lad, found the top of her box door wide open, when it's normally shut at night."

"What time?"

"Six. On the dot as always, in winter. But as for the CCTV—I could kick myself. Its film ran out three hours later. I should have checked and installed a new one immediately…"

His stiff upper lip wasn't stiff anymore. Sam passed him his own clean handkerchief and asked a tricky question. "Is your guard on duty all the time?"

"I wish. Eight a.m. to eight p.m. Union rules. Also, his wife has ME or something terrible like that, and could we find anyone to do nights here? No way."

So, the perp or perps had enjoyed a clear run…

"How many knew when the foal would be viable? Had enough colostrum at the ready?"

A pause, during which Sturt walked by, glancing in, holding Sam's phone like a trophy. Little did the officious creep know he was at the top of the list of suspects.

"We've no other mare who's just given birth. Our five other pregnant ones aren't due to foal until next March."

"Colostrum could have been brought in from another source?"

A reluctant nod. "Could be the wrong motive altogether."

"It's the one I prefer to dwell on, sir. That whoever did this wanted the foal to survive."

The owner-trainer wiped both moist eyes with Sam's handkerchief and handed it back.

"By the way, I noticed your front gates aren't electronically controlled," Sam went on. "Are they locked at any particular time?"

"No. We've never had any trouble with security before…"

Sam broke in.

"Any chance of speaking to your Harry Barr?"

Coleridge-Burton shook his tousled, gray-flecked head.

"He's too upset. His was the last shift that ended at one a.m."

"I'd still like to see him. Who else is normally found around here?"

"My wife, Laura, who loved this mare to bits. Our son, Rex; riding work out on the gallops; plus stable hands and riders…"

"How many?"

"Twenty altogether."

Sam sensed an impossible task looming and, not for the first time, wondered why Felix Coleridge-Burton or his wife hadn't simply called the cops. They'd have provided choppers with thermal imaging. The lot.

"Can we go somewhere to talk?" he said. "Get a proper list of names drawn up…"

His watch showed 10:00. How he missed the Mongoose. At least she'd have grilled the mucking-out brigade by now.

"To me, and I don't say it lightly, sir," Sam began tentatively, "but this crime smacks of being an inside job. We need to get everyone's alibis established. And fast. Oh, and I need to know more about the mare herself…"

***

The glass-domed swimming pool beyond the orangery glittered under the brightening sky. Sam thought longingly of Bondi again, then switched back to the crime, which was growing more complex by the minute.

Rosy Dream, sired by an unproven Dreamcatcher out of an equally unimpressive Rosehill Girl, had been bought at Tattersalls in Ireland as a bargain two-year-old by Laura Coleridge-Burton in October 1973. Having proved her talent by winning the Musidora Stakes at York, she'd been put to stud as a broodmare. Not until last December had she finally conceived. The colt's sire, Pas de Deux, went on to became a Group One winner in France and twice favorite for the Prix de l'Arc de Triomphe.

"Who sold her to your wife?"

Felix Coleridge-Burton needed no prompting. "An odd setup, come to think of it. I'd gone to Newmarket with Rex, as Laura was feeling unwell. The filly was for him to develop. Irish lot they were. I'm no snob, Mr. Cottrell, but she was a real bag of nerves. Sweating all over. Not what the punters want at the sales. Everything spooked her. Took weeks to calm down, but we'd seen her potential…"

"You mean tinkers?"

"I wouldn't go that far." He pulled out some stapled sheets headed by the British Bloodstock Agency's logo. "It's all down here."

***

Although the orangery was warm to the point of stuffiness, Sam suddenly felt cold. And not just his skin. This went bone deep, as if he was back in the Moyle River that runs off the Mourne mountains. Where Calum had pushed him in and held him under, fifteen years ago to the day. A pre-Christmas treat…

Not for the first time did he want to run.

"Mr. Cottrell. Are you alright?" asked the older man. "Can I order you a brandy?"

"I'm fine, thanks." But he wasn't. Not since reading the vendor's name on the record of sale. Willing his voice to stay even, he added, "I know you want to keep this crime under wraps for all sorts of reasons, but sir, it really is a matter for the police. I'm impressed with a DS Mike Charlton at the Met. He can liaise with Chelmsford CID…"

Coleridge-Burton hesitated. Sam knew what was going through his mind, but all the while, the clock was ticking. Supposing he'd been followed? Supposing…

"You're not known for bottling out, Mr. Cottrell. Why I hired you." The toff peered at him with shrewd blue eyes. "So, what's going on? Who are these people? Have they connections to any of my staff?"

"It's not bottling out, sir. It's called…"

But before Sam could finish, a shaven-headed guy dressed like a butler pushed through the double doors from the pool, almost knocking over a tall, spiky succulent in its ceramic pot. A weird, wrinkled mask covered his face, leaving only those eyes Sam had hoped never to see again. Instead of a butler's tray, black-gloved hands gripped a police-issue Beretta 92C pointing in his direction.

Where the hell had that come from?

Then immediately, he knew…

***

Sam had kept up his workouts at the gym, and boxing down at the club, knowing that with just two slouches a day around the prison exercise yard, Calum would be unfit.

But here he was. Lean. Toned. Deadly.

In the mirror opposite, he glimpsed the owner-trainer getting to his feet and pulling out his phone. His face had paled. His hand shaking. "I need to call 999."

"Put that away and sit down, sir," said Sam, aware of his jumping heart. "This is my shout."

"No, mine, ye snivellin' worm," snarled the mask. "I done twelve fuckin' years for ye. Four thousand, three hundred and eighty fuckin' days…"

That same hateful voice last heard on a thunderous night in Killiemore Cottage when their mother announced she was leaving. Not to another man, but a simpler life on her own. She'd given up on her boys. Reached the end of her tether.

Sam had never forgotten her face as she'd spoken, or the tears not wiped away…

"Time I spiked ye good and proper, little brother," Calum added. "Burst yer fuckin bubble…"

"*You* were the reason she had to go," Sam countered. "A trigger-happy twat who never went to school, never brought in a cent to help out."

His next-of-kin moved closer. The weapon's hollow eye on his chest. Meanwhile, the middle-aged Coleridge-Burton grabbed a retro soda siphon from the sideboard before hurling it at the intruder.

"Holy fuckin' Jesus!"

Its steel-banded body had connected with the black-suited groin, bringing him to his knees with a roar of surprise. The Beretta thudded onto the tiles and skidded under a coffee table, out of reach.

"Gotcha."

Sam was on him, pinning him down as an alarm's shriek filled the room and a pair of brown corduroy legs rushed past. He smelled fart and fear. Suddenly, just as he was gaining control, a stab of ice penetrated between his shoulder blades, causing air to float from his lungs, leaving him gasping like a fish out water. Calum's mask had slipped sideways. His dog breath filled Sam's nose as a woman's voice eked into the huge room.

Who the hell?

"Your number's up, Mr. Flanagan," it said coolly. "Time you settled your debt, remember?"

He'd almost forgotten his old name, but remembered the perfume…

The Mongoose.

Impossible. But there she was. From the corner of his eye, he saw a blade in her hand, as red as her lips. In the other, the Glock he'd bought her for emergencies only.

Like now…

"You said your mother was dead," he murmured.

"Joke, thicko. More to the point, I found stuff out since Calum's trial," she went on. "Stuff I've already passed on. Did you expect him to suffer in silence while you grubbed your way upwards? Got rich on my efforts?"

"Why Sunny?" Sam could barely whisper. "She'd been *my* foal. I'd bottle-fed her and…"

"Why not? Eilidh had left nothing for you boys, but everything to her brother Seamus Nolan, who sent Sunny to Tattersalls in Wicklow. We tracked her whereabouts after that. Even as Rosy Dream. Easy to check on websites who's doing what and where. The one way you'd be taught a lesson."

"We?"

"That's right. I visited Calum in the Scrubs and we hit it off straightaway. The rest is history…" She pulled her lover out from underneath him and together they headed toward the orangery's outer door. Him stumbling. Her, purposeful as ever.

"You didn't have to kill her. You butchers…" Sam wheezed after them.

"Didn't we?"

"Is her foal still alive?"

"What d'you think? Ask Mr. Sturt. He kindly raked over the drive for us after we'd gone. Caiou, Declan."

Declan…

Sam's brain was furring up in advance of his body. Too much blood warmed his sticky hands while that long-ago storm again hurtled in from the Atlantic, cutting out the lights in Killiemore Cottage. Obliterating faces. He'd deliberately worn gloves. Nicked Calum's hunting rifle, only meaning to shoot him in the arm for giving their mother guff over growing pot, but got Eilidh Flanagan instead. In the heart.

He was clean, with no record, but not Calum. The Gardai had already cautioned him twice for misuse of a firearm.

Tough.

Then he'd legged it to Belfast without so much as a toothbrush. Got a new name. New ID. Lain low. What would anyone else have done in his situation?

But he'd never forgotten his pretty, affectionate, bright chestnut Sunny…

A wailing siren drew closer, and two armed uniforms followed by Felix Coleridge-Burton burst in. Their shouts for him to keep calm and keep breathing were fading. Everything was, save for his mother's ghostly scream rising above the wind's turmoil, suddenly burning his ears.

Year	Indictable Offenses	Non-Indictable Offenses	Total Recorded Offenses
1970	30,756	169,581	229,389
1971	37,781	198,157	235,938
1972	39,237	190,152	229,389
1973	39,000	192,451	243,426

1. The Indictable Offenses figure includes all offenses that became known to An Garda Síochána. The non-indictable figure counts the number of people against whom proceedings were taken. (Source: "Crime and Punishment in Ireland")

No Direction Home

Nick Quantrill

A Joe Geraghty Story

I was surprised to learn the woman at my door was a police detective. I'd taken steps since arriving in Amsterdam to keep a low profile and mind my own business. Anita Halberg was in her mid-fifties, a long overcoat on, a tired look on her face that told me she was overworked. Some things were universal.

"Can we speak inside, Mr. Geraghty?" she said.

"It's Joe."

"We're not on first-name terms yet."

I didn't like the qualification she'd added to her reply. I could resist, close the door, and hope she didn't come back. I could finish the book I was reading, enjoy the rest of my drink. Or I could let her inside, hear whatever she had to say. Experience told me it was pointless resisting. I stood to one side, letting her enter.

"Nice place," she said, walking in and looking around. "I often wonder if I could downsize enough to live on the water."

"You shrink your life down," I told her. It was calm and quiet on the canal. "It's surprisingly rewarding." There wasn't much for Halberg to see. My shelves contained a few books, notepads I doodled in. No personal touches.

She glanced at the mobile handset I'd placed on the small table in the corner. "You don't have a smartphone?"

"Don't need one."

"You don't have a laptop to access the internet?"

"Same answer." I didn't bother with a television, either, just a small radio set to keep me connected to the wider world. It was how I liked things. My preference was to avoid the news, preferring to do my job and return home. Books were the solace and escape I needed.

Halberg shrugged, looked out the window. "These houseboats weren't always so desirable, you know? They used to be for those who couldn't afford anywhere else, or maybe squatters. Times change, though. I understand they're very expensive now." She stared at me. "How can you afford to live here?"

"It's not mine. My employer rents it to me. There's no problem with that, is there?"

"You're a model citizen, so far as I know," she said, turning back to face me.

"Pleased to hear it."

"That said, things were different back in England for you?"

"I don't live there anymore." Hull was my home city, but I'd lost touch with the place.

"You moved here a couple of years ago, right?"

"It was too good an opportunity to miss." She was well-informed.

Halberg had her arms behind her back, a smile on her face. "A change of scenery must be nice." She picked up the book I was reading, a tattered George Orwell paperback I'd picked up from a flea market. "Good for the soul?"

"Something like that."

Halberg cocked her head slightly, not hiding the fact she was weighing me up still. "You were a private investigator?"

"A lifetime ago." I didn't like the way she'd stepped forward and closed the space between us.

She took a photograph out of her pocket and handed it to me. It showed a young woman, late teens, maybe early twenties. She was enjoying a night out in a bar with a group of friends, clearly drunk, a big smile on her face.

"Kayleigh Mainprize is from Hull like you, but also like you, she lives here now. She's nineteen years old and she's missing. The police in touch with her father in England are concerned, too."

"I'm sure they are." I tried to hand the photograph back, but she didn't take it.

"Kayleigh works in a bar in the De Wallen area."

I didn't take the bait, or jump to any conclusions. I knew it as the red-light district. I set the photograph down on top of the nearest bookcase. "I can't help you."

"Humberside Police said you'd be only too pleased to assist."

"I don't work for them."

"Detective Sergeant Coleman said you'd be happy to help us save our resources, maybe even find Kayleigh so it puts her father's mind at rest."

"That's very good of him, but I've already got a busy job."

Halberg made a show of looking again at my book and half-finished beer. "Looks like you've got plenty of spare time on your hands."

I moved toward the door, opened it for her. I was done at the mention of Coleman. Another reminder I didn't need of a previous life.

Halberg didn't move. She took out another photograph and put it on the table. "He said you should look at this."

I picked it up, looking at a shot of myself taken by a CCTV camera. This was where the conversation had always been heading. I knew exactly where and when it had been taken. It showed me outside a block of flats, close to the entrance. It related to a case I'd worked before leaving Hull. The job had been for a client desperate for answers and I'd broken into the building, crossing the line to get them for her. It had been impulsive and, it now seemed, damaging. Coleman had known about it all this time, sitting on the evidence until the right time.

Halberg pointed to it. "Maybe if you cooperate, it will be overlooked."

"I'm no longer a private investigator."

She smiled and took out a business card, placing it on the table before heading for the door. "It's in your blood, Mr. Geraghty."

***

I pedaled around Jordaan before approaching Centrum and the Canal Ring, the traffic growing steadily heavier. It wasn't a long journey, and I'd become accustomed to not using a car. Night had fallen, the trams slowing down, people sitting outside canal-side bars enjoying an evening meal, the sound of a hundred conversations as I pedaled by. Amsterdam was flat enough to remind me of home, another city that the water took as much from as it offered.

The streets grew busier as I approached De Wallen. Chaining my bike up, I remembered it was the kind of area that heightens your senses. The volume increased, neon signs assaulted your eyes. The city changed, the possibility of danger increasing without you even realizing it was happening. Human sharks circled outside clubs and bars, all wanting to empty your wallet. I watched as a small group of drunken men lurched toward one, the shark swallowing them up. I'd walked around the area once before, enough to satisfy my curiosity.

Head down, I moved deeper into the streets, the repetitive thump of house music leaking out of the buildings. The bar I was looking for was off the main drag. Standing outside, I stared at the dark windows, unable to see in. It was tempting to simply turn away, forget I'd come here, and let Coleman do his worst. It didn't have to be my problem. But Halberg's visit had unsettled me. The point of moving here had been to stay under the radar, live a quiet life, and figure out what came next. I'd left Hull thinking I could outrun any problems I had. She was proof that I couldn't.

I headed inside, knowing I had no real choice in the matter. The interior was dark, lights low. It forced me to stop for a moment to allow my eyes to adjust. A number of high stools had been placed in front of the bar, a few empty tables lined the room. A plasma screen showed the evening's football, the volume muted, no one paying it any attention.

A worker a similar age to Kayleigh took my order. I watched her take a bottle of beer out of the fridge and crack it open, figuring she maybe knew her. A man stood in the shadows at the far end of the bar, eyeballing me. He was in his thirties, dark-skinned, a couple of days' stubble on his face. Experience had taught me to quickly weigh people up, and I didn't like what I saw. The man was trouble. I pulled up a stool, still deciding how to play things. Push too hard, too soon, and you risk being shut down. Don't push hard enough, and you learn nothing. The trick is to quickly assess where the comfortable middle ground is, establish some trust.

"Cheers," I said, lifting the bottle to my mouth, offering a toast. "Not too busy tonight, then?"

"Makes things easier," she said, a local accent. "Do you want to listen to the football?" she asked, pointing toward the screen with the remote.

I shook my head, saying it was fine. "It's not really my game."

"You're visiting tonight with friends?"

"I live here now."

She smiled. "It's a nice city if you have money."

"Like anywhere," I suggested.

"You're English?"

I nodded. "I'm from Hull." There was a slight flicker at that, a pause as she composed herself.

"I've visited," she said. "It's nice."

"Not everyone will agree with you on that."

"Good and bad everywhere you go."

"The place or the people?"

"The people."

"Can't disagree with that."

She leaned in closer to me. "Which one are you?"

"I try to be one of the good guys."

"But you left?"

"Maybe I'll go back one day."

She straightened back up. "I'm hoping to go travelling soon with my girlfriend."

"Consider me jealous."

"Sometimes you have to get away, right?"

"Truer than you know." I toasted again with the bottle.

She moved off to serve another drinker. The thought of just disappearing, heading off travelling, had crossed my mind more than once. It didn't feel like something you did in your late forties. I should have figured life out by now.

When she returned, I showed her the photograph Halberg had given me. "I need to speak to Kayleigh," I said. "I'm told she works here." I explained I was a detective, an *ex*-detective, asking on behalf of her father. "He's worried about her."

The man at the back of the bar quickly walked over, ripped away the photograph. He said something angry in Dutch to the girl. I hadn't picked up enough of the language to understand, but the gist was clear. She moved away, with a quick glance back at me. The man jabbed a finger at the photograph, spoke to me.

"Who are you?"

"I'm looking for Kayleigh." I pointed to the photograph. "Do you recognize her?"

He slammed it down onto the bar. "I can't help you."

"I'm told she works here." The man shrugged, like it was no big deal to him. "Any idea where I might find her tonight?"

His smile revealed a golden front tooth. "Plenty of work around here for young women if they want it." He leaned in toward me. "Finish your beer, detective. You don't need to be here."

"I'm not police," I said, "but maybe I'll ask around, all the same?"

"Drink up and go home." The man moved away, hovering once again in the darkness at the far end of the bar. The worker who'd served me also kept her distance, eyes to the floor. I picked up my beer, thinking about my next move.

I finished my drink, kicked out the stool and stood up, headed for the toilets. The harsh fluorescent lighting contrasted with the gloom of the bar. I stood over the urinal, blinking, for a moment before I was thumped across the back of the head. Falling down face first, I hit the metal trough. I lashed out, tried to regain my footing and haul myself back up, but it was futile. My head was gripped from behind, one arm forced roughly up my back. I shouted out, my head thrust forward, bouncing off the wall in front of me. The room started to spin, a fireworks display going off in front of my eyes.

"Who are you?"

I recognized the voice of the man from the bar. I spat out blood before answering. "I'm no one," I said, trying to work myself loose of his grip. A hand went to my pockets, rummaging through them. I tried to kick back, but was pinned to the wall, unable to move. It didn't matter. Old habits die hard. I never carried ID with me when I was working.

"You don't come into my bar and ask questions," he said. "Who are you?"

"I'm just someone trying to find Kayleigh for her father."

"There's nothing here for you."

With that I was pulled away, too disoriented and weak to resist. Dragging me to an unmarked door, the man kicked it open and pushed me outside, laughing as I collapsed in a heap on the pavement.

"Come back and I will really hurt you," he said.

The door closed, leaving me to gradually sit myself back up, the cold air helping to clear my head. I looked up as I heard footsteps approach. It was the girl from the bar.

"Let me help you," she said.

A hand went out to me, helping me to my feet. I leaned against the nearest wall so I wouldn't fall straight back down, or throw up. She handed me a piece of paper, *Vondelpark 10am*, scribbled on it along with her mobile number.

"Let's talk tomorrow about Kayleigh."

***

I cleaned myself up in the toilet of a burger chain restaurant before retrieving my bike. I leaned over the canal bridge and peered down at the water, watching as it gently lapped against the side. I knocked back the energy drink I'd bought, wanting the sugar to kick-start my system again. I dabbed at my head, careful not to aggravate the place where it had hit the wall. The pain was settling into a low-level throb.

"Are you okay?"

I turned to look at the elderly man who'd walked over from a nearby cafe. I managed a weak smile, knowing I looked like a truck had hit me. "I'll survive," I told him.

"Do you need the police?"

I shook my head and thanked him for his concern. The police were the last people I needed to speak to at the moment. I threw the empty can into the bin, carefully got back onto my bike, and headed for an internet cafe I knew would be open, the night air starting to do me good.

A neon sign above the shop door advertised repairs and unlocking services, money transfer facilities and refurbished laptops for sale. I paid for the use of a computer and settled in, a handful of others at work, earplugs in.

I headed to the website for the Hull newspaper, the stories on the home page making me feel like I'd never been away. I read about traffic congestion on the main route in and out of the city, a senseless knife death on one of the city's outlying estates, the mess the city's football club was in. The news was as gray as the city I'd left behind. There was nothing on Kayleigh Mainprize's disappearance. I considered this, unsure what to conclude. Maybe she didn't spend much time in her home city, but it was still a human interest story, an easy piece that would gather all-important website hits via its local connection.

There were other ways to get background on Kayleigh, social media the obvious place to start. I was no expert, but her Facebook page was essentially open to view, giving me an insight into her life. A series of photographs told their own story, a steady succession of nights out in both Hull and Amsterdam with a revolving cast of friends. Her check-ins told me she regularly travelled on the overnight ferry from Rotterdam, the invisible elastic that connected the cities. The posts to her wall were largely inane; a mixture of photographs, inspirational memes, and music videos for songs I'd never heard before. Her more private details, the stuff I really wanted, were protected from public view. All in all, it was the life of a regular, fun-loving young person.

I went back to the photographs, looking at them in more detail. The woman in the bar who'd asked me to meet in the park tomorrow featured in many of them, including some of the Hull ones. Some showed just the two of them, arms around each other, heart emojis superimposed on top with other filter effects. Kayleigh had tagged her, so I had a name, Isa Kristiansen. Her page was more carefully locked down, no further clues, but it felt like progress. I understood why she'd passed me the note outside the bar and asked to meet. There was little else to be found on social media. Kayleigh had a Twitter account, but rarely used it, only following celebrities and showbiz accounts. Her Instagram page was locked down more securely, totally inaccessible to me.

I swallowed two painkillers. Google didn't offer me any obvious hits, but a story via the Hull newspaper grabbed my attention. It didn't contain a direct reference to Kayleigh, but a man sentenced to prison had the same surname. My head was still fuzzy, slow to make the connection. The face shown in the report was familiar. I cross-referenced to the photographs on Facebook, finding a match. I'd found her father. I placed my hands behind my head and closed my eyes, sure this wouldn't be news to Halberg and Coleman. There was more to the story, I was sure.

***

I took a seat outside the coffee shop in Vondelpark, blinking against the morning sun. The painkillers were barely touching the sides, a splitting headache after little sleep. I didn't want Hull intruding into my life at the moment. It was a stone that didn't need lifting up because I might not like what I found underneath. I wasn't a private investigator these days, but some people still wanted to fuck with me. The black coffee in front of me was helping a touch, the nearest thing I had to a magic bullet. The high-pitched screams of enjoyment from the children in the playground on the opposite side of the pathway weren't so helpful.

The day was starting to unfold. Joggers and cyclists carefully picked their way along the paths, the green space an escape from the stresses of the busy city it served. The tourists were easy to spot, their bikes branded with rental company signage, most making slow and unsteady progress as they passed where I was sitting. I watched as Isa approached and leaned her bike against the fence surrounding the cafe area. She made her way over to me, placing her rucksack on the free chair between us. A waiter hovering at the entrance moved toward us, but she shook her head, saying she didn't want anything.

"Nice to see you, Isa," I said.

"You know my name?" A small smile on her face. "Well done."

"I'm supposed to be a detective, remember?" I returned the smile. "Kayleigh really should be more careful about who can see her Facebook page."

"Maybe I'll let her know that."

"She's the girlfriend you want to go travelling with, right?" I waited for to her to signal her agreement. "You met in the bar?"

"In a club. Kayleigh got me the job in the bar with her."

"You live together?"

"Of course, but it is expensive here. We've got a small apartment for now."

"So what's brought on this urge for you to go travelling together?"

"Who doesn't want to see the world when they're young?"

It was a fair answer and one I couldn't find fault with, even if I suspected it wasn't the entire truth.

"You said you used to be a detective?" she said.

"A private investigator for hire back in Hull." I shrugged. "It makes you enemies."

"But you helped people?"

"I tried my best." I sipped at my coffee, happy to take my time, hopefully gain her confidence. "Your boss at the bar doesn't like me very much."

Isa didn't answer, choosing to fiddle with her mobile phone instead. She glanced over at the playground before taking a deep breath and turning to face me. "He's not a nice man."

I wasn't going to disagree with that. I had the wounds to prove it.

"Why do the police think you can help them?" she asked me.

"It's complicated." I wasn't sure it would make much sense to her. "Some trouble back home might go away for me if I help them on this." I shrugged. "Maybe that's true, I don't really know. I just don't like being used, though."

"Sometimes we don't have a choice."

I sat back in my chair, playing those words around in my head, wondering how much say we ever had. A picture was starting to form. She glanced across again at the playground, scanning the faces. This time, I did the same.

Families played, children enjoying themselves on slides and climbing frames, roundabouts and sandpits. The space was ringed with a bench, adults sitting down and checking their phones. It took me a moment to realize one of those adults wasn't doing that and was staring back at us. I took my time, wanting to be sure.

I stood up, pain shooting down my side. It slowed me down as I headed for the playground, ignoring Isa's shouts. It took Kayleigh a moment to react, standing up as I tried to increase my pace. She moved quickly over to a bike and climbed on, throwing a glance over her shoulder at me before pedaling away. I put my arm in the air, gestured to her, shouting that I only wanted to talk. It was futile. I'd spooked her. I rubbed at my side, the burning pain feeling like a hot knife being twisted inside me. Several of the parents in the playground turned to stare at me, no doubt mentally taking down a description, just in case. There was nothing to do but walk back over to the cafe.

"That hurt." Isa didn't meet my eye as I sat back down. "Can you call her?"

"No."

"It's to do with her father?" I said, looking at Isa. "I've read about him. I know he's in prison." I didn't get a response, so moved on to the question that was beginning to bother me, a thought that was taking hold in the back of my mind. "Is he really looking for her?"

Isa considered the question. "Kayleigh made a stupid decision."

"We all make plenty of those."

"A really stupid decision."

I noticed Isa kept checking her mobile, knowing who she was waiting to hear from.

"Have you done anything you regret?"

"Plenty." My mind wandered to the photograph of me that Coleman had sent via Halberg. I'd overstepped the mark on countless occasions, I'd let people down. I'd run away from trouble. It didn't matter how many times I told myself that I'd helped people, brought them peace, the failures and mistakes weighed more heavily on me.

"We need your help." This time she was looking me in the eye, the resolve coming from a decision made. "We think you're a good man." She smiled. "Someone has to be. You took on Martin in the bar and weren't scared."

I stared out at the park again, lost for a moment in my own thoughts. I'd dealt with far worse than her boss, but it didn't answer the question I was asking myself. Was I a good man? There was evidence weighing on both sides of the finely-balanced scales, plenty of people who'd make a case for one side or the other.

Isa stood up, collected her bike from against the fence. "It's important you know Kayleigh did it for her father. It was a mistake, but she didn't have a choice." She hesitated, unsure of what more to say to me. "She shouldn't have done it, but it's too late now. He owes money in prison to some very bad men. I don't know the details, but if Kayleigh helps them, it helps him. They'll leave him alone."

"They threatened her?"

"They came to her house in Hull." She paused for a moment. "I'm sorry to involve you."

I smiled, said it was okay. I knew how it worked. You found a weak spot and you applied pressure. It was the same on both sides of the law. Kayleigh's father had nowhere to run to in prison, no one to help him. Someone had seen his daughter as a weak spot, someone they could exploit. It angered me, lit a fire in me.

I watched Isa pedal away, not moving for a moment. I stood up, waited for the wave of pain to pass, and left some money on the table. Glancing down, I saw that Isa had left her rucksack behind. I looked around, but she was out of sight. Sitting back down, I knew I could take it back to the bar, use it as another excuse to ask around. But curiosity is hardwired into me. I couldn't resist. I pulled open the drawstrings and looked inside. The rucksack was empty apart from a single padded Jiffy bag at the bottom. Taking it out, I turned it over in my hand. Looking inside, my stomach lurched, understanding why she'd apologized to me. I was staring at a sizable quantity of cocaine.

***

I stepped off the tram at Centraal Station, staring up at the imposing Gothic gateway to the city. Heading inside, I knew that trying to chase Kayleigh Mainprize in the park had stiffened my body up. My bones were aching, pain shooting through my muscles. Looking around, the main concourse was a whirlwind of activity. I carefully made my way through the crowd, people coming and going, heads down with earphones in or suitcases rolling behind them.

If it hadn't been my problem, it was now. The danger of what I was doing hit me like a hammer. The contents of the rucksack would be enough for me to receive a substantial prison sentence if caught with it. There'd be no talking my way out of the situation, but I couldn't just leave it in the park; the wrong hands might pick it up. I stared at the departure boards, tempted. I could dump the drugs down the toilet and be at Schiphol Airport in less than thirty minutes, leave this entire mess behind me and move on. A police officer walked past, a routine patrol of the station, a nod and a smile in my direction. I rubbed my face, telling myself to act normal. It wasn't so easy. My heart was beating faster, a sheen of sweat on my forehead.

My mobile still contained all the numbers I had collected from what felt like a previous life. I stared at Coleman's number for a moment before pressing the button to call, moving off to a seat in the corner. He answered by stating his name, my name and number not being stored in his handset.

"I think you owe me an explanation," I said.

It took him a moment to make the connection, the noise of a busy office in the background. He left the line for a moment. When he returned, the background noise had gone. I heard a door close. "You still there, Joe?"

"I am, and I don't like being threatened."

"Who's threatening you?"

"Halberg paid me a visit last night."

"She was asking for your help."

"Don't take the piss."

"What did you make of her?"

"I don't have an opinion, why would I?"

"That's not like you."

"I'm not a private investigator these days."

Coleman sighed, paused for a moment. "It's not always that simple, is it? Actions always have consequences, tabs that need to be paid eventually."

"And you thought you'd remind me of that by sending a photograph you'd been sitting on for a couple of years?"

He ignored the question. "Have you found Kayleigh yet?"

"I'm not a resource you get to decide to use if it suits." I didn't feel inclined to tell him I'd seen her in the park, that she was lying low in the city.

"We're working together here. I hope Halberg made that clear to you?"

"Crystal clear." I glanced around the concourse again, no one paying me any attention. "I'm not interested in working with you."

"You'll want to come home at some point, and I'm trying to help you here."

"Maybe I don't want to come home. Maybe I like it just fine out here."

"It's only natural. You'll need a clean slate."

"You think your photograph is proof I did something wrong?"

"I'm not talking morally, I'm talking legally. You might look at it one way, I'm looking at it the other way."

"And if I don't help you?" I wanted him to spell things out for me.

"You really need me to say it? Senior officers way above my pay grade have got a hard-on for you. Take the piss for too long and you make enemies. They're keen to make an example of you."

I didn't doubt it. I changed the subject back to Kayleigh Mainprize. "Her father's worried, right?"

"As you'd expect him to be."

"Maybe you could set up a chat with him for me?" Coleman didn't have an answer. I was beginning to get the upper hand, pushing him in a direction he didn't want to go. "I assume he won't have too much difficulty getting hold of a mobile in prison."

"I thought you said you weren't an investigator." He paused. "Maybe Halberg didn't fully understand what I told her."

"She speaks better English than both of us." He didn't deny it. "I'll give you a theory, shall I, given that I've spoken to Kayleigh's girlfriend? Maybe Kayleigh's found herself in a situation she can't get out of. Maybe it relates to her father. How am I doing so far?" Coleman stayed silent. "Kayleigh's on and off the ferries all the time and we both know the security there isn't all it should be. Maybe she was persuaded by someone to take over some items with her, drop them off with a guy at the bar she works at. Maybe someone leaned on her via her father in prison." Still nothing from Coleman. "Maybe it was a test run, maybe it was something more serious, I don't know, but am I getting warm here?" He didn't answer, no doubt running the calculation about how much to tell me. Weighing up how much he could trust me. Or control me.

"It's a fair theory," he eventually conceded. "But let's not forget a serious crime has been committed here."

"It's not black and white."

"It never is with you. You think you're better than the law?"

"You're putting words into my mouth."

"We want Kayleigh Mainprize and we want the hand luggage we know she brought into the country."

"You and Halberg have tried to play me from the start."

"Don't see things that aren't there."

"Nothing wrong with my eyesight. You might think I'm some of kind of weird hermit you can manipulate, but I can access the Internet and do my research." I wasn't buying it. "You're happy to burn a young girl for this?" I said to him. "Because her father is in prison and you can use her as a stepping stone?"

"Don't be naive."

"I'm not the one who's being naive here."

Coleman took a deep breath, not rising to the bait. "Maybe that's always been your problem, but you've never realized it? Am I being clear enough here? It's time to put yourself first, Joe, and stop chasing lost causes."

Maybe it was true, not that I was going to admit as much. "I do things for the right reasons." I cut the call, put the handset back in my pocket, and walked over to the ticket office. I couldn't lie to myself; the rucksack felt just that little bit heavier on my shoulder after Coleman's words. He wasn't wrong that I'd pulled enough shit over the years for it to catch up with me, an ongoing irritation to the police during the course of doing my job. But this was different. This was none of my doing. I hadn't asked to involve myself, and he wasn't prepared to help further. I didn't really owe anyone anything. I was being asked to offer up a young woman in exchange for guarantees about my own freedom.

I watched as a counter in the office came free, the man behind the plexiglass tapping his pen on the desk, beckoning me forward. Kayleigh and Isa wanted to go travelling, disappear and reinvent themselves. What was to stop me doing the same? Coleman had told me to put myself first. It came down to me or them, and I'd made my decision. I sent Isa a quick text message before walking over to the desk, the decision made.

***

I walked out of the bar I'd been beaten in the previous night, the wheels set in motion. Isa had replied to my text message, saying Kayleigh had agreed to meet. I'd set the time and place. I'd insisted on it. They couldn't argue. I was the one carrying the rucksack and all the risk.

Sitting down on a bench, I waited. The area had a different feel by day. I watched as tourists posed for photographs, guided walks and coach parties passing through, all viewing from a safe distance. I didn't have to wait long; Anita Halberg arrived on time.

"What happened to you, Mr. Geraghty?"

"Turns out the bar owner isn't keen on making new friends."

"You've spoken to him?"

"The conversation was a bit one-sided for my liking, to be honest." I'm sure Halberg smiled at the update. She told me I'd done the right thing by calling her. "I'm glad you think so."

She sat down next to me. "You might think my city is pretty liberal, but we're not that liberal."

"You've been watching this place?"

"We're aware of it," she said. "And the owner." Halberg took her mobile out, checking for new messages before giving up and talking to me again. "So you and Coleman are friends really?"

"I wouldn't say that. It's complicated."

"I thought this was mutually beneficial."

"That's the theory."

Halberg shook her head. "What are you doing with your life, Mr. Geraghty?"

It was a good question, one I didn't have an answer for. "It's complicated back home," I settled for saying.

"It seems it's always complicated for you. Sometimes things are just black and white."

I stood up, flexing my leg. Halberg was wrong about things being black and white. Things were nearly always gray in my world, no such certainty. I paced in a small circle, glancing at the bar. "I spoke with one of the workers. You probably know Isa, seeing as she's Kayleigh Mainprize's girlfriend?" Halberg didn't answer.

We both watched as a car pulled up, four men in dark clothing getting out. The leader headed straight for Halberg, but my Dutch wasn't good enough to follow the conversation. It was clear she was in charge, issuing the orders to them. I watched in silence as the men made their way inside the bar. It didn't take them long. They were back outside within a couple of minutes, the rucksack concealed within an evidence bag. It was held out to Halberg for her to look at. Another conversation in Dutch I couldn't understand followed, but the tone was clear. They were all pissed off. Halberg looked at the Jiffy bag. I'd taken the liberty of writing Martin's name and address on the front of it.

"There was no sign of Kayleigh Mainprize inside," Halberg said, turning to me. "The officers searched for her."

I didn't reply. The men headed back to the car, quickly pulling away.

"What's going on?"

"I don't know."

"I won't let it drop."

"That's up to you."

Halberg stared at me, barely able to contain her anger. "We're done, Mr. Geraghty. Go off and find yourself a purpose again, that's my advice to you. You should also think about doing it in another city, as you don't want to come to my attention again."

I did as I was told, walking off with my hands in my pockets, one last glance at the bar. Heading down the side of it, I looked at the emergency door I'd been thrown out of, the back street opening up into a network leading away from the main area.

The police had taken some drugs off the streets with the added bonus of wiping out a dangerous establishment. I wouldn't shed any tears for Martin. The police would crawl all over him for a time, and it was a fair bet that plenty of nasty secrets would come to light. It would keep them busy enough. Maybe Halberg would look for Kayleigh and Isa, but if she had any sense, she'd take the easy win. It was still a result. She'd eventually see it was a good day's work. Coleman would have to swallow it down.

I headed into the cafe, scanning the room. Isa and Kayleigh were sitting in the far corner. I headed across to them and handed over the tickets I'd bought earlier at Centraal. I told them to travel light and stay away long enough to let things settle down here. Kayleigh didn't deserve to suffer because of her father.

I wished them well and returned to my bike, looked around. Life went on. Coleman could do what he liked. If he wanted to make life awkward for me, I'd return the sentiment with interest. Maybe Halberg was right and being a private investigator was in my blood, but for now, I just wanted to go home.

Our Evie

Ricki Thomas

Hidden behind net curtains, the shimmering dawn sun blinding her momentarily, the neighbor gasped when she spotted Mary next door asleep on the bench at the bottom of her garden. She often mentioned it was her favorite place in the world, but not to sleep. The icy dew and sharp shards of dew-tipped grass; the old woman must be freezing.

Then Brian appeared, thundering along the path with clenched fists, ranting words she couldn't hear. Shocked, she tensed as he shook his wife awake, trampling carrots underfoot, and dragged her toward their home. The poor woman seemed distressed, confused, and stumbled to keep up with him.

The neighbor had always been suspicious of Brian. Lazy, unkempt and utterly miserable. A drinker to boot. What with dear Mary being so sweet. Her decision made, she picked up the phone and dialed 999.

***

Luke glanced around the incident room at the hardened officers, tired after the weekend and whingeing about having to work, and felt like he'd come home. He recognized some faces, knew a couple of names, and they all seemed to know of him despite largely ignoring him. Every step of promotion took bribery of some sort, and for Luke this was the distribution of bacon sandwiches to those who wanted, given with the cheeky smile he had mastered. A full-fledged detective at last, working with experienced tough lads on cases that required intelligence and commitment. After a lifetime of dreams, he was finally on his way to the top.

A door slammed somewhere outside the room and a hush descended, the no-shit-taken detective inspector striding through with a snarl. She nodded to Luke, her stiff updo unmoving. "You must be Hamby. My office. Now."

He followed her, pleased to shut out the sniggering detectives behind him. "Don't mind them. They'll make your life uncomfortable for a couple of weeks and get bored."

"Thank you, ma'am."

Sitting, she shuffled through the files on her desk and chucked a buff one his way. "It's an odd situation. Old lady was reported by a neighbor who's concerned about spousal abuse."

Irritable, he clasped his hands firmly to keep calm. He'd studied hard to be a detective because he was bored with mundane cases. "Surely that's a matter for social services."

"The uniforms had to respond, the witness saw him manhandling her. They arranged for social care to be contacted as she seemed quite agitated, but she denies her husband is violent."

"They always do."

She glared, silencing him. "The reason we're involved is because she was babbling about a woman named Evie McGrath, who went missing in 1950 in suspicious circumstances. Her body was never found and the case is still open. Anyway, she insists Evie was her mother, said she's buried in the garden, but the officers couldn't find anything to back up her story."

"What am I after, solving a cold case?"

"Just take a statement, ask her what she's on about, and rule it out."

Luke scowled, wondering if they were playing a newbie prank on him. He ate his sandwich, reviewed the basic details on the woman and her husband, and set off, reaching their cottage in the picturesque village just after lunch. Mary led him to the kitchen, chattering mindlessly about this and that. Luke was mesmerized by her skillful knifework on some tiny twisted vegetables, hacking away signs of dirt or insect infestation… pleased she wasn't preparing dinner for him. "You grow them yourself?"

She grinned proudly. "It's what I'm best at." He considered how bad her worst talent would be. "Those officers yesterday didn't tell me to expect another visit."

"It's your lucky day." He grinned, playing to her harmless flirting. "Do you want to tell me what's been happening with your husband?"

"What do you mean?"

"We've had reports that he's mistreating you."

"Piffle," she said, peeling the few rescued carrots with more vigor. "He's got a mouth on him, that's all. I can handle him well enough."

Luke was unsettled by the strange twinkle in her eye. Squinting against the brightness, he peered through the window at the stunning garden, the deep greens, leaves starting to turn now that the weather was colder. "That bench out there, what a lovely place to sit."

She dropped the carrot, her mood spinning on a knife edge. "A stream runs at the bottom of the garden and I love to listen to the water, the wind in the trees. Brian doesn't like me doing so and hustles me back inside. But I feel less lonely there, with nature's song and my mother's whispering voice."

Luke thought of a hundred nutty-as-a-fruitcake jokes, but kept a straight face. "Tell me about your mother."

"She's buried out there, I'm sure of it. I hear her singing at night. You policemen need to dig her up."

"And ruin your vegetables?"

Her stare made him wilt, and he replaced the playful smile with an expression of concern he didn't feel. The woman was clearly in the early stages of dementia; she should be seeing a doctor, not a copper. A commotion came from the hallway, an inebriated man staggering against first one wall, then the other. "Who are you?" he growled. "What are you doing here?" Shaking an angry but useless arm.

"Brian, control yourself. This is Policeperson Something-or-other, and this is my husband Brian."

"Called out the loony police, have they?" Brian glowered at Mary, eyes flaming.

"Mr. Clark, I understand you've lived here for over twenty years. Do you know anything about a woman named Evie McGrath?"

"You've got to be kidding me!" Snorting, Brian grasped a book from the side table and shoved it at the bemused officer. "This is where she gets her rubbish. From this pile of trash. Here, keep it, I don't want this crap in my house."

Mary grabbed wildly at the thin book, bending the tattered pages further. "Give it back."

"Let go, Mary," Brian shouted as if she were a mile away. Luke made his escape. But, as the car's engine chugged to life, the notorious paperback landed beside him on the passenger seat and Luke watched Brian storming back inside. "I said keep the bloody thing, it's putting ridiculous ideas in her head." The door slammed and Luke heard the drunken caveman screaming at his wife.

He drove away, questioning his lifelong wish to be a detective. Eager to breathe clean air. And going over his visit to the strange cottage.

"I've had enough of your amateur dramatics. Give the stupid book to PC Plod here and get me some sodding lunch," Brian had said to Mary as he was leaving.

Humiliated, she shrank back to the carrots, but not before Luke noticed the defiant, withering glare she'd given her moronic husband. The tense undercurrent raged, suggesting more than he'd witnessed, but this mismatched couple's relationship problems were nothing to do with him. He shook himself uncomfortably and kept driving, not wanting to see the oddballs or the spooky house ever again.

***

Barely sober, Brian grumbled at Mary in his boorish manner before heading back to the pub and, once the house was spotless, she shuffled up to the bedroom her grandmother had used.

Mary hated to sleep there, the dark and gloomy room that was a relic of years past. Murky floral wallpaper yellowed with age and curling at the corners, and paintwork a dreary forest green. Not to mention the atmosphere, a malevolent hangover from the cruel woman. The rusting iron bed had been there for as long as she could remember. It was where the harridan had died.

Mary's grandmother had raised her after her parents died, but had been vicious, beating her into behaving, quelling any inkling of an individual streak. She'd encouraged her education, but not if it got in the way of the many chores the child was burdened with. Meeting Brian had been a blessing, but her grandmother had gone crazy, demanding Mary stop the fledgling romance.

Instead, Brian had a stronger personality than Gertie had expected, and he whisked Mary into marriage and a new home, far away from the dragon. Those halcyon years as they raised their family had been wonderful and, although they worked endlessly, life was always cheerful and loving.

Then one by one the children left home and, pleading illness coupled with loneliness, Gertie insisted they return to the family home. With a heavy heart and sore, scabbed hands from keeping house while her husband got drunk and grandmother lazed around moaning and groaning, Mary settled into being a nobody.

Sadly, Gertie's dominant behavior had an effect on Brian. She would never make demands on him the way she did Mary, cosseting him like a spoiled prince who could do no wrong. Over the years he changed, and not for the better. By the time her grandmother died, Mary had become timid and submissive, and Brian lorded over her with menacing eyes and a filthy mouth.

Snapping out of her memories, Mary sank onto the foul bed, the unsettling creaks increasing the sensation of evil eyes watching, haunting her. She wanted to sleep in the marital bed again, on a mattress that didn't sag, with pretty floral bed covers. But Brian had banished her, told her she didn't deserve the comfort.

In some ways it worked, for nowadays Brian sounded like a freight train rumbling through the night, an alcohol-enhanced roar, and the chance of a good night's sleep away from him was marginally more important than the fluffy duvet. Knowing her place in life, Mary settled under the unwelcoming covers and slept.

***

Disappointed that his first day as a detective had been no more exciting than working as a regular constable, Luke was equally disturbed that his social life was nonexistent. Another night of a few beers on the sofa in front of mind-numbing television, channel-switching between mouthfuls of takeout fried rice.

It was no good. However hard he tried, he couldn't get Mary out of his mind. He left the food on the coffee table and reached into his work bag for the tattered book he didn't want. *Our Evie.* Passing the delicate volume from hand to hand, reading the blurb, the acknowledgments. Almost seventy years after its publication date, it was old and worn at the edges, initially badly bound and paying the price now, as several pages threatened to drop out when he opened it. He flicked through, skimming the over-explanatory tale that he couldn't be bothered with…but after reading the first page, he was hooked.

The post-war world was so different from the way Luke had grown up, and the story of the mother who'd tried to bring Evie back to life in the only way possible touched him. Penned by Clara McGrath as she wallowed in confused and bitter grief, the frustration of her fight against the police stonewalling was palpable. Sadness floated from every page. Of course, the accusation was pure speculation on Clara's part, for Evie had never been found. But Luke understood the desperation for an answer, good or bad.

The first few chapters, short and concise, were about Evie's early years, how she'd been funny and sweet, generous to a fault, trusting and loving. She sounded like the perfect child. Luke sipped his beer as the story of Evie and Timothy's romance unfolded, how they met at a dance when he returned from service in Europe after the war.

She'd been nineteen, he twenty-one, and for both it had been love at first sight. They soon became betrothed and were excited about the wedding, but fate stepped in when she found she was pregnant. His mother, Mrs. Stanley, took charge, insisting Evie move to the house she shared with her son, despite her unreasonable hatred for both the Irish girl and the Irish in general. It didn't matter about the wedding; Mrs. Stanley would tell people they had married in London, not willing to admit the girl's Celtic background despite her strong accent. She gave Timothy an inherited gold ring for his fiancée's finger to solidify the lie.

Happy for the offer of support, and pleased that she wouldn't be an outcast in the village for being the unmarried mother she was about to become, Evie packed her few belongings and moved in.

Disturbingly protective, Timothy's mother made Evie's life a living hell for taking her son away from her, as she saw it. Shy and under constant threat of being outed as a single mother in the days when it was unacceptable, Evie had toed the line and done as she was told. But after the child was born, a girl, she became more demanding, insisting that they find a place to live away from her partner's unpleasant family. But the unhealthily close mother-son relationship took precedence and Timothy refused, insisting there was no reason to uproot from a perfectly good and large home. Plus, his mother had been lonely since her husband died in the war.

Evie had no choice: they would raise the child there.

At first, she eagerly told anybody who'd listen about the baby, patting her bump, talking to it, but soon her almost-mother-in-law berated her for being crude. Such unfortunate bulges were to be hidden from sight under clever clothing. Pregnancy was a condition to be ashamed of, not to glorify. What on earth would God think of the behavior? Nevertheless, Mrs. Stanley was sure her son would be a wonderful father, and she couldn't wait to meet her grandchild.

Clara, however, felt nothing but unease about the situation, especially as she received increasing numbers of letters smudged by tears, describing the abuse Evie received at the hands of Mrs. Stanley and her son, how she kept house and cooked while he smoked and read newspapers and his mother lazed around. By the time the child was a month old, the last few letters had complained of extreme nausea and abdominal cramping alongside dramatic weight loss—possible signs of poisoning, thought Clara.

She begged Evie to leave the house. "*She packed a suitcase and told me she was going to come home with the baby, although I wasn't so sure, Mrs. Stanley being so dominant. She intended to get the bus from Eton Wick to Slough, and make her way north, get the ferry to Ireland.*"

Evie never arrived, although Timothy and his mother swore she had travelled as planned. What made no sense to Clara was that the baby remained with Mrs. Stanley and Timothy—surely Evie would never leave her beloved daughter.

And that's the last anybody would admit to knowing. On paper, Evie had simply disappeared with no trace. No sign of trouble or disarray, no letter of explanation.

Just gone.

Everything pointed to foul play, but the officers in charge of the case were placated by Mrs. Stanley and her son, who badmouthed the missing woman as flippant, loose, and money-hungry. The strenuous efforts Clara made to visit her grandchild were rebuked with scorn.

Convinced that weak and lily-livered Timothy, who died shortly after, had been responsible for Evie's disappearance, Clara pestered the police, protesting the lack of care or regard for her daughter's well-being. But they asked questions and were confident of his innocence. Eventually the only solution was to delve into the details herself.

It was a dirty tale, sordid, and deep emotion and anger flowed from the pages, but Luke thought as he put the book down for the last time that it was only useful as a piece of fiction. The gripping and heartfelt catharsis of a grieving woman.

Luke tucked the book back in his work bag and rubbed his tired eyes, then drained his beer.

Evie McGrath's case was open officially, though unlikely to be reinvestigated after all this time unless significant evidence turned up. As far as he was concerned, his involvement with the pleasant but nutty woman was over. And he was glad.

***

Someone was shaking her shoulders and she gasped. Shivering. It was cold. Too dark to see, even without the dreamt dirt that clung to her eyelashes. She wiped her face, shuddering when she made out a shadowy figure looming above her.

"Wake up, you silly cow. You're having a bad dream."

Still semi-conscious, Mary scrabbled up against the headboard, sweat dripping from her brow to her clammy pajamas. Disoriented and horrified, catching her breath.

"Yet another night's sleep ruined."

"I'm sorry, Brian." The images were sharp in her mind. He'd been the one burying her. She hated him more than ever. His persecution and aggression. A tyrant, that's what he was. A slave-driving slob. Useless lump of lard.

With a disgusted harrumph, Brian stomped to his room and fell on the bed, snoring like a warthog in seconds.

Mary waited until she was sure he was asleep and slipped on her dressing gown, locating her slippers with her toes. She headed through the darkness to the kitchen and poured milk into a mug, nuked it in the microwave for a couple of minutes. Outside the wind howled, the clouds spitting raindrops at the windows in blustery bursts. The shadows raised by intermittent moonlight through the window seemed dangerous, every creaking floorboard or pipe a stranger waiting to pounce.

On her deathbed, Mary's grandmother had sworn she would never leave the house, and on nights like this Mary could well believe the woman hid somewhere and everywhere, shrouding the house with a blanket of doom. Gertie had been a manipulative menace when she was alive, belittling Mary's every move and pandering to Brian. Getting what she wanted whichever way.

Quietly, Mary opened the door, the autumn breeze icy at her ankles, whistling through shrubs and trees, plaintive and distressing. The thin moon cast barely-there specks of light across the lawn, and she found her way through the beloved garden by memory alone, tickled by fluttering leaves.

Settling on the treasured bench by the angry stream, the dense, elegant branches of willow shielded her from the hammering rain.

Mary closed her eyes, allowing the haunting melody to drift through her body and envelop her soul, heedless of the muddy water that seeped into her slippers. The breathtaking sound reached a crescendo, a blend of the stern downpour and the howling wind. Melancholy yet soothing. An angel's song of love.

***

"What happened with that old woman yesterday?" The DI sniggered as she passed Luke's desk, expecting a downtrodden scowl.

"Actually, can I have a couple of minutes to talk about it?"

She groaned inwardly as he followed her to the office and shut the door. Typical rookie, taking the job too seriously.

"I don't think she's as crazy as you think." Of course he didn't, she mused with disbelief. "There are a few coincidences I could check out, especially as Mrs. Clark believes we would find Evie's body in the garden if we looked."

"Forget it, she's lost her marbles. The neighbor reported her asleep in the vegetable patch this morning. Flattened the cabbages, apparently. Husband was a bit handy with her on the way back to the house, berated her for making a fool of herself."

"That's harsh. Thing is, I couldn't sleep last night, so…"

"Don't start."

"No, really, so I did a bit of research about Evie McGrath."

"Wait, what? It's a cold case, nobody told you otherwise."

"I read a book about her last night."

"For God's sake, what book?"

"Evie used to live in Mary Clark's house. It was the last place she was seen."

He told her about the book, how it had landed on the passenger seat when he was backing out, and the DI sighed, feeling like a babysitter. "It's still theft if she didn't want you to have it. Or it could be seen as a favor. You need to give it back."

He should have nodded and agreed, but instead said, "I don't want to go back there, it's really creepy."

She laughed heartily. "There's your nickname from now on: Namby-Pamby-Hamby. Get out of here and grow a pair."

"What about Evie McGrath?"

The phone was buzzing on the desk and a colleague rapped at the door. The DI didn't have time for conspiracy theories. "I told you to rule it out. It was almost seventy years ago, get over it."

***

"Mr. Clark—Brian?" Brian nodded, holding the door between them as a barrier. "I'm from social services. The police called us yesterday about your wife."

He gave a toothless grin as he let her pass, indicating the stairs. "I told her to get to bed. Spent the bleeding night out in that storm. I can see the nosy buggers next door tweaking their curtains, watching us. She's an embarrassment, I tell you."

It was common for carers of dementia patients to tire of the condition, and the helpful woman disregarded his irritation. "Has she seen a doctor?"

"They say there's nothing wrong with her. Said she's a bit eccentric, but nothing wrong medically."

"Can I see her?" Brian again showed her the stairs and grabbed a beer from the fridge as she looked on in confusion. "Are you not concerned about your wife, Brian?"

"She can go to hell." The social worker hurried upstairs, just as the doorbell chimed, and Brian swigged the beer, grumbling. Opened the door. "Not you again."

"I need to see Mary."

"You lot may as well have a party up there. She's in her bedroom, the gaudy one that stinks of lavender." He grabbed another beer, ignoring the still-half-full first bottle, and staggered to the living room.

Greeting each other over Mary's dilapidated bed, the social worker conveyed her interest and questioned Luke's presence. He dug the book from a leg pocket and passed it to Mary, who clutched it to her heart. "Did you read it?"

"In one night."

She grabbed his sleeve and he felt a spider crawl along his spine, her dirty nails gripping, desperate. "That baby was me. Evie was my mother. I barely remember my father before he died, and he never talked about my mother. My grandmother banned me from asking about her, said she was an Irish floozy who didn't want the bother of looking after me so she went off with another man."

Luke stared at the sketch of the attractive woman on the cover of the book, able to see where Mary had become confused. They looked alike, the baby had a similar name—Mhairi—and he knew from the scant search he'd done before visiting that her parents, both deceased, were Eve and Timothy. Plus, Mary and Brian lived in the cottage. Mary must have noted these coincidences and, as she read, replaced the details in the book with those of her own life. But still it was intriguing.

The doorbell rang and broke the moment. The social worker, Luke, and Mary listened carefully to the botheration of Brian complaining and an authoritative, well-spoken boom silencing him with manners. Footsteps came up the stairs and a tall, suited man with broad shoulders entered. "Good morning, ladies, sir." He honed in on Mary. "I hear you've been getting yourself in a little trouble, young lady. Tell me what's been going on."

Mary wasted no time. "I get nightmares, I think I'm being haunted. I feel earth filling my mouth and nose. My throat. Gets in my eyes. I try to free myself but I'm restrained, the ropes dig into my wrists and ankles. When I breathe I inhale mud. It's gritty, slimy. Then I start to choke, my head is about to explode. By that time, I've usually shouted and Brian wakes me up, gets annoyed at me for ruining his sleep."

The carers exchanged surprised glances until the doctor persevered. "So why sleep in the garden?"

"Because I'm close to my mother there. He," she pointed to Luke, who shrank back, "needs to arrange to dig her body up. Then the nightmares will go."

Daft talk of hauntings and nightmares was not Luke's forte, and he was certain the DI would never agree to the cost of Mary's suggestion. His job here was done, and he slipped away.

***

Luke's third day as a detective was busier, more stimulating, and he didn't think of Mary until he received a complimentary call from the social worker at the end of the day, telling him that their unruly pensioner had again slept in the vegetable patch, although luckily the night had been warmer and dry. Not interested but not wanting the health professional to know, he made chit-chat. "Did you stay for the doctor's visit?"

"There doesn't seem to be anything physically wrong, but he suspects she's a little depressed. It's more common than one would think in the later ages."

"Is it a placebo jobby?"

"Pardon?"

"Is he giving her vitamin C for the placebo effect?"

"No, I'm sure it's the real deal. Why would you say that?"

He thought about sharing the woeful words of Clara McGrath regarding poisoning, but decided against it, not wanting to be involved in the aged woman's dream world. "What about the husband? He treats her pretty mean."

"She insists he's never been violent."

"And you believe her?"

"It's hard for him, trying to cope with her like this. He's not so young either. Maybe he's depressed too, who knows." Luke wryly raised an eyebrow. Everybody and their dogs seemed to be depressed nowadays. How on earth had they coped a hundred years ago? Or was modern life and its different set of issues the cause? Her perky phone voice continued. "I'm popping by to see her on my way home, do you want an update tomorrow?"

"Case closed for me unless anything further happens, so no thanks."

***

The doctor's advice to rest was amazing, and Mary spent most of the day on the bench, enjoying several crossword puzzles under the cool autumn sun. Peace and quiet except for the tinkling stream. "What the hell do you think you're doing? Where's my sodding dinner?"

Mary dragged herself from the seat, bending and stretching out her seized joints, and trudged to the kitchen. "I'm sorry. The doctor told me to take it easy."

"Doctors and their fandangled rubbish, what do they know." There was no point mentioning that their GP had prescribed tablets—Brian didn't believe in such things—so Mary took a tray of eggs from the fridge, along with a block of cheese, and started preparing an omelet. "Get me a beer, will you, I'm parched. Oh, and I'm off to the pub for darts in a minute, so get a move on."

She waited for him to gobble his food, eager for him to leave. Needing silence to collect her thoughts, find a way of making people believe her. As the door slammed barely seconds from her serving dinner, she sat and stared at the drawing of Evie. Like a twin of herself at the same age. Somebody had to listen. It was important.

Someone had to dig up the garden.

Resolute, she snatched the telephone, dialing. Ringing. Tuneless and repetitive. Fifteen, sixteen, seventeen… She put the receiver down, weary. "I've three children and four grandchildren, one of them must be home." The second household didn't pick up either, so she tried the third. "Mel, it's me, how are you?"

"Sorry, Mom, can't stop, I'm on my way out. Got a million and one things to do, you know how it is."

"Is Katie there?"

The silence registered, and Mary could picture her third child asking her own daughter the same question. Her thoughts were validated when she heard a whispered *no*. "She's at her boyfriend's all night, Mom."

"I see." She didn't see, or understand. Was she really such a terrible person that nobody had time or inclination for her? She said goodbye and cut the call, sadly accepting that she was alone in a busy-whizzy world.

Mary washed the dishes and locked up, about to go to bed, when the phone rang. She snatched the receiver as if it were the last cake on the planet. "Mom, it's Steve, I've got a missed call from you."

"I'm so glad you called. I'm having a bit of an elderly moment. I need the police to…"

"…and so I dropped Jack and Zane off for soccer practice, then had to zip to the hospital to see Angie's dad—he's a lot better, by the way—and then we had to go shopping and…"

"Steve, I have to go or the bath will overrun." She ended their conversation with the sad realization that he'd not heard a word, too busy with his own life and strife to care for her silly problems. Taking to the awful bed her grandmother had died on, the absence of her husband's rumbling soon saw Mary asleep.

***

Until Brian arrived home. Inconsiderately drunk—again. Stumbling and crashing as he made his way up the stairs, turning the house into a light show. He flopped onto the marital bed across the landing from her, a sweaty, inebriated heap, and rattled like a pneumatic drill.

Only then did Mary open her eyes. Slipping from the bed, she donned her robe and padded downstairs, into the garden. To her favorite place under the willow, the gentle breeze ruffling her mussy hair. Autumn was definitely underway, but if this was what it took to make people hear her, this was what she had to do. Wrapping her gown tight, the water trickling a lullaby sang her to sleep.

"I don't believe this. Get up, you old bag. Four nights in a bleeding row. This has gone too far."

Mary banged her head on a hefty marrow squash as she sat, disoriented. "I don't understand."

Muttering, Brian was already storming back to the house. He shouted over his shoulder, "I'm ringing Steve. Going to tell him you've gone nuts."

Apologizing to her brassicas and head to toe in mud, Mary dodged this way and that, trying not to flatten more vegetables than she already had. And from the house Brian watched his wife, her face etched with confusion. His son answered. "Any chance of taking your mother to the hospital? I seriously think she needs to be institutionalized." Brian briefly described her new take on beds to the son whose stress levels were already at breaking point.

Mary agreed to visit the hospital willingly, and Steve stayed a full five minutes before zooming back to his hectic life, suggesting that, if by the remotest chance they set her free that day, there was a bus stop by the main door.

Again, a physical cause for her unusual behavior was ruled out and they asked her to see the mental health team. Waiting. Bored, she dug into the bag that her son had hastily packed for her, finding some mismatched pajamas and a pair of frilly knickers that hadn't fitted for years. No book or magazine, no puzzles. Mary wasted two hours at the window watching the ambulances come and go, had three cups of coffee, spoke to a fellow patient before she was taken for an operation, and asked endless nurses how long the doctor would be. Finally, she gave up and sat on the chair, closing her eyes, snoozing.

"Mary?" She jumped, turning to a man in a white coat. "Your son is concerned that you've slept in your garden for four nights in a row. Can you tell me why you do this? Are you having problems with your husband? Is he violent?"

The barrage of questions was not what she'd anticipated, and she faltered. "No. Brian's a domineering control freak with a crude mouth, but he's never laid a finger on me. Well, not much, anyway."

"Do you feel unsafe in the house?"

"Not really."

"So, you choose to sleep in the garden?"

"No, I don't know how I end up there. All I know is that I'm not going mad. It's the dreams, they make me do it. I feel secure there."

She told him about Evie, about how nobody would take her concerns seriously. That she was certain her mother was buried in her place of sanctuary. Her worries that he would commit her drained when he took her hand, giving it a reassuring squeeze. "You're right, Mary. I'm pretty sure you're not suffering any form of mental illness."

She gaped at him. Still they weren't listening.

"My concern is why your husband and son were so quick to rush you here. A bad rash, it seems; they couldn't get free of you soon enough."

She certainly hadn't foreseen that and intended to milk the attention, filling the following ten minutes with details of the book, of Evie's disappearance. To summarize, she told him, "I need my mother to have a proper burial."

"Forget Evie for now. Do you think it's possible that sleeping in the garden is subconsciously a way of attracting attention?"

"I can't say for certain, but I don't think so." Still wary that the psychiatrist might suggest locking her up and throwing away the key, she said quietly, "I'm scared I'm being haunted."

He diagnosed on paper that she had too much time and not enough activity to stop her dwelling on an overactive mind, and prescribed sleeping tablets for seven days. "Is there somebody to take you home?"

Fed up, she lied. "Yes."

***

The rumbling hippo was in bed by the time Mary arrived home after catching several buses to reach her village. His snoring shook the foundations of the house and she could smell alcohol. Not a single call to the hospital to see how she was, of course. To avoid waking him, Mary kept the lights off and opened the back door, inching carefully across the lawn to the beloved bench.

Nobody intended to listen, so she would have to do something herself. It was time to dig.

She took a shovel.

Lost in the arduous job, she didn't hear Brian approach. "I just don't believe this. You really have lost the plot. Don't you realize that the neighbors see you out here? That they hear you talking to your pathetic plants? You're loopier than a sprung coil."

It had been a long, hard night, and her mind was fuzzy with exhaustion.

"Get inside." Brian tugged her, but this time she was having none of it. "Why didn't the blasted doctors keep you in?"

"Why won't you listen to me about my mother?"

"For God's…" The steeliness in her eyes perturbed him and he stammered, "It's all a coincidence, that book, everything. She'll be long dead by now, so why does it matter?"

"My grandmother killed her, of that I'm sure."

"You don't even know she's dead."

"Yes I do. She's here. I'm digging her up now."

"You're kidding me. This is unreal. Is the NHS so bad nowadays that they can't spot a lunatic when they see one?"

"You can't bully me anymore, Brian. The doctor said I don't deserve to be treated this way."

His face hovered close to hers, eyes challenging and lip curled. "You get everything you want, woman. I pay for your food, the bills, the roof over your head. And you just give me whingeing in return. Ungrateful, selfish cow."

"I collect a pension and the house is mine. Now I want you to help me get my mother."

He'd had enough. Either he'd beg the men in suits to give her a straitjacket and lead her away, or he'd stop this craziness for good. Grabbing a spade, he dug with vigor at the patch she'd already started, grumbling under his breath with every clump of soil he threw aside. She watched with hidden glee as her plan came to a head, even fetching a bottle of beer to help him on his way.

Three a.m. The witching hour. Brian's back ached, but he was pleased with his progress, now a good few feet down. He waved an arm at the hole, issuing a victorious grin. "See, you silly cow, there's nothing down there."

No response. He glanced at the bench, but Mary wasn't there.

The loud crack of the spade against his skull took him by surprise and his knees buckled, falling forward into the pit, but he was still conscious when the first clump of soil landed on his head. And the second. Third.

***

Mary had seen the coincidences in *Our Evie*, but knew from even the remotest of research that the Irish lass was not her mother. All she'd wanted was someone to dig the hole, and figured the police would do it with ease. Shame the ploy hadn't worked, but the result was the same regardless. Used to grafting in the garden as she was, covering the body hadn't been troublesome, and when Mary saw the curtains twitching next door, she beamed as brightly as the morning sun, waving.

The neighbor warily stepped outside. "Are you okay, Mary?"

"Couldn't be better." She patted the soil against the sapling she'd been meaning to plant forever and stood, clutching the small of her back.

"No Brian this morning?" Still suspicious.

"Nope, I gave him his packing orders, he left last night. The doctor made me see reason."

"Oh, I see." The neighbor was nonplussed. "You realize you've planted a tree in your veggie patch?"

"I'm a bit too old for all this digging and growing grubby produce, thought it was time to slow down." And with a cheery smile and a skip in her step, she disappeared into the house she'd inherited from her real grandmother. Gertie had bought it after Mrs. Stanley died.

It was time to sleep, in her own bed this time, and without the thunderous rumbling from a clammy mound of alcoholic coma. Closing her curtains against the promise of a beautiful day, flopping onto the cornflower covers, Mary settled into her new life. Alone.

Closure

Russel D McLean

A J McNee short story

The man who walks into my office has an uncertain expression on his pinched face. Late forties, thinning hair, dressed in blue jeans and a checked shirt. Heavy boots. Lumberjack chic, you might say. Minus the beard. He's clean-shaven, with smooth skin that looks like he takes care of it.

"Mr. McNee?" he says when he sees me.

I stand, offer my hand. "Everyone just calls me McNee," I say.

"Even your friends?" He says it awkwardly, like he's trying to make a joke.

I give him a smile, putting him at ease. A practiced smile, of course. Comes as instinct after all these years in the game. "Even them," I say, neglecting to mention that, after the last few years of my life, my friends are few and far between.

I offer him a seat. He takes it. Still awkward. When he sits, he takes the weight on his right. Discomfort. Not recent. Something he's lived with a long time. I noticed when he first walked in that there was a kind of stiffness on his left side, but now it's obvious.

"I have to admit, your email intrigued me."

He nods. "I guess most of your clients, they walk in here, and they ask you to find someone who's gone missing."

"Not everyone asks me to find themselves. Most people, that kind of thing, they go to a therapist."

He raises his eyebrows. "Ten years," he says. "Ten years, and I don't know that I can live with the gap anymore."

He seems normal. I've had people walk in before, claim to be suffering from amnesia. When I ask them what they want to know, they claim to want proof of having been abducted by aliens or other flights of fancy. Not like Scotland is Roswell, New Mexico, but we have our share of believers. In 1996, two men claimed to have been abducted while driving along the A70. In 2016, the Ministry of Defence confirmed that they had taken the claim seriously.

Clearly, the MOD are more open-minded than me.

But Lucas Clayton doesn't strike me as someone given to flights of fancy. His email was direct and clear. In person, he makes easy eye contact. And when he talks about his experience, there's a sense that he's aware of how he sounds, that he's worried about whether I really believe him.

My gut says I should.

But I have to go through the procedure. My gut's been wrong before. "And you don't have any idea what happened?"

He shakes his head.

"I mean…" I try to tread as carefully as I can. "As I understand it, from what you've told me, this is like a pure form of retrograde amnesia. There's a period of your life that is missing completely."

"Forty-eight hours."

"Forty-eight hours," I say. "It's a long period. Especially with no concrete explanation as to what happened."

"It's not that long," he says. "There are people who've had it worse. One lad I met when I was attending group sessions, he lost ten years. Just like that."

I try to imagine losing a period of my life, having a gap in my memories. Maybe it's like sleeping through something, but even when you're asleep, you're aware of that fact. To simply blink and be somewhere else… To know that time has passed, but not know what you did… the idea seems fantastical. Dizzying.

"In cases like this," I say, "I need to understand what you want. I mean, you want me to trace where you could have been, what you could have done?"

He nods. "After I lost my memory, I also stopped dreaming. Completely. I mean, dreams are vague things at the best of times, but this isn't that I didn't remember dreams: there was an absence. A gap."

"Like your memories?"

"The same," he says. "It's disorienting when you think about it, when you try and find something that just isn't there. There were times I tried so hard to remember that I actually vomited."

"And now you're dreaming again?" Not exactly the most difficult conclusion to draw.

He smiles. "You sound like my psychiatrist."

Maybe I do. After Elaine died, I attended mandatory counselling. For a while, at least. I was a police officer back then, and after she was killed in the hit-and-run, the force encouraged me to seek help. I know now it wasn't simple compassion, so much as the fact that I was losing control; it was affecting my work.

Looking back, I now know how much the doctor was trying to help me. Some days, I think I might empathize with him more now than I ever did back then. Working as an investigator, if you do private cases as opposed to corporate work, a lot of the jobs you get are deeply personal to your clients. And a lot of the time what you have to do is read between the lines of what they tell you.

After a moment, Lucas takes a breath and talks. There's something a little prepared about what he says, and I realize he's been thinking a lot about how to explain this to someone. I can imagine him, the night before our appointment, rehearsing how he's going to be, what he's going to say. Trying to second-guess what I might find useful, or what might persuade me to take on his case.

***

"I worked for a cash-and-carry business," he tells me. "What we did, we supplied bars, corner shops, restaurants. Food, drink, whatever. I was a rep, travelled the country making sure customers were happy."

"Scotland, or down south, too?"

"Used to be Scotland only. Then, you know how it is, there were cutbacks, doing less with more. Which translated to work harder, or have your arse handed to you." He takes a breath. He's looking red round the cheeks and there's a slight sheen of sweat on his forehead. It's spring, and there's no heating in the office. Shouldn't be too hot for him. Something else happening, and I don't know that he's even aware. "The doctors, they wondered if that was part of what happened. There'd been layoffs through the company. I'd been there for twenty years, right out of school."

"Unusual," I said, "the whole job-for-life idea, even back then."

"Oh, aye," he says. "Always telling my wife how lucky I was." That makes him stop. I know what he's going to say next, but I let him do it anyway. "Ex-wife, pardon me."

"Before or after the blackout?"

"After."

I nod. File the information away. Know from my own experience that trauma can sometimes affect people badly, make them push away the ones they love.

Memories push up. I push them back down, listen to my client. His story. His problems.

"The last thing I remember before… well, before… I was coming out of the Kirkcaldy depot, having just heard about another round of layoffs due. I felt sick. Had a headache. My own job was in danger. It was like the nightmares I'd been having for years had bled over into the real world."

"How bad?"

"The headache? Little floating circles at the edge of my vision. A constant crack of sharpness across the left side of my skull."

"Like a migraine?"

"I guess. Other people have said that. Never had it before or since, so I have no idea, really."

He shifts in the seat. Again that discomfort on his left side.

"The injury," I say. "Recent?"

"Had it back then," he says. "Part of why I'm here. They think I got it during the time that vanished."

He chooses his words carefully. Anyone else might have casually used the word "blackout," but since he doesn't, I guess he knows the connotations behind the word. The link to drinking issues. He doesn't strike me as a twelve-stepper, though. Just someone who might have considered whether he had a drinking problem.

"After leaving the depot, next thing I'm aware of is that I'm in hospital. They found me in my car in the driveway of my home. Passed out, head on the steering wheel, honking that horn away. The time from walking out the door, seeing those dots, through to waking up in the hospital… that was all gone, all blank. But I must have at least travelled home during that time."

"Who found you?"

"My wife."

"Did you have children?"

"No. Just me and her. We were thinking about kids."

"Did she know about your issues at work?"

Now he's getting uncomfortable. More shifting. "I didn't tell her. Not until later. When they were trying to work out what happened, when they suggested it could be related to stress."

"Do you believe that?"

"No."

"What else did they suggest?"

"Drinking. I'd been drinking more than usual."

"You were drinking that day?"

"They said I had been, yes. My blood alcohol content was high."

He's being open and honest. Only shifting when he has to admit something he now regrets. But that's reluctance, not avoidance.

"But you don't remember?"

"No. I mean, I got home from the depot, so there's that period of time… The front of the car was damaged. I mean, nothing serious, but…"

"You said it was forty-eight hours you lost. Did your wife know where you were? Or did she have an idea?"

"Apparently, I called her and said I was doing a run up north, that I was too tired to drive much further and that I was stopping in at a hotel. But apparently I'd told everyone at the depot I was going home." He licks his lips, clears his throat. "And before you ask, I wasn't having an affair. I know that much. I'm certain of that much."

I don't say that it's interesting he chooses to mention that. The thought must have crossed his mind. I wonder if it's why he and his wife are no longer together.

"Tell me about the dreams," I say.

"Just flashes. Fragments. Images. I'm in the car. I'm driving. But everything is off-balance, like the world's slipped to the side. I can't hold the car straight on the road. And then, it's like an earthquake, like the world crunches to a halt for a moment. I'm aware of something heavy pushing back against the car. And then…" He pauses, as though unsure of how to describe what happens next. "I wake up."

I nod. "You want me to find out what happened to you. You don't think the memory loss is down to work, do you?"

"No."

"I can't promise I can find the truth. Ten years is a long time."

"I read about you in the paper. Back when you found that girl, the one who was being hunted by her mother's psycho ex?"

Mary Furst. The case still haunts me. A missing-daughter case that turned into a nightmare of old domestic abuse and ended in a brutal murder.

I find myself shifting position this time. I wonder if he notices.

"You've got a reputation for these unusual cases, is what I'm saying. That story, it stuck in my head."

I lay out my payment structure. He agrees with everything I say. I could double it, and I don't think he'd bat an eyelid. But that's not who I am. He fills out the form carefully, his handwriting neat and controlled.

***

When he's gone, I draw up a plan of action. I'm waiting for some information to come in on other cases. Most of them are routine jobs. Can do them with my eyes closed. A lot of eye work is basically checking paper trails, waiting for people to get back to you. It's dull. Cases like the Furst girl, they're rare in the day-to-day.

I check the information he left behind. Look at the precise dates of when he blacked out.

I see the date he was found, with no memory, in his dented car.

Get a sick feeling in my stomach.

***

Driving out to Kirkcaldy, I pass through a small village called Dunshalt. From there, I hit a long road guarded by trees on either side. Driving during the daylight, I hope that this might make me feel easier. It doesn't.

If I have to drive to Kirkcaldy, I tend to use alternate routes. But given what I realized when I saw the dates that Lucas Clayton lost his memory, I knew I had to come this way. Spark my own recollections. Convince myself that I'm being paranoid.

The car he drove—a gray Merc—was the same make and model I remembered driving Elaine and me off the road all those years ago.

Driving between the trees, I try not to remember the argument we had, instead focusing on the good times.

When I emerge from the trees, there's a field to the left. I slow down, stop at a section of wall that was replaced a long time ago. It's weathered now, no longer as new as it once was. I get out of the car, touch the stones. They feel too smooth and too new to me.

I look across the field.

Close my eyes. Remember the taste of blood in my mouth, the crushing weight of the car. I remember pulling Elaine out from the wreck, thinking there was a chance she was still alive.

No. Focus on breathing. On the here and now.

What's the technique?

Focus.

Five things I can see

Four things I can hear.

Three things I can feel.

Two things I can smell.

One thing I can taste or remember tasting.

And breathe.

I open my eyes again. The field is empty, crops growing silently. They wave gently in the breeze. The sun shines over the hills in the distance.

The world has moved on.

I have moved on.

I stopped looking for the other car years ago. Someone told me long ago that I was killing myself by thinking the world worked out like it did in books. Closure doesn't always happen, he said. You have to deal with it.

At the time, my response was to punch him in the jaw.

I consider him a friend, now. Back then, things were different.

***

Clayton's wife still lives in the house they owned together when they were married. When I tell her I'm here to ask questions about him, she rolls her eyes. I tell her that he's started to remember some things, and that I'm helping him piece together what happened.

We go through to the kitchen. I lean against the breakfast bar. She pours herself a coffee.

"So what does he remember?" Getting right to the point.

I almost appreciate the change of pace. Usually, I'm the one with the questions.

"He doesn't remember much," I say. "But he thinks that maybe the car… It was damaged in something more dramatic than a wee dunt down the street."

"Oh, aye?"

"How bad was the damage?"

"Few hundred," she says. "I mean, beating out the panels, replacing the headlights. Paintwork, too. Then there was resetting the tires. They'd been knocked out of sync. I noticed that, when I took it to the garage. Bloody thing kept listing to the middle of the road. Either there was something wrong, or I was drinking the same as him."

"He was under pressure at the time."

"That man's always been under pressure," she says. "Even when things go well, he finds an excuse to wind himself up. I think he gets off on it, like? Is that a thing? Like, a sexual thrill that comes from being under the cosh all your life?"

"I'm a detective, not a psychologist," I say.

She shrugs. Makes this face, then folds her arms. "Does he remember who the tart was, at least?"

"You thought he was having an affair?"

"I never believed that shite about not remembering. I always thought it was his way of getting out of something."

"I've seen the doctor's reports," I say. "The amnesia is genuine, even if the cause is unclear."

She makes a face. The kind that doesn't believe a word of what I'm telling her.

"If he did have an affair," I say, "why do you think that person never came back into his life?"

She turns away from me, and looks out the window to the back garden.

I change tack. "How were things between you, otherwise?"

"You mean, in terms of our marriage? We still slept in the same bed. Slept, mostly. Not much else. He'd been having problems getting it up. But he didn't beat me, if that's what you mean. He wasn't a violent person. Even stepping on a bug concerned him, you know?"

That bit hits me hard in the stomach. I want to tell her I have my suspicions that his amnesia is related to a blackout from drinking. I want to tell her that I think he might be responsible for killing the woman I loved.

I want to tell her these things, but I say nothing, and excuse myself from her home.

***

What I need to be sure about is how he got from the depot to his home. There are a number of possible routes, but where did he go for two days?

He told me he usually kept a good wad of cash on his person in those days. He'd never been a big fan of cards, and liked to pay for things in cash where he could. It was, he said, how he funded his drinking. Funny little detail; after he lost his memory, he also lost his taste for the booze.

Cash. Great. Makes him even more invisible.

I mark the boozers and hotels between the depot and his old home. Google Maps gives me information, but I know that ten years could see any number of pubs and hotels close and open. What I'm doing is looking for a needle in a haystack.

There's a phrase I read in a novel years ago. New York detective, used to be a policeman until he accidentally shot a kid. Leaves the force, becomes a private eye, and also an alcoholic. Should have been cliché, but something in the way the author wrote rang true as anything I'd ever read. Both the investigation work and the drinking.

There's a scene that always stuck with me, where he's explaining how you start looking for something when you have no idea where to start. How he had this word for the method: GOYAAKOD.

Stands for Get Off Your Ass And Knock On Doors.

Of course, in the modern world, you can sit on your arse and get the same results. I let my fingers do the knocking.

It's a big list, so I narrow it down by keeping them to within a mile or two of the depot, and then looking for the cheapest rates. If what Clayton remembers about his behavior during those days is accurate, he'd be spending more on the booze than the accommodation.

Six tries, then someone says, "Are you from the police, then? Fuck me if you aren't the slowest bunch of arseholes in the universe."

"I'm not police," I say. "But I guess what I said rings a bell?"

"This is my place, I remember every dickhead who stayed here. This one, he paid for his room, then he got pissed in the bar. And then I threw him out on the street. No refund, either. He blackened my eye. I called the police, they came round, then said because I couldn't give them a name that there wasn't anything they could do."

"Are you online?" I ask. "If I was to send through a picture, do you think you could identify him?"

"Christ," he says. "They can barely keep the phones working here, never mind the internet."

"Okay," I say. "Then I'll come to you."

***

When I walk into the bar at the Minstrel and Raven, the first thing I think is how the place probably hasn't changed since the day it opened. There's a bar with Tennents, McEwans, and an alleged selection of wines that runs to one red and one white. A couple of no-brand whiskeys. There's a sign up behind the bar about how rooms are available at decent rates. An old duffer looks up as I enter and says, "You'll be McNee, then."

Which means he must be Mr. Newman, the hotel's proprietor.

He nods to the young girl who's cleaning glasses, and then comes out from the bar. He says, "You drinking?" and, when I shake my head, says to the girl, "Get me a pint, and this one'll have…?"

"A black coffee," I say. "I'm driving."

"The new laws," he says, "have been a killer for passing trade."

"Good for road users, though."

He shrugs. We grab a table in a corner.

"This guy," I say, "he must have made an impression. You say you hadn't seen him before?"

"Look, it's over a decade ago, but even then I hadn't seen him that I'd remember. He could've been in before, but most of the ones I remember are the ones who want to be remembered, you know what I mean?"

Our drinks arrive. I sip at the coffee. Tastes like dark water served at boiling point.

Newman says, "Show me the picture."

I bring out my phone. "Bear in mind," I say, as I show him an image of Clayton, "that it's been ten years since—"

"That's the prick."

"You're sure?"

He taps just above his left eye. "I know, son. Like I say, I remember the ones who want to be remembered. And he wanted to be remembered. Making a bloody scene, looking to start a fight."

I thought about what Clayton had told me about his drinking, about how he felt it dulled his anger regarding his position at work.

"Do you remember anything else?"

"Aside from the black eye?"

"Aside from that."

"I remember thinking he shouldn't even have been capable of driving."

I nod. "Look," I say, I gave you two dates when I called. I need to know if you remember specifically which night it was that you threw him out, that you saw him drive off the way he did."

He tells me. He's certain.

I think that I wouldn't be able to finish my coffee, even if it had a taste to it.

***

Back in the car, I do the maths. Work out how long it would take him to drive from the pub to the stretch of road where Elaine was killed.

At one point, I start to shake. Close my eyes. The Five to One technique. But I don't even get to four. For the first time in years, I see Elaine's face clearly behind my eyelids. I've never forgotten her, but over time her face has become less defined in my mind. To see her so clearly, it's a shock to the system. My heart beats faster. My breathing catches in my throat.

Her lips move.

She's saying something.

I open my eyes. Focus on the task.

Do you want this to be true?

I don't answer the question. I can't. If I stop to think, I know I'll break down.

I track the route. Work out the average speed.

I think about Clayton bombing along the road. What was going through his mind? Was he finally ready to tell his wife the truth about what he'd learned that day? Or was he drunk enough to think he could pretend nothing had happened?

She told me earlier that day that he was the kind of person who got high on being nervous, on being in situations that made him wired. The way she spoke, he enjoyed being the underdog, the one that everyone was kicking around. Maybe that was why he turned to drink.

Did it matter? Alcoholics don't always need a reason to start drinking.

I'd seen the doctor's notes about his memory loss. Although they didn't have a definitive answer, they made it clear they believed that his drinking could have affected his memory, could have been responsible for a mini stroke or similar that somehow affected his recall of those two days.

I trace the journey over and over again. He could have taken other routes. Anything could have happened that night.

And yet it seems too much of a coincidence.

I open the door of the car and vomit on the side of the road.

Lucas Clayton was driving the car. The car that ran us off the road.

Lucas Clayton killed my fiancée.

He's the man they never found.

And he doesn't even remember.

***

Two days later.

I pick Clayton up outside his flat in the Blackness area of Dundee. He gets in the passenger seat, says, "You have something to show me, you said?"

"I'm piecing things together," I tell him. "Slowly. But… those memories you told me about… what do you think was happening?"

"They were dreams more than memories," he says. "I mean, dreams represent something, but I'm not so sure they're always literal."

Or maybe he doesn't want to admit what we both know. "You said you didn't dream for years." I start up the engine, pull away slowly, heading toward the town center, and from there the Tay Bridge that will take us over to Fife. "I have to wonder."

"Where are we going?"

"I've been trying to figure out what you did for two days," I say. "No one's really sure about what causes this kind of complete memory loss, but you've seen the doctor's reports. Your drinking… combined with physical factors… there's a good chance that maybe you just blew a gasket that night."

We both go quiet for a while. On the bridge, we race seagulls to the other side.

When we're across, I say, "You were trying to do the right thing, I think. You came out of the meeting, like you told me, and then you decided to go to the closest pub and drink away your worries. Maybe thinking you'd try and gather your thoughts. Maybe a little Dutch courage for talking to your wife."

"Not a huge stretch," he says. He looks out the window as we talk at the countryside flashing by.

"But you overdid it. You already told me how you were drinking more and more due to worrying about the stability of your employment. So what I'm thinking is that night was a real bender. You got in a fight," I tell him. "You were chucked out. You'd actually paid for a room for the night, but they weren't having it."

"Jesus," he says. "So where did—"

"You drove off. Half-cut and all, but you drove."

"Jesus," he says again.

I press the accelerator down just that little bit harder.

***

I don't think about that night as often as I used to. There was a time I relived it every time I closed my eyes. We were driving home. We were arguing. Something stupid. That was what hurt so much later. What we were arguing about, there was no need for it. And I'd been the one at fault, even if I didn't see it at the time.

Then the car came out of nowhere. Wrong side of the road. Beams on high.

Crash.

Flip.

Flip.

Crash.

In the field. Crawling out of the wreckage. Looking at the road. Seeing that gray Merc parked there. Trying to call out. Watching it drive off.

Going back.

Pulling Elaine out of the wreckage.

Realizing that she was already gone.

I wanted to find whoever was in that car. I wanted to find them. I wanted to show them what they had done. I wanted them to see the woman I had loved lying there, her face bloodied, her clothes torn. I wanted them to see her, to understand what they had done.

And then I wanted to beat them to death.

***

For a long time, I wasn't grieving so much as I was angry. Anger kept me going. It allowed me to feel like I had a sense of purpose.

Not exactly a healthy attitude, but at the time it seemed the only thing I could do.

Eventually I moved past the anger, came out the other side.

I thought less and less about what I would do if I ever found the driver of that car. I let myself say goodbye to Elaine. I believed that the wound had sealed up.

***

"What are we doing here?" Clayton asks.

We're parked at the side of the road, next to the patch of wall that was repaired months after our car had smashed through the dyke, and rolled through the crops.

I stand a little away from him, leaning against the car. The bodywork feels cool against my flat palms.

"This is the route I think you took home."

"But why stop here? This… this doesn't mean anything to me."

He's looking at the field where she died. Right at it. He's looking at the place he should have been looking at on the night he drove home, damn near blackout drunk.

All the excuses he has in the world, all the stress he claims he was under, it doesn't matter. Because his actions cost someone else their life that night.

"I thought…" I have to stop for a moment, gather myself. "I thought it might help, maybe, to take a moment. Maybe see if anything stirs memories."

He's silent for a second. Doesn't look back.

I watch him. I think about walking up, taking a rock, maybe, smashing in the back of his head. I think about whether I could kill him.

I've killed before. Self-defense, but I've done it. I can take another life if I have to.

But what about if I *want* to?

I think about a man I used to know. A crime boss. Thought he saw something of himself in me. He once told me that, if I allowed myself, I would find it easy to take a life.

I had believed then that he was wrong.

But now?

I'm not so sure.

Would it restore balance to the universe? If I killed Lucas Clayton, would that make up for her death?

Justice is about redressing balance. If I submit a report to the police, I know that all the evidence I have is circumstantial. Nothing will happen. Nothing that will bring Elaine back, or make my wounds close up again.

There has to be some justice, doesn't there? Natural and legal justice don't always seem weighted equally.

He turns to face me. There are tears in the corners of his eyes. "You know, I keep trying to remember," he says. "I always thought that something happened like you told me. That I got flat-out drunk. I mean, driving in that state..." He takes a breath. "I could have hurt someone."

I can't look away from his eyes. He doesn't remember. He has no idea what happened that night.

I feel something on the back of my neck, suddenly. Like a breath. Or a kiss. Gentle. Reassuring.

I break eye contact. "The worst part about this job," I say, "is that sometimes you can't give people the answers they're looking for."

"We've got something," he says.

"Do you really want to know?" I ask. "If you hurt someone, would you really want to know? What would you do? What would you say to them?"

"I'd tell them I was sorry," he says. "It wouldn't be enough, I know. Not for them."

That breeze again. And something on my arm. Like fingers brushing against my skin.

***

Back in Dundee, I drop him off outside his flat. I tell him I'm sorry there's nothing else I can do for him. I just don't know that I can give him the answers he's looking for. I tell him I'll refund his advance. He tries to refuse. I insist.

I go back to the office. I think about going home, decide that I can't. Not yet. I find a box at the back of a cupboard. I open it, pull out things I could never move to my new place. Old photographs. Old memories.

I look at a picture of Elaine.

I think about the invisible fingers touching my arm.

Not a ghost. I don't believe in ghosts.

A memory. A reminder.

When I'm done, I put the box away.

A Wonderful Time

Lavie Tidhar

In another time and place, Shomer stands with his back to the wall of the ghetto. He turns the precious postcard over and over in his hands.

"Having a wonderful time," it says, and nothing more—nor can it, for even the mere arrival of this missive from the outside is a miracle. It is signed Betsheba, *and hidden in its bland exterior—a picture of the Niagara Falls, in distant America beyond the seas—is a world of meaning. For she has made it, Fanya's sister, she has escaped the war in Europe and the murder of the Jews and she is in America, she is safe, she's free.*

And Shomer marvels: how a small rectangle of paper can offer so much hope. He will take it home and show his wife, and they will celebrate. For himself he has no more concern: if only he could get out Fanya and the children…

But the ghetto is encircled by the German soldiers, and more and more the trains come to the Umschlagplatz*: they depart laden with Jews and they return empty. And more and more they come.*

And Shomer hides the postcard on his person, and he measures out his steps like a prisoner in the prison yard. For he does not yet know how much time they have left.

Only his mind is free, and in his mind, as always, he constructs a story, a cheap and nasty tale of shund *or pulp. For only in his fantasy can he escape this time and place.*

***

The postcard said, "Having a wonderful time." I turned it over and over in my hands. It was addressed to me in a girlish hand. The address read, "Herr Wolf, Detektiv. Above the Jew baker shop, Berwick Street, London."

It was dated 15 March, 1938. It was a month out of date.

"You don't look much like a detective," the policeman said. His partner sniggered. I could smell fresh bread from the bakery downstairs, and *Kaiserschmarrn mit apfelkompott*, a Bavarian specialty—it is like a rich torn pancake served with applesauce. It made my stomach rumble. I have always loved sweet things.

I swept my hand across the bare office. "I have a desk and two chairs, one for visitors, a hat stand and a typewriter–" I said, then gave up. The typewriter was out of ink, anyway, and only my hat hung on the hat stand. It was a nice hat. A fedora. It was a little beat-up by life, just as I was. But it was still hanging.

"Who is it from?" I said.

"This is what we hoped you would tell us," the policeman said. His name was Redgrave.

"And since when do the fuzz deliver the mail?"

They looked at each other, then looked at me.

"What?" I said. I had a sudden bad feeling about all this. "I don't know nothing."

"Do you not," the other policeman, Lockwood, said.

"Says he doesn't," Redgrave said.

"You believe him?" Lockwood said.

"Seems a trustworthy sort," Redgrave said, and they both chuckled. Then Lockwood dangled handcuffs at me with his index finger.

"We'd like you to come with us, Mr. Wolf."

"But I didn't do nothing, I told you!"

"Come, come, Mr. Wolf."

Redgrave's hand went to his night stick and stayed there. I gave up.

But I was most certainly not having a wonderful time.

***

There's a certain righteous cruelty in the face of your typical Bavarian schoolmistress, as though she had seen everything in the world and found nothing but disappointment, yet was still determined to carry out her duty. It was the sort of face to put fear into old men and young boys alike. There was just one small thing: she was dead.

In death she looked equally disappointed—as though when the big moment finally came it was nothing but a letdown. I'd seen people die before and helped a few more on their way, but that kind of a death mask was new to me.

I said, "I don't know her." I stared some more. That face, there was something about it, like a horse one once rode in somebody else's stables.

"You sure, gumshoe?"

I nodded, slowly.

"Then why was she carrying a postcard addressed to you in the pocket of her coat?" Redgrave said.

It was a not unreasonable question.

I'd been wondering the same thing myself.

"Where did you find her?" I said.

"Tossed in the back of the picture house on Shaftesbury Avenue," he said, "by the bins."

"The Avenue Pavilion?" I said. I knew the cinema vaguely.

He nodded.

"And with a .43 slug in the back of her head."

"Nasty."

Execution style, I thought. Neat and professional. I liked things neat. And I appreciated a professional.

"German?"

"Refugee, probably," Redgrave said, with a little distaste in his voice.

"Illegal, most likely," Lockwood said. He shrugged. "Not much we can do, then, I suppose," he said.

"What do you mean?" I said. "This is a murder!"

He just shrugged again. "Do you know how many of you there are now?" he said.

"Too many," his partner said.

"Coming over here, like rats from a drowning ship."

"*Germans*," Redgrave said, with loathing.

"Illegals. More and more of you each day. Well, we did the best we could."

"Best we could."

"If we were going to arrest anyone, it would probably be you," said Lockwood.

"Me?" I said. "But I didn't *do* anything!"

"Oh," he said. "But I'm sure you have, Mr. Wolf." He looked at me, almost curiously. "Didn't you used to be somebody, once?"

I had nothing to say to that. He smiled, thinly, and covered the woman's face.

"You can go," he said.

And that was that.

***

Back in 1923, briefly, I had been somebody. Standing in the huge hall of the Bürgerbräukeller in Munich, with the smell of spilled beer and damp coats and cheap cigars and women's perfume, I gave a speech. I had been good at giving speeches. There had been an anger then in Germany that was palpable, as thick in the air as the fug of cigarette smoke is during Oktoberfest. Girls in dirndls served the patrons, and giant swastika flags hung from the walls under the glass chandeliers. I told my audience that Germany was suffering. That Germany needed saving. That the Jews were the cancer and that I was the cure.

Oh, they cheered. How they cheered! It was time, I told them. It was time to take back *control*!

They loved it. They lapped it all up.

Then we marched on the Odeonsplatz and everything went to shit. Someone shot Max Scheubner-Richter through the lungs and the f–ker fell and, since we had linked our arms together, he brought me down with him. I'd dislocated my shoulder and was in quite great pain. I almost wished he would come back to life just so I could shoot him myself.

After the firefight I ran. We had a getaway car, but it broke down on the way to the Alps and so instead I headed to this little village called Uffing, on the shores of the Staffelsee. It is a very pretty place.

***

I stared at the postcard in my hands now. The two police officers had left it with me. Neither snow, nor rain, nor heat, nor gloom of night stayed these couriers from the swift completion of their appointed rounds. As Herodotus would have said.

The postcard showed a view I knew well. It was the Staffelsee.

It is a charming lake. I had once gone boating there in the summer. It had been a beautiful, sunny day. But back in 1923, I made my way there in the dark, and at last knocked on the door of the Hanfstaengls' house in Uffing. The money-grabbing Hanfstaengls, some called them. Putzi and Helene. Putzi had been with me in Munich, but he ran just as soon as trouble started. He'd be halfway to Austria by now, and snorting Pervitin in Piesendorf before the night was out.

Helene opened the door.

By God, but there was a woman! She had the sort of legs you could suck for popsicles and the bush of a French prostitute. She was American, but of good Aryan stock. What she was doing married to a Hanfstaengl was anybody's guess.

"Adolf?" she said. Her hand rose to her mouth—too theatrically, I thought. You know those *hausfraus* and their flair for amateur dramatics. "I heard the news on the wireless, is Putzi—"

"Putzi's fine," I said—cursing him inwardly. "He should be halfway across the Alps by now. I would be too if it weren't for the d—n Maybach breaking down."

"You poor thing," she said. She ushered me in. "You're wounded!" she said.

"I bleed for Germany," I told her.

"Oh, Adolf!"

She busied herself around me like a bitch in heat. I could smell the foliage of her garden getting all moist.

I knew she wanted me. Women always did, back then, you see.

I let her minister to me.

***

Later, the G-d d—ned village policeman came to arrest me.

***

"That's it!" I said.

Two pigeons flew away, startled, and an old homeless woman, pushing a cart filled with dirty clothes, leered at me.

"What's it, ducky?" she said. "Come give old Mildred a kiss."

She stuck her tongue out at me through broken black teeth.

"Get away from me, you filthy whore!"

Old Mildred lifted her skirt at me and leered some more. There were broken red veins in her nose. I tried not to look at what was under the skirt. "You'll come around, ducky," she said. "Sooner or later, they all do."

I shuddered and walked away.

I knew who the dead woman was, after all, I realized. Anna or Marta, one of those names. She had been the Hanfstaengls' maid back in Uffing.

How she turned up dead, in London, and with my name on her person, I had no idea.

It really wasn't my business to get involved in. I wasn't getting paid. Though someone must have had a reason to off the old woman, and in London, in this cold year of our Lord 1938, that reason was more often than not hard, cold money.

People died just as much from the simple reason of being a foreigner, of course. But that usually involved a beating, not an execution.

"*Schiesse*!" I said, to no one in particular. A pigeon came and landed by my feet and stared up at me with the dispassionate gaze of an SS Rottenführer.

I was out of work and I was out of luck and I was going to take on this s—tshow of a case, just on the off-chance there was something in it for me.

***

It took me three tries and on the fourth I struck lucky. I'd gone through Soho, to those boarding houses I knew where they hired out rooms to foreigners. There had been an influx of refugees from Germany after the Fall, when the Soviets took over and my former cause was stomped under the boot of Jewish communism. The communists had thrown me in a concentration camp and, though I managed to escape, my leg still ached in cold weather—which, in London, was always.

I passed a shop with a sign that said "No Germans, No Dogs." On the wall I saw a poster of my old friend, Oswald Mosley, the leader of the British Union of Fascists. He had a thin moustache and a mouth like a smiling rat's. Word was he was going to run for Prime Minister and, if so, he might just get in.

The last boarding house was on Greek Street. It was run by a Madame Blavatsky—not the one who talked to ghosts, though she claimed to be a distant relation. I had run into this Blavatsky on a previous case. Now she glared at me suspiciously from behind her tea service.

"You again? What do you want?"

"It's nice to see you too," I said. "Nice weather we're having, what?"

"What?"

"What?"

"*What*?"

"I *said*, nice weather we're—oh, forget it," I said. "Listen to me, you old crone, I'm looking for a woman who might have been staying here. Bavarian, late fifties. As ugly as a bulldog and twice as vicious, at a guess."

"Anna Maria Fischer," Madame Blavatsky said. I was a little taken aback.

"Really?"

"Found her, didn't they," she said. "Knew it had to be her. Someone stuck a bullet in that gob of hers. She still owes me two weeks' rent." She looked at me with mournful eyes. "Who's gonna pay me now, Wolf?"

"Don't look at me," I said. "I haven't a farthing to my name."

"Listen, you f—king kraut," she said. "You wouldn't be here at all if you didn't think there was something in it for you down the road. So I'll tell you what. You can go up and rummage through her knickers drawer to your heart's content, but if you find any money later on along the way, you bring it here, you hear?"

"You'd trust me to do that?" I said.

She shrugged, lifted a dainty foot, and farted. "Got nothing to lose, have I," she said.

She reached for the radio and twiddled the knob until the Lord Haw-Haw Half-Time Show came on. He was spouting off as usual.

"*England for the English! For too long have we lived under the yoke of Europe on our doorstep, the encroachment of foreigners onto our sacred soil! No more! It is time to take back con—and now for a word from our sponsor.*"

I left her there and went up the stairs as angelic trumpets played on the wireless and an angelic voice entreated me to *Smoke Chesterfields—The Way To More Smoking Pleasure*!

"*F—king* Lord Haw-Haw," I said, with feeling.

I found the room. It was more like a closet. The bed had been made and some cheap undergarments hung to dry from a string tied between the bedpost and the wardrobe. When I looked in the wardrobe, I found a copy of my single book, *My Struggle*, in the original Franz Eher first edition, with both volumes bound together in a later binding. Quite a nice little copy, I thought. When I opened it to the title page, I realized with some surprise that it was inscribed.

Well, well.

It had been a very long time since I last signed a copy of one of those.

So horse-faced Anna Maria was a National Socialist. I barely remembered the woman—most of my attention on visiting Uffing that time was to my wound, and my fetching American-born hostess—but at some point I must have signed a copy for the help.

How the help turned up dead in London was still a mystery, but at least I was getting warmer.

There was no cash lying around, and I was sure Madame Blavatsky had already cleaned up anything of value. They always do, these landladies. They are as greedy as my old friend Goering, and usually just as fat.

Still, I tossed the room. I turned the sheets and looked under the thin mattress. I emptied the wardrobe. Anna Maria wore cheap clothes and even cheaper shoes.

It was when I bent down to look under the bed that I saw a small sheet of paper poking out from underneath the dresser. I cursed, straightened, and tried in vain to shift the heavy lump of wood. At last—with a creak that could have been the wardrobe and could have been my back—it moved. I reached down and stared at the page.

The Saturn-Film Company
Cordially Invites You
to a Night You Won't Forget!
Exclusive Screening
Bar Service
Private and Discreet!
MEN ONLY
The Avenue Pavilion Picturehouse, Shaftesbury Avenue

I stared at the flyer.

This was not what I had expected at all.

***

"The cinema night is for members only, sir."

The usher had the shiny face of an excited teenage boy who'd grown to a disappointing manhood. I'd seen faces like that in the trenches, during the war. Hairless rats, we called them. They never made it long out there in Ypres. Of the nearly four thousand men in my regiment, a mere six hundred survived that battle.

"How does one become a member?"

He looked at me dubiously. "There's a process," he said. "A committee and so on."

"I just want to see the movie."

He looked from side to side and then stared at me with those big bulging eyes of his. "You're not with the pigs, are you?"

"Do I look like a policeman?"

"You look like a bum," he said, and laughed, and it took all my willpower not to slap the teeth out of him. "And it's ten shillings."

"Ten!" I grabbed him by the shirt and pushed him against the wall. "You little weasel—"

"This isn't an ordinary picture!" he squeaked.

"I don't have ten shillings."

I barely had the money for a slice of bread, and my rent was overdue.

"*Five*, if you let me go *now*."

"You let me in and I don't call the fuzz on you."

He all but laughed in my face. "You think they give us trouble? This is a gentlemen's club and gentlemen don't get raided."

I sighed and let him go.

"All right, then."

"All right?"

"Sure."

And I clocked him with a coal hammer straight out of the famous Frank Klaus-Billy Papke fight.

I dragged the unfortunate usher into the cloakroom and left him under a pile of evening coats. Then I sauntered into the cinema proper.

The room was dark and the show had already started. Men sat avidly in the rows. Their eyes were fixed on the screen. They wet their lips. They wriggled uncomfortably in their seats, much like an SS trooper trying to make room for his gun.

I watched the show. The movie was called *Slave-Girls in the Harem*. As a documentary it had little to recommend it. The movement was jerky and it was a silent picture. It was shot in a large room with a large bed by the wall and too many pillows. Four girls stepped into the room and quickly disrobed. They began to perform questionable actions on each other. Then a couple of young men joined them.

I'd seen worse in Vienna in '13 when I was living on the Meldermannstrasse. This had no art. It was mere filth.

I turned my back on the screen. In my younger life I had wanted to be an artist. I was a decent enough painter, I thought. But I had not picked up a brush in years. The men in the audience grunted like the pigs they were. This was no use to me. I sidled past the curtain and made my way up the stairs. The manager's door stood open and a thick cloud of cigar smoke wafted out.

How I loathed the smell!

I came and stood in the doorway. The man behind the desk was fat and had small greedy eyes.

"Hey," he said, "you're not supposed to be h—"

He squeaked in alarm as I went at him like Hermann Goering with a sponge cake.

"Are you ready to talk?"

He whimpered and spat out blood. It dribbled down his chin. I was kneeling on the floor, looking right into his eyes.

"Do you know Anna Maria Fischer?" I said.

He looked at me blankly.

"Who?"

"German, in her fifties, face like an Ascot winner?"

"No idea, mister."

"Found dead behind your picture house, by the bins."

"Oh, her."

"What was she doing there?" I said.

"No idea, mister."

I socked him a couple more punches, just as a reminder.

"Look, I don't know nothing! She came round a couple of times asking for work. Or so she claimed. I tried to brush her off, but she made a nuisance of herself. Finally… Well, you'd be surprised, but there's a market for everything.

Some punters really get their kicks watching old ladies get it on, so I finally sent her to the studio."

"The studio?"

"Saturn Films. They produce all our pictures."

"And where can I find them?" I said.

He tried to crawl away then. "I can't tell you that," he said. "I'd get in trouble."

"You're in trouble now," I pointed out.

"What you gonna do, beat me up some more?" he said. "Still better than a .43 in the back of the head."

I had to acknowledge he had a point.

"Seems we're at an impasse."

He spat some more blood. "Seems so."

I got up. His cigar was still burning in the ashtray and a box of matches sat on the desk. It bore the picture house's advertisement. I shook it and it was half full. I stuck it in my pocket.

"Stay where I can see you," I said.

"What are you—"

I smiled at him and started opening drawers.

"Hey, you can't *do* tha—"

"Shut the f—k up!" I said. Then, "Hello… What do we have here?"

"I'm dead," he said.

"I hope so," I said. I smiled at him and waved the invoice at him. It is as I always say. One cannot conduct a criminal enterprise or a genocide without paperwork.

I looked at the address on the invoice, then back at the man.

"*Surbiton?*" I said. "Where the f—k is Surbiton?"

***

The Surbiton train station was a pleasant building done up the year before in an Art Deco style. I took a moment to appreciate the workmanship. The place itself was some fifteen miles out of London. It was a leafy sort of suburban village, with a greengrocer's and a butcher's on the high street, several pubs, and a picture house called the Coronation Hall directly opposite the station. It had a high stained glass window of a Star of David, for no reason I could see. It just went to show, Jews were everywhere. Had I had my way back in

'33, things would have turned out very different. But the Communists took control of my beloved Germany, and now Europe groaned under the heel of international Jewry and their Marxist faith.

How I hated Jews! And gypsies, Poles, Slavs, mimes, smokers, and the French. I really hated the French! And British trains. I hated British trains. I had had to get one from Waterloo to reach Surbiton, though I dodged the fare.

"Excuse me," I said to a passer-by. "Could you direct me to this address, please?"

The man stopped and glared at me. He wore mutton chops and a vest and had the ruddy complexion of a country drunk. He stared at me like I was a piece of dog s—t he'd found on his foot.

"Not from around here, are you?" he said.

I had nothing to say to that, so I didn't.

"Word of advice, my friend. Go back to where you come from. We don't like foreigners here, much, unless you're here to cut the lawns."

I glared at him in hatred. I used to *be* somebody!

Once upon a time, all of Germany marched to the beat of my drum!

"Up the hill," he said, relenting. "Can't miss it."

"Thank you."

"Don't mention it."

With that he stalked off, no doubt to feed his pigs or screw the help—it was that kind of place.

I walked up St. Mark's Hill. Oak trees grew thickly and hid stately Victorian homes. Who knew what kind of depravity they hid? A squirrel ran past me and climbed up a tree. Like Sherlock Holmes before me, I could not look at these scattered houses without the feeling of their isolation and of the impunity with which crime may be committed there.

Surbiton! I thought, savagely. What a f—king sh—thole!

I found the house. It looked like an old hospital. The gates were closed. There was no sign to suggest an occupancy.

It is an old truism of the detective trade—when in doubt, try going through the back.

I went round until I found the entrance. There was a wide low gate for deliveries and I pushed it and went in. Then I jimmied the back door and let myself into the house.

It was the sort of grand old home the British love which is full of cold drafts and no one's cleaned the carpet in years. The sash windows let in the murky gray sunlight. A mouse darted past me and vanished into a hole in the wainscoting.

I tiptoed along the corridor—and came straight to the orgy room.

It was the same room I had seen in the earlier picture. The four-poster bed was still there, only now it had two naked men with oiled bodies on it, and they were doing things to each other that would have made even Ernst Röhm blush.

Bright lights were set up around the room and they generated so much heat that everyone was sweating. *Everyone* was the film crew: there were several of them standing all about, and there was even a buffet table set against the far wall.

A camera mounted on a dais was pointed at the two rutting men, and a large, imposing man over six feet tall was barking orders.

"Thrust harder! Thrust harder! That's it! Now turn him over, Carl! Now gently massage the buttocks!"

I recognized that voice, and the imposing figure, and the toothbrush moustache like I myself used to sport. He was as ugly as a mastiff with an erection.

"*Putzi*?" I said.

***

Ernst "Putzi" Hanfstaengl turned and looked at me with utter surprise. It was as though one of his actors had suddenly sprouted a second *schwanz*.

"*Adolf*? But…but how?"

"It's Wolf, now," I told him. "Just Wolf."

"But my dear fellow!" He went to embrace me. We had been close, back in Munich. Back then he had been a follower, another devotee of National Socialism and the cause.

Now he was just a pornographer.

"It is so good to *see* you!" he said. "But what are you doing here? How on earth did you find me?"

"Anna Maria," I said, tiredly. The room smelled like a public bath. One of the actors turned and stared at us with his *schwanz* still in his hand.

"Mr. Hanfstaengl? I'm losing wood."

"Take five, boys. There's cold cuts and potato salad on the buffet tables." He waved them away. The cameraman and the lighting technician and the actors and all the rest of them lit up cigarettes and went off for a bite to eat and a cup of tea. I guess all that hard work made them hungry.

"Anna Maria, Wolf?"

"Anna Maria Fischer. Your old maid."

He grimaced. "What about her, Wolf? Come, come, dear fellow. Let's adjourn somewhere we can talk."

He led me out of the orgy room, down a corridor, and to a cool, dark storage room filled with film canisters. Posters on the walls advertised other Saturn pictures: *Robin's Wood, Gunga Dick, Triumph of the Willies, Follow The Yellow Prick Road,* and *Lust of the Swastika.*

Warning signs said *Do Not Smoke—Highly Flammable Material.*

"Must you bring up this old business?" he said to me then. "Wolf! Forget this nonsense. Come and work with me! I am making money hand over fist!"

He gestured rudely with his fingers, miming an intimate act.

"She had my name on her person, Putzi," I said. "I was visited by the pigs!"

He made a dismissive gesture. "She always had the hots for you, Wolf. Forget Anna Maria! Since when did you care for the help?"

"Who do you work for, Putzi? You do not have the sort of juice to run this kind of operation by yourself."

At that he grew somber. "There are questions one should not be asking," he said. "Not even you."

I let it go. My silence drew him in.

"She just wasn't no good, Wolf," he said. A whiny note entered his voice. "The bitch was going to rat us out. I had no choice, you see? No choice at all."

"Tell me."

He shrugged. "What is there to tell? She followed me and Helene to London and somehow found out about my little enterprise. Next thing you know, she shows up here and starts blackmailing me. What was I to do, Wolf? You've always said it yourself, after all: there are few problems one can't solve with a gun."

I felt so very tired then. "How is Helene?" I said.

"Good, good," he said, distractedly. "Misses the Fatherland, though, as do I. It is terrible, what happened, Wolf. Terrible."

He looked less than upset at the humiliating defeat of National Socialism. Just imagine, had I won! I would have changed the *world*!

I took out the box of matches that I had liberated at the picture house. I shook it and it made a little rattling noise.

"Oh, there's no smoking in here, Wolf. On account of the film stock. It's the nitrates, you see."

"I don't smoke."

A confused look came into his eyes. "That's what I thought," he said. "Then what—?"

I smiled at him almost kindly as I struck the match and held it. The flame was very bright. A look of horror came into his eyes then and he said, "You wouldn't—"

I began to whistle the Horst Wessel song. Putzi barrelled past me in his haste to escape. I turned and tossed the match and, still whistling, left the room.

Behind me, without much fuss, the film stock caught fire.

***

I stood under a rather lovely oak tree that must have been standing there a hundred years or more, and watched the studio burn. It burned with all the dedication of a race theory scholar reading Hans Günther's *Short Ethnology of the German People* for the first time. I mean, intensely.

I did not believe in justice, which is for the weak.

But I believed in order—order above all things.

I believed in the manifest destiny of the Aryan race, in Kaiserschmarrn and apple strudel, and that dogs were better than cats. I was definitely a dog person. I believed in vegetarianism, and that smoking was a filthy habit and that the only thing worse than a Pole was a Jew. I believed *I* should have won in 1933, and that the swastika flag should have hung over the Reichstag building—but it wasn't.

I believed in Geli Raubal until she killed herself to spite me. I believed I should have been paid a higher advance than the measly £300 my British publishers, Hurst and Blackett, paid me for *My Struggle*. And I believed the *f—king* trains should *f—king* run on *time*!

I believed in doing the right thing—whatever the cost.

I stood and watched the firemen arrive and the hoses go, and the black smoke rising. Then I crumpled the postcard from Uffing and let it drop to the ground, and I made my way back down the hill.

***

In another time and place there's Shomer, walking back. The night is cold and there is no firewood with which to light a fire.

Meeting his friend Yenkl by the Yiddish Theatre, Shomer shows him the postcard from America. After a moment, his friend chuckles without mirth.

"There is a story told of the writer, Ödön von Horváth," he says. "He was walking in the Bavarian Alps once when he discovered the skeleton of a hiker with his rucksack still intact. Von Horváth opened the bag and found a postcard that said "Having a wonderful time."

Shomer nods, for all that he is distracted. He thinks of Fanya and the children, and of what the next winter will bring. If there is another winter.

If it is not, already, too late.

"What did he do with it?" he says.

"What?"

"With the postcard."

Yenkl nods, sagely, and shrugs.

"He posted it," he says.

Historical Afterword

The detective who calls himself Wolf first appeared in my 2014 novel, *A Man Lies Dreaming*. I never wanted to revisit him—or so I foolishly thought. This is his fourth outing since then—the interested reader may find his previous adventures in the pages of *Apex Magazine*. He seems to come back to me every Christmas. All I can say is, sometimes there is a man. He is the man for his time and place—and we live in a time that in many ways bears extraordinary similarities to the 1930s in which Adolf Hitler's poisoned seed grew fruit.

The young Adolf Hitler spent several years in Vienna, where he lived for a time in a homeless shelter and then in a men's dormitory. He was well familiar—though disgusted—with the red-light district, and would have likely been familiar with the Saturn Film Company. Cinema was effectively invented in 1895; almost immediately it gave rise to the pornographic movie. Saturn-Film, established by Johann Schwarzer in the early 1900s, was the first film production company in Austria. Among their pictures one can find *Forbidden Bathing*, *At The Slave Market*, *Female Wrestlers*, and *In The Harem*, all of which are listed in their 1907 catalogue. The films were regularly shown in *herrenabende*, or "night shows for men," much as described here.

Harvard-educated Ernst "Putzi" Hanfstaengl was one of Hitler's confidants during his Munich days. Following the failed Beer Hall Putsch in 1923, Hitler fled to Uffing, a small village in Bavaria, to the Hanfstaengls' home. The story is that when the village constable was sent to arrest him, a pale and wounded Hitler opened the door and surrendered, saying, "You must do what you must for your country." Hitler went on to spend time in Landsberg Prison, where he wrote *Mein Kampf*. The rest, sadly, is history.

About the Editor

MAXIM JAKUBOWSKI is a London-based former publisher, editor, and translator. He has compiled over one hundred anthologies in a variety of genres, many of which have garnered awards. He is a past winner of the Karel and Anthony awards. He broadcasts regularly on radio and TV, reviews for diverse newspapers and magazines, and has been a judge for several literary prizes. He is the author of twenty novels, the last being *The Louisiana Republic* (2018), and a series of *Sunday Times* bestselling novels under a pseudonym. He has also published five collections of his own short stories. He is currently Vice Chair of the British Crime Writers' Association. *www.maximjakubowski.co.uk*

About the Authors

KEITH BROOKE's first novel, *Keepers of the Peace*, appeared in 1990. Since then, he has published eight more adult novels, six collections, and more than seventy short stories. His novel *Genetopia* was published by Pyr in February 2006 and was his first title to receive a starred review in *Publishers Weekly*. *The Accord*, published by Solaris in 2009, received another starred *PW* review and was optioned for film. His most recent SF novel, *Harmony* (published in the UK as *alt.human*), was shortlisted for the Philip K Dick Award. Writing as Nick Gifford, his teen fiction is published by Puffin, with one novel also optioned for the movies by Andy Serkis and Jonathan Cavendish's Caveman Films. He writes reviews for *The Guardian*, teaches creative writing at the University of Essex, and lives with his wife Debbie in Wivenhoe, Essex.

ERIC BROWN has won the British Science Fiction Award twice for his short stories, and his novel *Helix Wars* was shortlisted for the 2012 Philip K. Dick award. His latest books include the crime novel set in the 1950s, *Murder Served Cold*, and the SF novel *Buying Time*. He has also written a dozen books for children and over 150 short stories. He writes a monthly science fiction review column for *The Guardian* newspaper and lives in Cockburnspath, Scotland. His website can be found at: www.ericbrown.co.uk.

DAVID STUART DAVIES is the author of eight Sherlock Holmes novels and *Starring Sherlock Holmes*, which details the detective's film career. David's two successful one-man plays, *Sherlock Holmes: The Last Act and Sherlock Holmes: The Life & Death* have been recorded on audio CD by The Big Finish. His new play, *Sherlock Holmes: The Final Reckoning*, premiered in Edinburgh in February 2018. David is the author of other works of crime fiction including six Johnny Hawke novels. His latest books are *Blood Rites* and *Oliver Twist & The Mystery of Throate Manor*. He is a Baker Street Irregular, a member of The Detection

Club, and edits *Red Herrings*, the monthly magazine of the Crime Writers' Association.

Born in New Orleans, O'NEIL DE NOUX is a prolific American writer of novels and short stories with forty books published, over four hundred short story sales, and a screenplay produced in 2000. Much of De Noux's writing is character-driven crime fiction, although he has written in many disciplines including historical fiction, children's fiction, mainstream fiction, mystery, science fiction, suspense, fantasy, horror, Western, literary, religious, romance, humor, and erotica. Mr. De Noux is a retired police officer and a former homicide detective. His writing has garnered a number of awards, including the United Kingdom Short Story Prize, the Shamus Award (given annually by the Private Eye Writers of America to recognize outstanding achievement in private eye fiction), the Derringer Award (given annually by the Short Mystery Fiction Society to recognize excellence in short mystery fiction) and Police Book of the Year (awarded by PoliceWriters.com). Two of his stories have been featured in the prestigious Best American Mystery Stories annual anthology (2003 and 2013). He is a past Vice President of the Private Eye Writers of America.

JANE FINNIS lives in Yorkshire and has been fascinated by Ancient Roman history ever since, as a child, she walked the straight Roman roads that still cross the countryside there and saw the historic remains in cities like York. Her mysteries are set there, but in Roman times when Britain was a raw frontier province of a mighty Empire. Her amateur and rather reluctant sleuth is Aurelia Marcella, who runs the Oak Tree Inn on the road to York, where she receives all sorts of visitors bringing all sorts of problems. Aurelia appears in several short stories and also in a series of novels: *Shadows in the Night*, *A Bitter Chill*, *Buried Too Deep*, and *Danger in the Wind*. www.janefinnis.com.

MARY HARRIS is a writer (published in fiction and nonfiction), editor, and screenwriter; she understands the struggle to get the idea from the head to the paper. Her main mantra is, "It's all about the story." She has worked for several large publishers, including Sourcebooks and Loose Id, and is the executive editor of Hidden Thoughts Press. She is a passionate believer in the Oxford comma but allows nothing to interrupt the flow of the story. She lives in North Carolina with her family and Diggz, the best cockapoo ever. www.maryharriswriter.com.

RHYS HUGHES has lived in many countries. He currently splits his time between Britain and Kenya. His first book, *Worming the Harpy*, was published in 1995, and since that time he has published more than forty other books, eight hundred short stories, and numerous articles, and his work has been translated into ten languages around the world. His most recent book is *Mombasa Madrigal and Other African Escapades*. His fiction is generally fantastica.

ALISON JOSEPH is a crime writer and award-winning radio dramatist. After a career in television documentaries, she began writing full time with the first of the Sister Agnes series of crime novels. She is also the author of a series featuring a fictional Agatha Christie as a detective. She is currently working on a standalone thriller about genetics. Alison was chair of the British Crime Writers' Association from 2013–2015 and is a member of the Killer Women collective.

RUSSEL D. McLEAN is the author of seven crime novels and several short stories, which have run the genre gamut from crime to SF to horror. His debut novel, *The Good Son*, was shortlisted for "Best First Novel" by the Private Eye Writers of America in 2010 and was the first appearance of Dundonian PI, J McNee. After working as a bookseller for over ten years, Russel now splits his time between writing fiction and work as a freelance editor. His latest book, *Ed's Dead*, is a darkly humorous, standalone noir set in Glasgow. www.russeldmcleanbooks.com.

PAUL MAGRS lives and writes in Manchester. In a twenty-five-year writing career, he has published novels in every genre from literary to Gothic mystery to science fiction for adults and young adults. His most recent books include the concluding volume in a science fiction trilogy for kids, *The Heart of Mars* (Firefly Press), and *Fellowship of Ink* (Snow Books), which continues the multi-volumed saga of Brenda, the long-lost bride of Frankenstein. 2019 sees the publication of his book on writing, reading, and creativity, *The Novel Inside You* (Snow Books). He has taught creative writing at both the University of East Anglia and Manchester Metropolitan University and now writes full time.

NICK MAMATAS is the author of several novels, including the murder mystery *I Am Providence* and the supernatural thriller *Sabbath*. His short crime fiction has appeared in *Best American Mystery Stories*, a number of Akashic Books' City Noir anthologies, and his short science fiction and fantasy was recently collected in *The People's Republic of Everything*. Nick lives in Oakland, California.

SANDRA MURPHY is an extensively published nonfiction writer and the author of several short stories including "Sharon Leigh Takes Texas" featured in *The Book of Extraordinary Amateur Sleuth and Private Eyes* anthology and her own crime collection in *From Hay to Eternity: Ten Tales of Crime and Deception*.

NICK QUANTRILL was born and raised in Hull, an isolated industrial city in East Yorkshire. His trilogy of Private Investigator novels featuring Joe Geraghty are published by Fahrenheit Press and he's hard at work on a fourth. Nick is also the cofounder of the Hull Noir festival.

Born in Wales, SALLY SPEDDING was a sculptor and artist until words took over. Her short stories and poetry have won awards and continue to be widely published. Sharpe Books is publishing seven of her noir crime chillers, beginning with *The Nighthawk*, set in the eastern Pyrénées and featuring newly retired DI John Lyon from Nottingham. For thirty years, she and her artist husband have been inspired by their bolthole near Perpignan where timeslips occur. www.sallyspedding.com.

RICKI THOMAS is a scriptwriter and author with seven crime thrillers and many short stories in print. From Oxford, she has travelled extensively and now lives with her youngest son in Hertfordshire. Ricki's biggest interests are criminal psychology, music, and comedies.

LAVIE TIDHAR is the author of the Jerwood Fiction Uncovered Prize winning and Premio Roma nominee *A Man Lies Dreaming* (2014), the World Fantasy Award winning *Osama* (2011) and the Campbell Award winning and Locus and Clarke Award nominated *Central Station* (2016). His latest novels are *Unholy Land* (2018) and first children's novel *Candy* (2018). He is the author of many other novels, novellas, and short stories.

YVONNE WALUS's heritage is intercontinental. Communist Poland taught her never to trust newspapers, how to play the game within the system, and to value uniformity. South Africa's apartheid taught her never to trust newspapers, how to play the game within the system and to value diversity. New Zealand has so many lessons to teach, Yvonne is planning to stay put for a while. Crime fiction is her passion. Her childhood hero was, predictably, Hercule Poirot. For a time, she was totally into Jack Reacher, but her current favorite is Benedict Cumberbatch. Her own books are available on Amazon and you can connect with her here: www.yvonnewalus.com.

Mango Publishing, established in 2014, publishes an eclectic list of books by diverse authors—both new and established voices—on topics ranging from business, personal growth, women's empowerment, LGBTQ studies, health, and spirituality to history, popular culture, time management, decluttering, lifestyle, mental wellness, aging, and sustainable living. We were recently named 2019's #1 fastest growing independent publisher by *Publishers Weekly*. Our success is driven by our main goal, which is to publish high quality books that will entertain readers as well as make a positive difference in their lives. Our readers are our most important resource; we value your input, suggestions, and ideas. We'd love to hear from you—after all, we are publishing books for you!

Please stay in touch with us and follow us at:

Facebook: Mango Publishing
Twitter: @MangoPublishing
Instagram: @MangoPublishing
LinkedIn: Mango Publishing
Pinterest: Mango Publishing

Sign up for our newsletter at www.mango.bz and receive a free book!
Join us on Mango's journey to reinvent publishing, one book at a time.

CPSIA information can be obtained
at www.ICGtesting.com
Printed in the USA
BVHW080830220819
556334BV00001B/1/P